YOUR HAND

Dennis Boyle

Contents

Chapter 1

"Raise your hand. Put a finger down if you have at least one friend. Put a finger down if you're married. Put a finger down if your spouse is a monster. Put a finger down if your one friend helped make a plan to escape. Put a finger down if the plan ended in failure."

Play back. Watch. Erase. Even the attempt at making a TikTok was a failure. Why even make one? Was she out of her mind? Making this wasn't the answer. Trinity bit the inside of her cheek, her eyelid twitching from lack of sleep. Maybe it was lack of sleep giving her idiotic ideas. Surely, her husband had the popular app too. What if he stumbled upon her one minute video? Then what? Was it even a question, because the answer was plain and simple. It was one word. Death.

Then there were the suggestions. Get help, Trinity. Run away, Trinity. Stay with me, Trinity. Even...call the cops, Trinity. One problem. He is the cops. Cops are a brotherhood. They protect one another. So the last suggestion her bestie made was probably the worst one the good intentioned girl had yet to date.

Their last escape attempt, the stay with me one, only led to Trinity's husband coming to her only friend's house. Sure, he had been cordial.

He kicked down the door, grabbed her by the hair and threw her into the truck. No need to guess what happened next. A sound beating was a surefire way to keep a wife in her place.

A week had passed since then. One would guess she wouldn't be thinking of new ways to get away. Fantasy sure was a useful means to stay alive. It provided entertainment, she mused.

"I wonder what Becky's doing," Trinity whispered to herself plugging her phone into the charger and setting it onto a small table situated next to her chair in the tidy living room.

All the chores for the day had been completed. A pot of chili boiling on the stove created a mouth watering aroma. Warm bread was baking in the oven. The meal should make for a quiet night. Only thing left to do was freshen her makeup and hair, and don a clean dress. David liked a well put together woman.

Brushing out the tangles, Trinity swore at her appearance. Slaving over the stove all day melted her makeup from the morning. She would need to start the entire application process over again. Great. Thank goodness for makeup wipes.

Once her face was clean, she was ready to reapply. Moisturizer, primer, foundation, concealer, setting powder, contour, blush, highlight, brow gel, eyelid primer, shadow, mascara, eyelashes, lipstick, perfume. Done. Nope. Not done. Deodorant. Trinity squinted her eyes at her reflection in the mirror. Was that sweat breaking through her setting powder?! Oh, hell no. Not today. What gives? Trinity looked over all the makeup spread over the bathroom vanity. Crap. She forgot setting spray. That's fucking why. Son of a bitch. Exhausting.

Grabbing the powderpuff, she dabbed at the sweat til her face was matte again, then finished with the setting spray. Never forget setting spray. There. Perfect.

Becky would think she belonged in a magazine. She'd heard it all before from numerous people, including her husband, about how gorgeous she was. When the makeup was off, the mask, she looked pretty average in her estimation. What was all the fuss about? Two eyes, a nose and a mouth. Everyone has the same parts, yet some are deemed more beautiful than others according to society. Dumb.

Sighing, she quickly cleaned up, put her makeup away and went to her closet to pick out a dress. Her makeup was warm earth tones. Maybe a sexy black dress. Not that she was in the mood for what the dress would undoubtedly elicit, but it would happen sooner or later. May as well get the deed over with. Now for strappy stilettos.

Looking back at her reflection in the full-length mirror mounted on her closet door, she nodded. Her appearance would please her husband tonight. The black dress was made of silk with spaghetti straps, plunging neckline accentuating an ample cleavage, a tight waist showing off flared hips and round buttocks, with a hemline ending mid-thigh. Show time.

He should be home soon, Trinity glanced at the stove clock. Five o'clock. Rarely was he late. Like clockwork, headlights shown in the driveway.

Dragging in a deep breath, she pressed her palm against her stomach to still her nerves. Tonight will be okay. Quickly, she unlocked the door and went to the stove to carefully spoon the chili into David's bowl. The bread was next. A few slices on a plate and centered onto the table. Oh! His beer. That would have been disastrous.

Placing the food and his beer onto the table, she worked on filling a small bowl for herself. She had eaten earlier so he wouldn't think she was eating too much. That conversation never went well. Just as she was placing her bowl down, the front door opened and closed softly.

This was positive. Usually when the door slammed, it was an obvious sign for when he was angry. Softly shut doors were good. The rattle of his keys being placed into the bowl on the hall tree was next. Now was her cue.

"Hi honey," she smiled brightly coming around the corner.

"Holy fuck. You look hot." David stopped untying his shoe a moment.

"Thank you," she blushed.

"Come and give your husband a kiss, baby."

Swallowing hard, she moved until she was in his arms. His lips claimed hers soft. So soft, it sparked a memory from when they first met. He had been so tender then. The tender side of him was who she had fallen in love with. Of course, that had been a mask much like her makeup.

"Mmm. What's for dinner?"

"Chili," she smiled.

"Let's get it then."

The slap to her behind was nothing new, but it hurt. His slaps were playful in his mind, maybe.

"Delicious," he eyed her. "So what's with all this?" he gestured at the table and then to her with his spoon.

"All of this? I don't...I don't understand?" What was he getting at? Making dinner was something she always did. So was dressing up for him. Her heart started to thrum in her chest. His eyes didn't look right.

"Yeah. The dinner. You. What's up?"

What did he want to hear? What answer was going to be the right one? This game was impossible. She was going to be the loser if she chose wrong. Think!

"Well...I was cleaning and came across our wedding album."

"And?"

"Seeing you in your tuxedo made me feel, I don't know," she shrugged. Trinity glanced up. A playful light was back in his eyes.

"You don't know?"

Taking a steadying breath, Trinity boldly stood up and neared her husband til she was standing next to his chair. "It made me...want you," she whispered.

David's hands were at her hips, skimming her sides. "Damn, baby, if you're horny just say it. I can accommodate. Sit down. I wanna eat first."

"How was your day?" Trinity breathed a sigh of relief. She skated out of his suspicion. It felt like only a few minutes had passed since they first sat down to eat, but an entire thirty actually went by. A headache started to bloom.

"Usual. That asshole, Jimmy, was caught fuckin' 'round with the cashier again. I mean, what a jackass. If you're gonna mess around, do it where you're not gonna get caught," he laughed.

How often did he mess around on her? Did he have any diseases? It wasn't like she could ask that. If she did, he would beat her. But what if he did have an std? She would catch it for sure. So what was worse? Having an std or dying by his hand? Both could be a death sentence. Only one was faster than the other.

Maybe she should let him beat her to death. Then it would all be over with. She would be out of her misery. There was no other way. She tried. Cops were not the answer. Again, he was the cops. Running away wasn't the answer, he would find her. And if someone helped her, they got hurt too. It was hopeless.

"Get me some more, would ya?" he held out his bowl.

"Of course."

Trinity quickly filled his bowl and brought it back to the table. She better make it look like she was eating a little even if she wasn't hungry. He'd soon notice.

"So what did you do with yourself today besides the obvious dinner and getup you're wearing?"

Didn't he just call her hot a few minutes ago? His mind was warped.

"Oh, um, I went to the grocery store and then came home and cleaned before making dinner. Uneventful really. I'm just glad you're home now."

He didn't respond, only kept eating his food. He was wolfing it down. Trinity couldn't stop watching him. She didn't like judging people on their looks. After all, she was just thinking about how looks didn't matter. But, his actions had truly turned him ugly. People always said he was handsome with brown curly hair and light brown eyes. He had a little boy face giving him an innocent appearance. But she knew better.

"Go upstairs. You can clean up after."

"Ok."

She hated having to clean up after. It was tiring. There was no choice in the matter.

"Take off your dress. Leave on the shoes."

Doing as told, she stood naked near the foot of the bed and waited for his next instructions with a shiver. When the instructions came, her mind separated from her body. Her favorite place to put herself was at an imagined cabin in a forest filled with tall trees, small animals, a gentle stream and flowers.

It was her favorite place to retreat to. No one knew about it and no one could take it away. No matter what happened to her physical body, her spiritual one was always able to go home to her forest. Sometimes, little forest nymphs would come to chat with her. They would tell her of their explorations of the world, their secrets of their existence and all the new places they themselves hoped to go.

The air was always clean and warm in her forest. Usually, one only needed a light sweater if it were evening like it currently was. Fireflies, paired with a full moon, provided the evening's light. Clear and starry. Beautiful.

It was an easy thing to sit on the porch swing, as she was, and stare up at the constellations giving them new names. The Little Dipper was visible from where she sat. Instead of Little Dipper, it could be called Little Sugar Scoop. She laughed soft in her mind. Silly.

The evening had a light breeze to it affording her a sample of the wild flowers growing among the trees. Breathing in deep, she captured and memorized the earthy scents around her. So lovely. Yes, she could definitely sit here forever without complaint.

A stinging slap to her bottom jolted Trinity out of her safe haven.

"Go clean up downstairs."

It was over. Blinking away the water filling her eyes, she pulled herself up, picked up her dress and put on a robe. It was over. By the time she came back to bed, he would be snoring. Tonight was a success.

Tomorrow it would all start again. Experience told her that the day after a good day was always bad. Tomorrow, she wouldn't be so lucky. If she wanted to escape what was coming, she would need to think of something. But what? She couldn't do anything that would raise suspicion. She tried that before. It only ever ended in disaster.

Taking her time with packaging the leftovers for his lunch and washing the dishes, she wracked her mind. What could she do tomorrow that would earn her another reprieve? Maybe if she asked him if he wanted her to do any extra chores, he would forgive her shortcomings. Whatever those would be for the day. There was no guessing what they were ahead of time.

The last item in the sink was a butcher knife she had used to chop the tomatoes for the chili. Gingerly, she picked it up and turned it over in her hand mesmerized when the light reflected off of it. It would be a simple thing to do. He wouldn't know what hit him. He'd be asleep.

It would take a strong person to commit murder. Setting to wash the blade, she knew she wasn't strong enough. There was no way she could commit murder. That stain would be on her soul forever. It was too horrible to think about. Moving to rinse it, she didn't notice at first. She hadn't felt the slice of her own palm until the water turned a pinkish red.

"Shit," she whispered.

This cut wasn't shallow. It was fucking deep. She'd need stitches for sure. Feeling a little lightheaded from witnessing her own blood, she closed her eyes and took a cleansing breath before grabbing a towel to staunch the blood flow.

"What the hell is taking you so long?"

Trinity jumped startled. "Dave, I...I sliced my hand open. I...,"

"What the fuck? Why the hell did you do that? God dammit, Trinity. Lemme see."

Trinity winced when he grabbed her hand. Yeah, it needed stitches asshole! Biting her lip, she stuck with breathing.

"You need stitches. Get in the truck. I'll fucking take you. Move!"

Trinity did as told and waited for him to come out of the house. Yeah, tomorrow wasn't going to go well.

"I can't believe you fucking cut yourself. Did you do it on purpose?"

"No! Why would I do such a thing?"

She shouldn't have asked that. He was angry. There was no telling what that would earn her later on. Stupid!

"Shut up. Don't fucking question me. And don't think this little cut is gonna relieve you from your responsibilities at home. I'm the man, I earn the money. I provide you with everything you need to live. So don't forget it. You gotta do your part."

"Yes. Thank you, David."

The drive felt like a woozy blur. Once the hospital was in sight, he pulled up to the emergency department's sliding glass doors.

"Go on, get out. I'm gonna park."

He wasn't going to help her inside. It didn't matter she was feeling light-headed. It didn't matter her robe wasn't securely fastened around her naked body. It didn't matter there were people inside who would possibly see her in such a disheveled state. None of it mattered because he didn't care.

Trying in vain to tighten the belt of her robe to close the gap to her exposed cleavage, Trinity squared her shoulders. She needed medical attention. Now was not the time to worry about cleavage.

When she approached the front desk, a young lady glanced up at her from her computer but quickly refocused on what she was doing.

"Name and date of birth."

"Trinity Fallon. June first, two thousand."

"Insurance card."

"I...I don't have it with me. I should be in the system."

"I still need to scan your card and see your id."

"I don't have it with me," she repeated. "My husband will be here soon. He's just parking the car."

"What do you need to be seen for?" the girl asked popping her chewing gum.

Was this girl for real? Sure she herself was only twenty years old, but this chick couldn't be that dumb. Her hand was in a freaking bloody towel!

"I sliced my hand open with a knife."

The girl entered the information into the computer and soon a medical identification bracelet printed out. Suddenly, a set of double doors opened.

"Step through."

Thank God she didn't have to sit in the waiting room with the rest of the people in her half-dressed state. She met the girl around the corner where she fastened the bracelet around Trinity's wrist and gestured for her to sit.

"Someone will be in to triage you."

Unsure of what to make of the abrupt treatment, Trinity decided to let it go. She had much to be thankful for at the moment with having been accepted without her license and insurance card. David was going to blame her for not grabbing her purse before they left.

"Hi there. I'm Casey. You're Trinity Fallon?"

Trinity nodded.

"I'm just going to take your vitals. Are you able to keep hanging onto the towel for me?"

"Yes."

"Okay. Let's get your blood pressure."

The automatic cuff tightened to an uncomfortable degree for a few moments before the air let out in a gush. Then a thermometer was placed under her tongue for a few seconds.

"Temperature is ninety-eight, six. Blood pressure is a little elevated at one thirty-five over eighty. Pulse is elevated at one ten. Is it normally like that?"

"Everything is usually within the normal range."

"Alright. Well, let's get you into a room right away so the doctor can take a look. Are you able to walk?"

"I believe so."

The walk to the room was down a hall and around a corner. Farther than she had anticipated. Her dizziness definitely increased. It didn't matter once she sat down onto the bed.

"The doctor will be right in."

"Thanks." Trinity glanced around. There wasn't a hospital gown to change into or a robe. And what about her blood pressure and pulse? If the numbers weren't within normal range, were they going to do something about it? Maybe the numbers weren't too bad.

A few minutes ticked by. Trinity took in the small private room. Two visitor chairs sat against one wall, a rolling table for the patient to utilize, a door leading to a probable bathroom, a computer, a television, a sink, a bunch of monitors, a weird looking chest of drawers, a huge overhead light, and a dry erase board with a diagram to explain pain scale laid out from happy to sad to screaming faces, made up the room. She would say her pain was the grimacing middle face. So, level five maybe.

Where was David? He said he was only parking the car. Did he abandon her here? No. Why would he do that? He told her she had to take care of all of her chores tomorrow like she usually did. This injury was no excuse for not having chores done. He didn't abandon her. Maybe he just couldn't find a parking space.

"Trinity Fallon? Hi, I'm Dr. Logan."

Dr. Logan was extremely good looking. Of course he was. Why did he have to be? Embarrassment for her state of dress flooded her, and she shifted trying to close her robe against her breasts.

"What happened tonight?" he gestured.

"I was washing dishes and sliced my hand open on a knife."

"I see. Let's have a look."

Gingerly, he removed the towel to see the depth of the wound and nodded his head. He then flexed her hand in a few different directions causing her level five to shoot to a level eight and earning a whimper the doctor apologized for.

"You did a good job keeping your hand elevated. Makes my job easier as far as blood is concerned. Looks like you'll need about ten stitches. There doesn't seem to be any tendon damage. Trinity, forgive me, can I help you tie your robe for you?"

"Yes, please," she sighed relieved.

"No problem. I'll have my nurse bring you a gown," the doctor said.

"What's going on here?" David's voice was stern as he entered the room.

Trinity gulped, flinching away from the doctor. She did not need David's suspicion right now. Unfortunately, she seemed to gain the doctor's. His gaze fell on her for a few seconds.

"Your wife's robe fell open, Mr. Fallon."

"You people don't have hospital gowns? What the fuck?"

"I'm having my nurse bring one, sir. But, no worries, we'll have her stitched up in no time. So, how did this happen?"

The question was directed at David. Trinity knew better than to open her mouth while the doctor moved about the room gathering the proper supplies.

"Didn't she tell you already? I would think you would've asked that question."

"It's been a long night," the doctor chuckled. "I've forgotten your wife's answer. Refresh my memory."

"She cut herself doing the dishes. Any other questions, doc?"

"If I have more, I'll certainly let you know."

"Good. Now how long is this gonna take? I have to get some sleep."

"This is going to sting a bit. It's a numbing agent called lidocaine so you don't feel the procedure."

Trinity nodded then cringed from the injection into her palm. That did not feel good. However, soon her palm was completely numb and the doctor worked on the much needed stitches.

"I asked you a question, doc."

"Trinity, the sutures I'm placing will need to be removed in about five to seven days. You can see your primary care physician to have them removed or you can come back here. But, if you return here, the cost will be much more than simply making a regular doctor appointment."

"I understand. Thank you."

"Well, I guess I'm invisible. That's real nice. I'm gonna be in the truck, Trinity. Hurry the fuck up."

"Mr. Fallon, you do realize that if I feel this injury was done by your hand, I will report you for domestic violence."

"Yeah? Try it. See how far you get," he clipped.

When David walked out of the small room, the heaviness of the air left with him. Trinity's shoulders sagged. She couldn't stop the tears. How embarrassing! This was not good. She may very well need more medical attention tonight. He wasn't going to wait with her beating. She could feel it.

"Mrs. Fallon, do you need a safe place to stay tonight?"

"He'll find me. I need to go with him."

"Often times, people who suffer from domestic abuse feel hopeless. They're not. There is hope and help."

"No. He's a cop. He'll find me. I have to go. Please, doctor, please hurry."

"I'm within my legal right to report him, Mrs. Fallon," the doctor warned.

Trinity's face paled. It was a mistake to come here. "I-I n-need to go. I can just tape my hand. I shouldn't have come," she tried to scoot off the bed.

"Let me finish. You're almost done."

Before Trinity was released, he handed her discharge papers and a pamphlet for domestic abuse looking torn.

"Thank you, but I can't take this. If he sees it...I might end up back here tonight. Thank you for helping me."

"This department is open twenty-four hours a day. If you need us, you come right back. We can get you help, but I really wish you wouldn't leave."

Trinity stood up, tightened her belt and smiled, "Thank you, Dr. Logan."

Picking up the pace of her steps despite the dizziness sweeping through her head, she located David's truck in the parking lot and headed for it. It was a miracle she made it back to the vehicle and inside where she fumbled with the seat belt.

Finally, it clicked into place. She didn't dare risk looking at David's face. She could already feel his anger. Maybe there was a way to fix this.

"I can't believe that doctor. He sure had a lot of nerve, but backed down when you showed him who's boss."

"Shut up!" David's voice boomed. "What did you tell him?"

"W-w-what?" she stammered.

"What. Did. You. Tell. Him? Why was he insinuating that I fucking hurt you? Huh?!"

His voice was pure thunder. She was in the eye of the storm. No matter what answer she gave next, it wouldn't matter.

"I d-d-didn't tell him anything other t-t-than I sliced my hand doing the dishes, and I d-d-don't know why he assumed it was you."

"Well, Trinity, I d-d-don't fucking believe you. Why were his hands on you when I walked into the room?"

"My robe was coming undone, and I don't h-h-have any clothes on underneath it. He was helping me close it."

"Liar!"

A firecracker pop rang through the small cabin of the truck, a flash of light, then the sting from his palm coursed though her jaw. The blow rattled her teeth causing her jaw to feel unhinged. He was yelling again, but she didn't know what he was saying too caught up in waiting for the pain to ebb. Once it did, she slowly worked her jaw from side to side then pressed it against the cool glass of the window.

Too bad the ride wasn't longer. The truck was now silent as he drove them home. If she thought for one second this was over with, she'd be a fool. The reprieve would only last a few more minutes. Still, it was longer than boxers got between rounds.

Perhaps she could pretend to be a boxer. She just finished round one. Now was the small break before round two started. How many rounds would there be tonight? Was there going to be a knockout again? How exciting.

"Come on."

Unfastening her seatbelt, she was about to open the door when it was yanked open.

"I said come...on."

Grabbing a fistful of her hair, he dragged Trinity out of the truck. Her hand came up to clutch at his wrist, but that was a mistake. She winced against the tight bandages. Her palm was still thankfully numb, but the tape pulled against the tiny hairs on the back of her hand.

Trying to stop him from pulling her hair was no use. He used his grip on her head to drag her along behind him like a dog that had been bad. It was a miracle the follicles of her scalp didn't release to avoid the abuse. They didn't. Her hair was thick and able to handle the forceful tugging that was now starting to burn causing tears.

"Get inside and put some goddamn clothes on. Fucking slut."

Despite the pain and dizzying nausea, Trinity managed to run up the stairs to the bedroom. Round two was over with. This was her break. She needed to grab sweat pants, a t-shirt and dress as quickly as possible.

Frantic, she pulled open her dresser drawer and rummaged til she found a white t-shirt. She slammed the drawer shut then pulled open the very bottom drawer which was much deeper than the rest. Bingo! Her gray sweat pants were right on top. Perfect. One leg up, next leg up. Dressed. Round three.

Like clockwork, the bedroom door slammed open and she was once again face to face with her opponent. So that's what took him so long. He was strung out. High as a kite. Eyes bloodshot and pupils blown. What had he taken? Had he smoked something? Pot? Crack? Did he take pills? Didn't matter. This was dangerous. She would need to fight.

As if sensing her realization, David's contorted face shifted into an evil smile. He now knew she knew what he had done. He also knew she knew he was going to attack. She was at a disadvantage with her hand unable to curl into a fist. She would need to fight him off one handed. Better yet, she would need to dodge him.

Without further warning, he lunged at her. His fingertips brushed the hem of her shirt as she launched herself onto the bed and scrambled into a crouching position trying to judge his next attack. It made him laugh.

"You think you're so slick!" he screamed.

"No! I didn't do anything wrong!" she screamed back. It didn't matter anymore. No matter what she said, he would still hurt her and wouldn't remember any of it come morning.

"Bullshit! I'm gonna fucking kill you!"

Faster than him, Trinity ran off of the bed and down the stairs where she locked herself inside the bathroom. He wouldn't know exactly which room she was in for at least a few seconds. Glancing at the window, she contemplated jumping out of it. But if she did that, she would have nowhere to go and it was cold. Freezing to death wasn't the answer.

Tapping on the sink, she looked around. She needed a weapon. The medicine cabinet might have something in it to help. What could she use? Hair scissors. She could stab him. Stab him in the throat or the eyes. Kill him. She could kill him and it would be over with. She had a witness for tonight. The doctor could testify for her.

But what if he didn't? What if she had no good alibi, and she ended up in prison? Then what? She'd never last in prison. She couldn't risk that. The pounding on the door startled her out of her thoughts, and she shut the cabinet door.

With a boom, the door flew open hard splintering the wood and bouncing off the wall, then his arm. His smile was menacing, his figure larger than life from where he stood in the doorway.

"Little gingerbread girl, the water will surely get you wet."

What? What was he talking about? She blinked away nervous tears.

"Hop onto my tail and you can ride there while we cross the wide, wide river." David held his hand out and wiggled his fingers at Trinity. "Oh no!" he bit his fingernails, his eyes shifting back and forth in exaggerated worry. "The river is rising! Surely if you stay on my tail, you'll get wet. You better hop onto my back, little gingerbread girl," he warned stepping fully into the bathroom.

Trinity moved back til her thighs hit the edge of the tub.

"Tsk, tsk, tsk. The water is so nasty. Isn't it?" David pressed his body against Trinity's. His hand reached up under her t-shirt where he kneaded her breast. His other turned on the tub faucet earning a small whimper.

"The water rises still," he sighed shoving the stopper into the tub drain. "Whatever shall we do? Ah, I know. I know, I know, I know," he whispered. "Little gingerbread girl?"

David's forehead rested against Trinity's. The steam and loud splashes and gurgles from the tub filling were loud and troubling. What was he planning? Trinity couldn't help the shivers starting to wrack her body or the jolts of disgust shooting through her while his nose nuzzled the side of her cheek.

"The water is very high now. You must hop onto my head," he grabbed her hand and placed it against his stiff member. "Hop. On."

Trinity struggled under his tight grip, her heart pounding in her chest. A gasp slipped from her lips when his hand suddenly flew to her neck and quickly turned her, bending her body over so that her nose hovered above the high water in the tub. Oh God! He was planning on drowning her.

"No! David, please. Please let me go. I promise I'll never be bad. Please," her voice escaped with a strained crack.

"Shh. Shh, gingerbread girl. Climb up between my ears, sweet. Sit up as hiiigh as you can so that you...don't. Get. Wet."

But she was getting wet! Her nose was nearly immersed. The water was too hot! There was only a small pocket between the water and her mouth. Beads of perspiration broke out at her brow.

If she didn't slow her breathing, she wouldn't be able to fill her lungs with as much air as possible. Breathe in slow, exhale slow. Inhale, exhale. Inhale...

"Snip, snap! The fox strikes!" he roared.

David plunged Trinity's head into the tub of hot water. Instinct caused her to pull back and thrash against the tight hold. The heat from the water filled her ears, her nostrils and pressed against the delicate skin of her eyelids like an invisible strain infiltrating her mind. If felt as if every pore in her face was filled with lava.

Finally, David pulled her head out of the small hell. She heaved to find her breath, struggling against his hold.

"How did you like that, little gingerbread girl? Did that doctor make you feel just as warm? Well, just know your fox can make you feel hotter!" he shouted, spit catching in her hair.

Back into the heat. The slap of the water against her face, muffled the words David was spewing. One and two and three and four and five and six and seven and eight and nine and ten and eleven and twelve and thirteen and fourteen and fifteen and sixteen and seventeen and eighteen and nineteen and twenty...

Her shoulders started shaking and despite the bandages on her hand, she used it to press against the tub. To press against David's legs. She couldn't breathe! She needed air! Please!

Suddenly, he dragged her up and out. Her chest heaved. How much longer was he going to do this? How much longer could she withstand it? Her stomach started to riot.

"I'm sorry, David! Please! I'm so sorry!" she screamed. Except she wasn't screaming. Her voice was barely a whisper.

"Nope. Not gonna happen. Not this time, little girl. I'm not gonna fall for this apology," he smoothed his cheek against hers. His stubble a grater against her burnt skin. "You see," he whispered, "I was too soft last time you apologized. Yeah. Too, too soft. This time, you're gonna learn. Yes. Yes, you are. Back in!" he sang.

One and two and three and four and five and six and seven and eight and nine and ten and eleven and twelve and thirteen and fourteen and fifteen and sixteen and seventeen and eighteen and nineteen and twenty and twenty-one and twenty-two...

It's a funny thing when the body starts to run empty. On air that is. The lungs start to burn with the strain for oxygen. It's an imagined reach that stretches and stretches for something it can never touch. Yes, it burns. The brain panics and the body moves all on its own accord. Flailing and twisting. Convulsing.

It's hard to control the internal mechanism for survival. The body fights. Boy, does it ever when it's threatened with death. Even so, it takes a long time to die. It's as if each major organ shuts down one at a time. Agonizingly slow. So interesting. So dizzying. So soft. So quiet. So still.

So...black.

Chapter 2

In daily living, there are different considerations for the definition of silence. Some people consider the absence of technological noise silence. Some consider whispering silence. Others, total absence of noise is silence as defined by the dictionary. But where there lives a heartbeat, can never exist true silence.

A heartbeat is a rhythmic sound. Ba-dum, ba-dum, ba-dum. It's heard at the very door of the eardrum. That's why it's so loud. So clear. When all other noises are gone, such as television, music, animals, traffic, for example, the heartbeat is the loudest thing on the planet. It's so loud, it could wake a person. So it would seem.

That's what must have woken her from her slumber. It was the first thing she heard. Her own heartbeat. Ba-dum, ba-dum, ba-dum. Rhythmic, strong, steady. Then, the conscious inhalation of breath. A slight whistling noise dragging through the nostrils, disbursing into the lungs and exhaled on a sigh. Finally, the cold. But cold is silent. Silent until it causes teeth to chatter and limbs to twitch.

Trinity's arm jerked from the bone chill that coursed through her and tapped porcelain hard enough to cause her funny bone to zing. The rattle of the plastic blinds above her head caught her attention and registered with her brain the window was open. Cold air poured into the bathroom covering her like a blanket. The bathtub her bed.

He left her to freeze to death over the course of the night. In the fetal position, she flexed her feet to feel an inch worth of water swish under her body. The rest must have drained until her arm managed to form a stopper.

It was a wonder her heart was beating so amazingly strong and not frozen from the cold. Hell, it wasn't too late. Maybe pneumonia would settle in. Gingerly, Trinity uncoiled her body and struggled into a sitting position. She needed to get the window closed. She needed to get out of the blasted tub.

Hindsight was twenty twenty. She should have taken the good doctor up on his offer. She wouldn't be in this position if she had. Maybe, or maybe she already was in a good position. She was alive after all.

Summoning all of her strength, she hoisted herself up and managed to wrangle the window shut. Her fingers clung to the sash a moment before pushing away. She needed to assess her throbbing face. It felt raw and blistered.

Closing her eyes and swallowing hard, she opened them to see her skin was in fact very red and blistered in a few areas. A slight tap to one blister caused it to pop open. A clear liquid trickled down her cheek. Trinity grimaced with a whimper, pressing her fingertips against the onion thin case the blister left behind.

There were five more blisters just the same, easily giving way under the lightest of touches. It was probably a bad idea to probe at them, but she had to. If David saw her like this, it would cause more problems.

Pulling open the cabinet drawer, she sifted through the junk and thanked the heavens when she found some antibiotic cream and a half empty tube of green goo normally used on sunburns. This would have to do. Perhaps later she could apply some cool packs.

Cleaning up her mess on the counter along with the water on the floor from her dripping clothes, she realized David wasn't home. She could tell. It felt like mid-morning or early afternoon. Either way, she needed to get the house and dinner organized. It didn't matter her hand ached fierce, and her face burned like the sun kissed her far too hard. A few ibuprofen and ignorance would have to tie her over. There was work to be done. She had to go to the store as well.

She remembered she was going to make her homemade chicken soup today. Had she told him she was going to make that? Because she couldn't remember, she would have to. What would she need for it? One whole chicken, celery, carrots, onion, chicken broth, poultry seasoning, tortellini noodles. Also, an Italian bread with butter would be nice. Was there anything else?

Trudging back up the stairs to the bedroom, stopping once to settle her spinning head and stomach, she tried to focus her mind but couldn't seem to get it to work. No matter. Maybe once at the store, she'd remember. For now, she needed clean clothes.

After dressing, Trinity made herself a cup of coffee, to ward off her chill. She winced drinking the hot liquid too fast. Despite it, she took a few more sips before grabbing her keys and purse. Once in the car, she rummage around in the glove box for her sunglasses. She would need to make sure to have them on.

Maybe if people happened to look at her, they would think she just came back from vacation. A hot one. Hell, who was she kidding? She looked like she'd been through it. Maybe she should have put on some makeup. Yeah right. Makeup over her ointment greased face? What a joke.

With the car parked near the front entrance of the store, she opened the glove box again for a brush. How could she have forgotten to brush her hair? Shit. She even forgot to brush her teeth. She forgot everything. Brain cells must have died from the dunking she endured, she mused.

"Fuck!" Trinity groaned when the brush hit her scalp too hard. If her face was burnt as bad as it was, her scalp had to be the same. Tossing the brush down, she decided to finger comb her hair instead.

How was tonight going to go? Was he going to pretend nothing happened? That's what she planned on doing. Maybe she would even buy some flowers for the table. Make things look cheery and bright. How did her hair look? Checking the rearview mirror, it seemed to look okay. Naturally wavy hair definitely had its perks. Disguising a disheveled appearance for one. At least that's what she liked to believe.

Shrugging, Trinity grabbed her purse. Every muscle seemed to cry out with any move she made. Interesting how she was moving at all. At least no one would notice because no one knew her. So that was a good thing.

Once inside, Trinity grabbed a shopping cart and headed to the produce section. Much to her disappointment, the sunglasses were going to have to go. Despite the fluorescent lighting, it was hard to see with the glasses on. Into the purse for now. Alright. Carrots, celery and onion. Perfect trifecta to cooking. Anything was tasty with those three base vegetables. That's what her mother taught her.

Memories flooded to the forefront. Her mother started motherhood so late in life having Trinity at fifty. Why did she wait so long? Now her mother was in her seventies and retired with her father down south where the weather was warm. It was clear she had been an accident child. Her parents weren't too invested in her. Except when it came to food. That was the only time Trinity ever had an opportunity to bond with her mother. Her mother would cook and Trinity would watch.

Anyone lucky enough to try Trinity's cooking raved about it. It was the one thing she was proud of. Too bad she didn't have her own family to cook for. Instead, she had David. Too bad he turned out the way he did.

What else did she need? Oh yeah. A whole chicken and noodles. Moving was so exhausting. It escaped her attention the looks she received from the produce section until she turned for the meat counter. Yeah, yeah, the face was burned. Go ahead and stare. Jeeze. Hadn't their parents taught them staring was rude?

Where were the fucking noodles? Fresh tortellini was not in the grocery aisle. It would be in the refrigerated section. Duh. The brain definitely wasn't functioning right. That's okay. It'll catch up. Before heading there, the Italian seasoning should be in the next aisle over. Right? May as well go look.

A few people in the aisle grabbed their items and left until it was herself and another man with his back towards her. Good. Stay turned away. Don't look at me, she thought. Wait. Crap. The Italian seasoning was way up high. Too high. The man's tall. He would definitely be able to reach it. She didn't want to ask for help. But no seasoning meant another night of hell. One she wouldn't be able to handle. Better ask before he leaves!

"Um...excuse me, sir?" her voice rasped in a whisper. Her throat felt sore from having spent the night in a cold tub with the wind blowing down upon her. Yup. Gonna die from pneumonia.

"Yes?" he turned, hesitating a moment.

The man's suit was tailored to perfection. Tanned skin emerging from a crisp white cuff, fastened by onyx cufflinks. It must be designer. His shiny shoes too. Trinity's eyes traveled up his gorgeous clothing til she met the black-colored depth of his eyes. His hair, equally as black, was slicked back away from his face. The style held into position by some sort of pomade undoubtedly. There was smoulder to this man. He held power. There was no mistaking that. A powerful man in a grocery store.

He was easily the sexiest man Trinity had ever seen in the entirety of her life. Not only were his eyes spellbinding, his features reminded her of a statue. Perfectly carved from his straight nose to his angular jaw. Even his lips were the right balance of plump. Beauty personified.

"May I help you, miss?"

His voice. So deep. He could narrate a story.

But wait. What? Had she said something to him? Oh God. She did. She needed the seasoning on the top shelf. Oh no.

"Oh. I'm sorry. I'm so sorry to bother you, sir. I w–was just wondering if you could possibly reach something for me? But I–I'm sorry. I can, I can just get the s–store clerk," she breathed. She hated when she stuttered. Why was she doing it now of all times?

"What do you need?" his eyes followed hers to the Italian seasoning. "This?" he pointed at it.

Trinity nodded and watched as he plucked the small container off of the shelf and handed it to her. She shouldn't be looking at him. She's married. And if anyone from David's precinct saw her, they would tell him she was talking to a man. Diverting her attention to her shoes, she took the seasoning.

"Thank you, sir," she whispered.

This was bad. What if someone saw her? Maybe she should walk around to make sure no police were in the store. She needed to know.

"You're most welcome," his eyes dropped from her face to her bandaged hand.

She needed to get out of here. She needed to get to the next few aisles over and check out who the hell was in the store. Quickly, she left the aisle without looking back at the beautiful man and started checking. Her heart thrummed in her chest at an unnatural pace. She ignored the winded feeling. She could breathe later. For now, she had to know.

Aisle one, all clear. Aisle two, she was just in, all clear. Aisle three, all clear. Aisle four, all clear. A panicked lump started to rise in her throat. Aisle five, all clear. Aisle six, all clear. Two more aisles then the meat section, produce section, dairy section and frozen section. Come on.

A startled gasp ripped from her throat as she crashed into a hard wall. Except it wasn't a hard wall, but a person. No. She raised frightened eyes up into black ones. The beautiful man! A whimper leaked out of her.

"I'm so sorry."

The man's hands gripped her elbows, steadying her. She couldn't look at him. She had to look in aisle six or was it seven? Time was running out! She started to move away, but his grip held firm. Her eyes shot to his in a panic.

"P-p-please let me go. Pl...,"

"Miss. Are you alright?"

"Yes, yes. I'm fine. Thank you."

"I know that look. It's not a look of fine. Who are you running from?"

The question was simple. Straight forward. Direct. No beating around the bush. Worse than that was the commandment he held in his voice. He expected an answer.

"Please let me go. I-I-I have to...," Trinity licked her lips unaware of the tear that escaped down her face, "I have to check aisle seven and eight," her voice cracked.

Anxiety's cruel what if questions whispered into her ear, driving her from the store. Her cart was left in aisle two. She hadn't even checked out. All of her groceries left behind. On the bright side, there were no patrol cars in the lot. No one had seen her speak with the beautiful man. Relief swept through, banishing her panic attack.

She would need to drive to the next grocery store a town over, just in case. This put her behind schedule by an hour. Maybe if she purchased chicken soup already made, he would never know. That could save her some time because she still needed to clean the bathroom and bedroom. Luckily, yesterday she had vacuumed so that chore was done. Although, she forgot to sweep the basement steps. It would be difficult to do with one hand, but not impossible.

Once home and the chores complete, Trinity worked to get dinner on the table and the evidence of her canned soup tossed away in the trash. She even went so far as to take the garbage out to the trash cans so that he wouldn't notice. Everything appeared to be in order. Even the fresh flowers were cut and placed into a vase of cool water. Yellow daffodils.

The room had a spring feel to it now. That was good. Perhaps the little bit of cheer would dispel any foul mood David might be in. Lord knew she wouldn't be able to handle another night like last night.

Once David arrived home, she thanked the heavens the door closed soft. Kinda soft. Was it soft? Maybe it was a little forced. Shaking her head, she got up from the chair to greet him.

"Hi honey," she smiled.

Silence. Not even a look. He unlaced his shoes and placed them on the mat, threw his keys into the bowl and moved past her as if she weren't even there. This was bad. Smoothing her hands down her sides, she went to the stove and dished the soup into a bowl and placed it down softly, repeating the steps for her own dinner.

"H–how was your day, honey?"

"Fine. We're going out tonight."

What? Since when? He never took her out. Ever. Panic coiled tight her stomach. She didn't have the energy to go out. She needed to rest.

"What would you like for me to wear?"

"We're going to a club. The boys invited me out. They're all bringing their bitches."

This was bad. Just about as disastrous as it could get. Any place that had alcohol was bad news.

"Place is called La Notte. It's a classy place so wear that black dress you had on the other day and fix your goddamned face. Go on. I don't wanna be late."

Good. She wasn't hungry anyway. But how the hell was she supposed to wear the heels she had worn for him the other day? They were five inch stilettos. And what about her face?! Shit.

Making her way into the bedroom, she grabbed a thong, the dress and the shoes. The dress had an open back that dipped low. There was no room for a bra. She was going to look like a slut and be blamed for it.

Once in the bathroom, she quickly dressed, curled her hair and caked foundation, concealer and powder over her injured skin ignoring the pain. How should she do her eye makeup? David would want her to look good tonight. She can't embarrass him. Perhaps a smokey eye with a nude lip would please him distract from the rest of her face.

Her platinum blonde curls fell around her face and breasts, tumbling down to her waist. The reflection looking back at her was gorgeous. She could have been a makeup artist. A horror makeup artist. She wasn't quite sure how she managed to make her skin look as if nothing had happened. But she did, and that was all that mattered.

Finally, she removed the bandage from her hand to reveal the blood encrusted sutures. It was a miracle none of them popped after everything they had been through. Washing her hand with warm soapy water, she toweled it off and covered the wound with a smaller bandage significantly less noticeable. Hopefully, she would please him tonight. Popping another two ibuprofen, and another for good measure, it was now or never.

Making her way back down the stairs on surprisingly steady legs, Trinity waited in the living room for David who was in the downstairs bathroom. When he came out, she couldn't deny he looked handsome. Not as handsome as the man in the grocery store, however. Nowhere near.

"You look very handsome, David," she complimented.

"Yeah, well, you look fucking hot. Do not, I repeat, do not leave my side unless it's to go to the bathroom. And then you tell me. Got it?"

"I do. Yes."

"Good, because you know what'll happen if you don't, right?"

Trinity nodded her head.

"I should fuck you before we leave here tonight," David looked at his watch. "Fuck. We don't have time. We're already late. Let's go."

Relief.

Hopefully, he wouldn't make her drink tonight. With the ibuprofen she just took, it would be best to stay sober. Chances were high that after a while, he wouldn't even notice her.

"So there's gonna be a bunch of people from work at La Notte. The guys never met you before. My guess is you're gonna cause a stir, so just stick to my side."

"Yes. I understand."

Great. Just what she needed.

"There's valet parking here. Wait a second. I'll get your door."

David got out of the truck and handed his key to the valet, then came around to open her door and helped her out. He was different now. Where once a monster now a perfect gentleman. A loving and doting husband. She had seen a glimmer of this side from him when they first started dating. It died out once they said I do.

"Come on, hun. Let's go meet the boys."

The club seemed to have its own pulse with dance music and colorful lights. David wasn't exaggerating when he said the place was classy. The color scheme seemed to be black and red. Everything in the place looked very expensive from the tables and chairs to the people. It was like a magazine or a movie. Gorgeous and sexy.

"There they are. Come on, honey." David looped his arm around hers and made his way to the group of men and women joking and laughing. Everyone seemed to be having a great time. The women were dressed to kill and looked beautiful next to their dates and husbands. Trinity swallowed hard, nervous for what was to come.

"Hey y'all!" David yelled, slapping one man on the back.

"David!" They all cheered.

"Guys, this is my wife, Trinity. Trinity, meet the boys."

"Well, goddamn, David. How the hell did you convince her to marry your ugly ass? Holy. Shit!"

"Shut the fuck up, Jack."

Now she had the full attention of the entire group. The once beautiful women now looked different with their subtle sneers and upturned noses. They didn't like her. It was because of the men's reactions to her. She didn't need to start this night off with jealous women. Great.

"Nice to meet you," she said to a few who shook her hand.

"What are you drinking, sexy?"

Crap. If she answered that question, it would get her into trouble later. She looked at David instead. He would probably answer for her.

"She's gonna go to the bar with me."

David pulled her along with him through the thick crowd and up to the bar.

"I'm gonna order a beer. What do you want?"

"Sprite, please."

"Fine. Probably best you don't drink. Don't move."

Standing as still as possible, she took the opportunity to fill her eyes with the decor of the building. Everything was so beautiful and alive here. How fun it must be for those who were on a date. It made her smile.

"Hey, baby girl. How 'bout we take it up on the dance floor?"

A man was talking to her, but she looked up at the ceiling instead. There was no way she was going to be caught exchanging any syllables with anyone. Not one single peep of a sound. And if it meant she was a bitch, so be it.

"Hey. I'm talking to you sweet cheeks."

"She's mine. Back the fuck off."

The man held up his hands, then disappeared into the crowd.

"You talking to him? What did you say?"

"No, David. When he started talking to me, I looked up at the ceiling and didn't move. Just like you instructed."

"Good. Lemme grab our drinks."

Letting out a breath, Trinity looked over at the bar where her husband was when her eyes fell on a man sitting on a stool observing David. It was him! The man from the grocery store. He was staring at David with a peculiar look on his face. Before she could turn away, his eyes locked with hers.

Time was frozen. She was frozen. The beautiful man's eyes traveled from her shoes all the way up to the top of her head and then back down again to her eyes. He made no move to take her in, in a hurry. Did he recognize her?

When David neared, the man got up from his seat and approached. What was he doing? Absently, Trinity took the Sprite from her husband.

"Excuse me, sir."

"What?" David's shitty tone died in his throat when he turned to face the man.

"Would you like to join the VIP room with your date? I have a few spots available?"

"She's not my date, asshole. She's my wife. And why the fuck would I want to sit in a room with you?"

"Forgive me. I didn't know she was your wife. I'm the owner of this establishment. You look like a fine couple, and thought you would enjoy it. I'm mistaken then. Enjoy your evening."

Trinity closed her eyes unable to watch the man walk away. David just made a complete ass out of himself and her. Embarrassment had her cheeks on fire.

"Who the fuck does he think he is? I don't care if he's the owner or not. I saw the way he looked at you. I'm not stupid. Let's get back to the group."

Trinity followed her husband back, not before looking over her shoulder to find the beautiful man staring straight at her. He recognized her. There was no doubt in Trinity's mind. She knew he recognized her because his gaze dropped to the hand that had been bandaged earlier today.

It was his way of saying hello apparently. Just as long as it was a silent hello and nothing more. She didn't need his intervention. He was a smart man. He knew what was up. Hopefully, he wasn't planning on being a hero tonight. Glancing around told her, he probably wouldn't. Where did he go?

David's squeeze around her waist brought her back to the conversation. What were they talking about? She had no clue. Her attention was completely on the beautiful man who was also the club owner. That came at no surprise. His club was just as beautiful as he. All that remained to be seen was the man's girlfriend or wife. She was probably gorgeous too.

Men like him always had a beautiful person attached to their arm to show off or compliment. She didn't. She had a monster. A monster or a fucking demon. The label didn't really matter. Either way, she couldn't figure out a way to escape the current situation that was hell. Every time she came up with a plan, the nagging what if question shut her down.

Smiling and nodding, she again redirected her attention to the conversation. Taking cues from the people around her was all she had to go on to know when to laugh or smile. What the hell were they talking about? She better pay attention.

One of the women, what was her name again? Callie? Trinity couldn't remember, nudged her.

"So, like, are those real?" she gestured to Trinity's chest.

Was this woman for real? Why did she care if her boobs were real or not? Jeeze. These people were all weird and fake. When was this night going to end?

"What do you mean? My wife's tits are all real. What? Don't believe me? Feel 'em."

"David?" Trinity gasped.

"Go ahead, Callie. Give 'em a squeeze. What? It's the only way she's gonna know, babe," he shrugged.

Much to Trinity's horror, the woman took the invitation and placed her hand on her breast and squeezed. Trinity's body stiffened when the tips of the woman's nails dug into her skin under the harsh grip.

"Oh. I guess you're right. She's real," she sneered. "Mine are fake and perfectly symmetrical. You can feel mine, if you want to."

"No, thank you." Trinity brought her arm across her chest and clutched her shoulder hoping no one else would touch her. How could David do that? Did he not realize she was touched without consent? Why was she even surprised? He didn't care. He never would.

"David, I need to use the restroom," Trinity whispered.

David grimaced, but looked around spotting the bathroom sign. "Go ahead. I'll wait for you here. I'll be watching," he whispered into her ear.

Nodding, Trinity left the group behind for the bathroom while making sure to avoid eye contact with anyone. She didn't need that.

Once inside, she was relieved to see a chair against the wall. Perfect. She needed a breather. This night wasn't the worse, but it wasn't good either.

Who knew the beautiful man was the owner of this club? What were the chances of running into him again? He really was beautiful. So confident and sexy. His girlfriend or wife was sure lucky.

How must that feel? To be with someone so beautiful and kind. She wasn't entirely sure he was kind, but he seemed to be. Also, to be with someone as established as he presented. There would be no worry about how bills were going to be paid. There would be no worry about a beating. There would be no worry or wonder if each day would be the last. There would be no question of being loved or not. How would that life feel?

Trinity closed her eyes and, for the briefest of moments, allowed herself to dream. Freedom feels...wonderful. The flush of a toilet interrupted the moment, and she opened her eyes. That's right. She was in a bathroom. How fitting. She better go back.

Pulling open the door and heading into the dark hallway, she laughed to herself. This was the hallway back to her prison, she mused.

"We meet again."

She knew that deep voice. It belonged to the beautiful man. Nervously, she looked down the hall where she could see David in the distance. His back was to her. It wouldn't have mattered if it wasn't. This far down the hall was too dark to see her from where she stood.

"Oh, h-hello," she stammered, turning around to face him.

He smiled kind at her, "You were at the grocery store earlier today."

Trinity glanced over her shoulder. Good, he was still talking to the group. "Um...yeah," she breathed.

"How's your hand?"

He took her hand into his and flipped it over, smoothing his thumb gently over the bandage. Trinity pulled her hand away with a shiver.

"Fine. It's fine. Silly kitchen accident."

"The group you're with isn't pleasant."

It was a statement. One that wasn't wrong. Did he see Callie grab her? Probably. This man looked to be very aware of everything around him. There would be no dancing around with her answers.

"No. I suppose they're not," she smiled tight.

"Why don't you join me for a drink? Your husband hardly seems to notice you've gone."

"Eventually he will."

"Eventually. Then what?"

"Then...," she looked back. Now David was starting to look around for her. Of course he was. "Then is then," she smiled.

"What's your name?"

"Trinity."

"Trinity," he tested her name on his tongue. "Bellissima."

"I have to go. It was nice to see you again."

The man took her hand into his, then brushed his lips softly over her knuckles. She couldn't stop the shiver running down her spine.

"Carpe diem, Trinity."

"W-what?"

"It's Latin. It means seize the day. We all have one life, Trinity. Just one chance to make it count. It's alright to be selfish. It's alright to take what you deserve. It's also alright to leave behind whatever it is that's stopping you from your happiness."

"Not everyone has that luxury," she swallowed, her eyes darting between his.

"Perhaps not, but you do. Remember that, Trinity."

Kissing her hand once more, he left her standing by herself. Just in time too. Trinity blinked, dumbfounded by the strange meeting she had with the beautiful man.

"What the hell are you doing?"

David. She should have known. She must look strange standing by herself in the dark hallway staring into space. He's going to accuse her of being on crack.

"Well? Answer me?" he grabbed her arm in a tight hold and yanked it back.

"I...I thought I lost my contact lense, but it's in my eye. I'm sorry."

"Oh. Well, come on. We gotta dance one dance and then we'll leave."

Dance? Since when does he dance? He never dances. Great. She's not a dancer. Might as well get it over with.

A slower tempo song came on much to Trinity's relief. She didn't want to have to dance fast. On the other hand, she didn't want to be in David's arms. Maybe if she imagined it was the beautiful man, it would make it more bearable.

David's arm snaked around her waist and pulled her body flush against his. The smell of beer was heavy on his breath and sweat. Hopefully, he would pass out when they got home.

The rest of their group was on the dance floor. No wonder he wanted to dance. Why was he such a try hard? Why couldn't he just be himself? Maybe he wouldn't be so mean if he were confident. There would be no finding out that answer. He wasn't ever going to change.

Unexpectedly, David decided to dip her. Her body bent backwards over his arm painfully causing her to wince and flinch when his mouth came between her breasts to lick her cleavage.

Hoots and hollers came from their group. Closing her eyes, she prayed for the song to end. Prayed for David to remove his mouth from the valley of skin between her breasts. Prayed for him to remove his hands from around her waist. Why was he doing this?

When the song finally ended, he dragged her from the dance floor and said his goodbyes before exiting the club. Finally. She couldn't wait to get home. Couldn't wait to take off the skimpy dress and shoes. Couldn't wait to take a shower to feel clean again. Couldn't wait to go to sleep.

Hopefully, she wouldn't wake up.

Chapter 3

- -

Trinity woke up. Of course she did. Why would she think that anything like sudden death while sleeping would ever happen to her? She wasn't old, ate pretty healthy, kept her body up and didn't have any underlying health conditions. Of course she wasn't going to drop dead. Life wasn't nice to her like that.

Instead, she was wide awake. At least she woke up before the alarm. Getting up before David was always a good thing. She could get ready without any interruption and have his coffee made by the time he came down the stairs.

Maybe she would make some scrambled eggs this morning with toast and bacon. That should put him in a good mood. She made quick work of her shower and hair so that she may get to the task at hand. But, first, her face needed attention. Because it was still very tender, she settled with using some more aloe gel, then mascara and lipgloss to finish.

Into the kitchen, Trinity was happy to see the sunshine flooding in through the windows. The brightness always made things seem happier. Seem being the keyword. With the Keurig warming up, she whisked eggs, poured them into a hot pan, and popped bread into the toaster. Then, she lined a baking sheet with foil and thick bacon for the oven. The savory aromas would wake him.

A few minutes later, he sauntered into the kitchen. He was nearly dressed in his uniform finishing the buttons. Maybe if she helped him, he would be kinder today.

"Good morning," she smiled. "May I help you with those buttons. My fingers are much smaller than yours."

"Yeah. Thanks." He kissed her forehead while she buttoned the last few on his shirt. "You were great last night."

Trinity's eyes flicked up to his. "Thank you," she whispered. "Your breakfast is ready. Let me get it for you." She served his plate, then hers before sitting down. "I enjoyed dancing with you," she lied.

"Did ya now? What part did you like the best?" he grinned shoveling food into his mouth.

"That's easy. Your kiss." Why did she even say that? Was she stupid?

"Horny again? Don't got time to fuck ya now, babe. Tonight." David wiped his mouth, then tossed his napkin down.

Trinity gained her feet and cleared his plate, then walked him to the front door, "Have a nice day, David."

"I will. Oh, one more thing. I almost forgot," he pulled her to him. "I want tacos tonight. That's one. And number two, bills are tight. I need you to look for a job."

"A job?"

"Yeah. And not in retail or anything like that. Find a secretary job. You know, in an office. They pay more. Okay?"

Trinity nodded.

"Good girl. Gotta go. You're making me late."

The front door banged shut. It was a heavy door with a lever style door knob. One would think that a cop wouldn't have a lever style. It would be so easy to break and gain entrance. At least to her it seemed that way. Why not just a regular door knob? Trinity rubbed her temples.

He wanted her to find a job. How? She didn't have any skills. David told her to skip college to become a housewife with the hopes of later becoming a stay-at-home mom. He was supposed to take care of the bills.

There was no way a company was going to hire an inexperienced person for secretarial purposes. The most she could probably become with her lack of experience was a receptionist. But some receptionist jobs required computer work. Hopefully, she could find one where the computer stuff was light. Maybe Becky would know.

Sitting at the kitchen table, she dialed her best friend's number and asked her to come over. Since Becky was already out and about this morning, she would be there soon. Quickly, Trinity cleaned up the kitchen. It was seconds later the doorbell rang.

"Hey, girlfriend. What's news?" Becky plopped her bag down.

"I have to find a job."

"A job? Why? I thought he told you to be a housewife. Excuse me, domestic engineer," Becky gagged.

"Yeah, well, he said money's tight now. I'm supposed to find an office job."

"What a goofball," she laughed with a roll of her eyes.

Trinity frowned. What was so funny? And goofball? Was she serious? David was a fucking monster. Becky knew that. She'd seen it firsthand.

"You haven't been to school. You don't even know anything," Becky accused.

"That's why I called you. I was hoping you knew someone that would take on an inexperienced person?" Trinity clasped her hands and smiled with hope.

"Nope. We need the computer."

Dropping her hands, she pressed her head down onto the table. "He disconnects the internet during the day," she groaned.

"You can still type and print your resume without the internet, at least," Becky pointed out. "And what about your phone?"

"Oh yeah. Duh," Trinity chuckled. "Wait. I can't use data."

"We'll use mine then," she sighed.

An hour and two cups of coffee later, Trinity had her resume completed and a very short list of places to try. Two dental offices, one veterinary clinic and one office she hadn't heard of. Becky said it was some sort of transportation company.

This was impossible. Her resume had McDonald's and a cafe listed. She should really be applying for a food service job. No person in their right mind was going to hire her for an office position. Crap.

"Let's go. You won't know until you try. I'll be with you every step of the way."

"You can't go in with me, Becky. People will think there's something wrong with me."

"Well, that's how you'll weed out the assholes. The right company for you will be the one who doesn't make anything out of your bestie standing right by your side," she argued.

Really? Was that right? "Fine. Let's go."

"Wait. You're not wearing that are you?"

"What's wrong with what I have on?"

"You're wearing jeans, Trin. You gotta look like an office bitch. You need a dress. Something light in color and cheery."

"Light and cheery. Hmm. My pink with white polka dot dress?"

"That'll look gorgeous on you. Yes! Oh, curl your hair quick too."

Once finished, Trinity descended the stairs to Becky's cat calls. It was the first time in a while, she genuinely laughed. She did have to admit she felt pretty. A gift from her mother-in-law, the dress was a knee-length, flare style with short sleeves and a zip-up back and tie waist. Trinity finished off the look with black flats and a wristlet.

"Perfect."

"Are you sure women dress like this in an office setting?" Trinity held the skirt out at her sides feeling a bit doubtful.

"Mhm. Come on. You'll see. Let's hit up the dentist offices first."

"I doubt the people at the dentist and vet clinic dress like this though."

"Probably not. I usually see them in scrubs when I bring Floofy in."

"That name still gets me," Trinity laughed.

"Hey! Don't be making fun of my little floof, floof. She's my baby."

"Your cat doesn't even like being held."

"That's okay. I'm allergic anyway."

"How do you even manage your allergies with her?"

"It's a tough life, Trin. I do what I gotta do. Is that the place?" Becky squinted, then pulled into the lot.

"Yeah."

"Grab your resume. Let's do this thing."

Trinity dropped her resume off at both dental offices, the veterinary clinic and a hospital urgent care clinic they spotted. None of the women at the offices were dressed as fancy as she was. It seemed Becky didn't exactly know everything. Even so, most of the people behind the counters nodded their hellos and took her single sheet of paper. They were probably going to shred it the moment she walked out the door.

"The transportation company is the last one, girl."

"Yeah. I'm not too sure about it. I mean, David will kill me if I work in a office with truckers."

"Well, he needs you to make money doesn't he? Let's scope it out. We've got nothing else to do."

"Speak for yourself. I have to go to the store to get taco meat."

"You should try to poison his ass. It would solve all of your problems," Becky slid Trinity a glance pulling back onto the road.

"I'll go to jail, Becky."

"Doubt it. You think his friends really like him? Because if you tell me they do, I'll find it hard to believe. It would be so easy to off him. I bet no one would complain."

"His co-workers seemed to like him. I can't take the risk. As much as I hate my situation, I don't think I could make it in jail."

Becky scrunched her nose and nodded as she looked for the address of the transportation company, stopping in front of a high rise building.

"Looks like we're here."

"Here? How? This isn't a trucking company."

"I know. How weird is that? What did the ad say again?" Becky shoved a piece of gum into her mouth.

"Receptionist wanted? I don't remember."

"Well...let's go inside and see. Nothing to lose, remember?"

"Yeah right."

When Trinity and Becky walked into the building, they gasped. The inside was beautifully decorated in black and white marble, from floor to ceiling, sleek metal light fixtures hugged the walls and a large metal sculpture hung from above. The company name was fixed to the wall behind a simple black desk. The place reeked money. This was a trucking company? How?

Trinity took in the glass elevator she had missed along with the bustle of people. A young girl sat behind the big desk, curiously watching them. Trinity nudged Becky. They better go up to her before she calls security. As they approached, her smile grew wide.

"Good morning. Welcome to Venturi Transport. How may I help you?"

"Um...I saw your ad for a receptionist. I would like to apply and drop off my resume."

"Wonderful. Let me just get you an application." The receptionist leaned over to grab a piece of paper, then came out from behind her desk. She was sharply dressed in a black pencil skirt, light blue turtleneck and black heels. Her hair was in a sleek ponytail.

Trinity looked down at herself. Despite how pretty she felt earlier, now she just felt like a big cupcake compared to this young woman. Becky's advice wasn't so good. Maybe she should have worn something less...pink?

"What's your name? We'll head to one of the small conference rooms so you can have some quiet filling out the form. Oh," the woman looked back at Becky. "Isn't your friend coming? She can come too, you know."

"Trinity Fallon and she, I mean Becky, can?" Trinity raised her eyebrows surprised.

"Oh sure. The more the merrier! I'm Eugenia. Nice to meet you two."

Huh. What Becky said was kinda true. All the other places seemed to look at her a bit strange with Becky in tow. Not this woman. She seemed pretty cheerful. Maybe it was a good sign. She didn't seem uptight or snobby despite her luxurious surroundings.

The conference room was just as ritzy as the entrance with a heavy cherry-wood table and cushioned leather seats. Anyone could comfortably sleep in one of those bad boys, Trinity mused. Who knew a trucking company could be so beautiful.

"Have a seat. Would you like anything to drink?"

"Um, no thank you."

"How about you?"

"No thanks," Becky smiled, popping her gum.

"Alrighty. Any questions?"

"Um...if I were to get this job, where would my desk be? It wouldn't be with the truckers would it?"

Eugenia hesitated at the door, then turned wide-eyed. She stood for a moment before busting out with a belly laugh.

"I'm sorry. I'm so sorry. I don't mean to laugh. Oh my God, if he heard you," she bent over a little while continuing to laugh.

Becky exchanged a perplexed look with Trinity before rolling her eyes, "What is so funny?"

"Girls, this is not a trucking company. Trinity, after you fill out the application, Google our company and read up a little before you get interviewed. I'm going to pretend you didn't come in yet. No one has to know you're here. That way, when you get interviewed, because you will, you'll be better prepared. I like you Trinity Fallon. I think today's going to be your lucky day," she said with a wink and left, but poked her head back inside the doorway. "By the way, we're an import export company."

Trinity smacked herself on the head. How stupid could she be? She shouldn't have assumed the company was a trucking company just because the word transportation was in the name. Jeeze, she would have looked like a complete moron to whomever was going to interview her. Thank goodness for Eugenia.

"They must be looking to fill the position pretty quick if you're gonna have an interview on the spot like that. That's kinda weird for a place as big as this one, don't ya think?"

"Yeah, I guess? Maybe we should go."

"What?! No way. That chick is helping you out. Who cares if it's weird or sketchy. You want to help David out right? And if helping David helps you, I wouldn't leave. Besides, she's dressed good and seems to be happy. You could be like her. Hell, so could I. I should get an application too."

"I thought you liked your internship."

"I love it, but sometimes trying to think of articles to write is tiring."

Becky was the same age as Trinity. They met freshman year in high school and were friends ever since. Through friends, Becky had met David first and introduced Trinity to him after he asked about her. But, Becky seemed to be the one who lucked out with a great internship with a popular magazine agency that was set up for her through her college.

"I'm going to read about this company while you fill out that manuscript."

It looked like Eugenia had grabbed one piece of paper, but looks were deceiving. It was more like a five page packet. This was going to take forever.

Thirty minutes later, the packet was finally complete. It had the normal stuff like name, address, phone number, date of birth, social security number, previous and current employment and references. But it also had essay questions on how one felt about work ethics, life goals and how to handle certain situations. It was weird in a way, but at the same time not?

"Huh. This place has been in business a really long time. It was passed down through the generations. And, yes, it's an import export company as Eugenia said. Looks like it's still privately owned. It makes a shit ton of money every year."

"What does it export and import?" Trinity asked.

"I...don't know yet. Lemme keep reading. Ugh. This is really confusing. All I've been able to gather is that they have something to do with export and import. Sorry. I fail."

"No, no. Thanks for looking. I'll just be myself and go from there. Nothing to lose."

"Knock, knock. Hi guys. Did you get the packet filled out?"

"I did," Trinity smiled.

"Awesome. And did you look up the company's website?"

"Yes. It's a little confusing, but at least I know you're not a trucking company."

"Right," Eugenia laughed. "Well, the hiring manager just left on an emergency."

Trinity frowned, but stood up. "Oh. That's okay. If they're interested, they can always call me and I can come back."

"Oh, no. Sorry. I didn't mean to give you the wrong idea. I only meant, you're in luck. The owner of the company is here and when he heard his manager left, he said he would do the interview himself. He never usually does them. That's why you're lucky," she explained brightly.

"Are you sure?" Becky laughed. "Sounds like she should run for the hills."

"Oh, heck no." Eugenia looked around before coming into the room fully and closed the door. "You two definitely don't want to leave. If there are cameras in here I'm so getting into trouble for saying this, but you don't want to leave. The owner is super fine. Like, the sexiest man alive fine. Even if you don't get the job, at least you'll get to sit with him for a little while."

"Jeeze. How hot is he?" Becky asked.

"Like beyond a ten. Every chick here tries to bag him. He's like the world's most eligible bachelor. No offense, but do you two live under a rock?"

"No offense, but you're talking to us pretty familiar. What gives?" Becky braced her hands on her hips irritated.

Eugenia blinked twice before laughing, "Trinity, you seem to have a good friend here. I see why you brought her. Way to hustle, Becky."

Trinity looked between Eugenia and Becky. Eugenia seemed to be a very happy-go-lucky woman who was giving her a break. So why was Becky being so snarky? Trinity felt a ball forming in her stomach from the sudden tense air.

"Well, come on," Eugenia waved her hand ignoring Becky.

"Wait. I'm not being interviewed in here?"

"Nope. And, Becky, this is the end of the line for you. You'll have to slum it with me out front," she grinned.

"Slum it? For real?"

"Come on, Miss Fallon. We'll just stop at my desk up front, and I'll show you the map to his office. There'll be a small waiting room where you'll sit down, and he'll come out to greet you."

"Mrs. Fallon," Trinity corrected.

"Mrs. Fallon? How old are you?"

"Twenty."

"Girl. Please don't tell me you got married because you got knocked up."

"Inappropriate much?" Becky rolled her eyes.

Trinity's eyes widened at Becky. It was obvious Eugenia was being overly friendly. For what reason she didn't know. But she had no reason not to give Eugenia the benefit of the doubt. Eugenia was probably a very friendly woman who seemed to like her while Becky, her best friend, was being a bitch. And for what? Eugenia was likeable, funny and helpful. She needed someone like Eugenia on her side. She would definitely ask Becky about it later. In the meantime, she needed to get her head in the game.

Eugenia cringed, "Sorry. I put my foot in my mouth a lot."

Trinity smiled, "I just fell in love, I suppose."

"Pff. Trust me, she's not in love anymore."

"Becky!"

"What? It's true. Why keep it a secret?"

"Ugh!" Trinity rolled her eyes fed up.

"Why don't you just divorce him?" Eugenia suggested.

"It's complicated."

"Ah. I hear ya."

Thankfully, Eugenia caught the hint and changed the subject by pointing out the office Trinity needed to go to on a building map. With a wink, she sent her on her way.

Trinity was alone now. This was weird. Could it really be that someone could like her off the bat like that? So much so she was being interviewed on the same day as applying? Did stuff like this happen? She had little experience to compare it to. Well, except McDonald's. She did have a same day interview there, but that didn't count. It was McDonald's. They hired just about any teenager.

Another thing that kept playing on her mind was Becky's attitude. Was Becky being defensive because getting interviewed on the same day was suspicious? Maybe Becky was just being protective. Had to be.

Several hallways and a few turns later, Trinity found the elevator. All of the buttons were in order except for the one she had to press which was larger and labeled Forty Private. Why would it be labeled that rather than just the number like all the other floors?

When the elevator door opened, it opened to opulence. At least it seemed to be opulent with the same marble-covered floors as the entrance, and pretty wall sconces much fancier than the silver ones on the first floor. Several six-paneled doors lined the long hall set off by tall pillars between each one. Offices must lay behind all those doors. Offices with beautiful, scary views of the city. Despite her fear of heights, Trinity knew it must look gorgeous at night with all of the glowing lights from the bustle down below.

May as well enjoy the surroundings for as long as it'll last which would be as long as an interview. So about twenty minutes give or take? Twenty more minutes of being in an environment of normality. A place where people did their day and looked forward to going home. Unlike herself.

Looking down the hall, a set of double doors stared imposingly back at her. A large phoenix appeared to be carved into the wood, a wing spanning each door. Intimidating much?

Stopping short, Trinity gulped. This was it. She should probably knock. Raising a shaking hand to the door...

"Miss? Excuse me. Miss?"

Trinity dropped her hand, craning her neck to the side to see an older woman quickly approaching with a severe expression on her face. She definitely wasn't happy. Maybe it was because of her starchy, white blouse buttoned near to her chin with a snug blazer and skirt tight enough to give a sausage a run for its money. The woman needed oxygen. Still, she was kind of scary.

"I...I was just," Trinity pointed at the door.

"Oh. No, no, no. We don't ever knock on Mr. Venturi's door. No. No, we don't," she waved her finger with a disapproving shake of her head.

"I'm sorry. I was told to."

The woman's eyes bugged, "Told to? By whom? What's your business here, young lady?"

What was going on? Hadn't Eugenia said she was to interview with the owner? This was so confusing.

"Interview," Tess handed over the piece of paper Eugenia gave to her that was similar to a hall pass.

The woman's lips moved as she read it. Trinity couldn't help zeroing in on the fine details of her face. While her expression was pinched severe at the moment, she could easily see she was attractive. It was probably safe to say she was beautiful in her youth. Her hair was let go to allow for streaks of silvery white intertwined with the once black, and her eyes were a pretty shade of blue.

"I'm sorry, but I don't know why you would be given this when I'm here. You'll be interviewing with me. Come."

Oh boy. There was no way she was going to name Eugenia. She would hate to see her get into trouble. Hopefully, the older woman wouldn't ask. What was her name?

"E-excuse me."

The woman stopped abrupt causing Trinity to hop back a little lest she run into her.

"Yes?"

"M-m-my name is Trinity Fallon." Why did she have to pick a time like this to start stuttering? She never stuttered unless very nervous. Needless to say...she was very nervous.

"Oh! Excuse my poor manners. My name is Melanie Jewell. Ms. Jewell to you of course. A pleasure to meet you," she said and held out her hand.

Trinity took Ms. Jewell's hand and gave a smile she knew didn't reach her eyes. This woman was strange. "Nice to meet you."

"Come along. My office is just here. I'm Mr. Venturi's personal assistant in case you haven't guessed that already."

She hadn't. In fact, she thought Ms. Jewell was a manager of some sort. Well, knowledge is power supposedly.

The door clicked open and Ms. Jewell waved Trinity to a seat. As guessed, this office was beautifully decorated. Hues of blue and cream, leather and wood, made the room a dream.

Gingerly, Trinity sat down onto one of the chairs while Ms. Jewell took her place behind her big oak desk. All of the offices probably had big desks and leather chairs like the ones here. Gently, Trinity ran her hand over the soft leather cushion. It's cool surface soothing to her nerves.

"So, according to the document here, you've applied for the receptionist position. Is this correct?"

"Yes."

"One moment. Let me login to my account. Your resume should be up-loaded by now for me to take a look at."

Maybe the interview would be less than twenty minutes. Trinity wanted to groan in embarrassment. She was a waitress not a receptionist. How was she supposed to explain her husband insisted she apply for an office job and if she defied him, he would beat her for it?

"Your work experience is very limited. Mrs. Fallon? You're very young to be married."

What was up with the personal questions today? It was one thing coming from Eugenia, but coming from Ms. Jewell felt like quite another. Trinity was pretty sure the question and statement weren't ethical.

"Um...yes, I'm married."

"I see. Do you have children?"

She shouldn't answer the woman. Her questions had nothing to do with the job being offered. Yet, looking at Ms. Jewell's expectant eyes, it was hard to resist.

"No."

Her brow wrinkled at the answer. Why did she look surprised? Why does everyone assume children are involved when someone gets married young?

"Pardon my intrusive questions, but I'm having a difficult time under-standing why a high school waitress is not a college student but rather married."

Seriously?

"I w-w-would prefer not t-t-to answer if it's not going to be used against me, Ms. Jewell."

"Used against you? This isn't a court of law, child. I'm simply asking."

"Oh. Well, I chose to join the workforce rather than school. I would like to move from the food industry and into a more p-p-professional setting. I decided to apply because r-r-receptionist positions don't require s-s-schooling," Trinity swallowed hard against her dry throat. "Perhaps if I get my feet wet in reception, I can then d-d-decide if I enjoy an office setting and then spend my money on schooling to f-f-further my career goals. B-b-but, for now, my goal is to move away from blue collar toward white collar."

Ms. Jewell eyed her with interest. It was as if she could sense Trinity had more to say. "Go on."

"Not everyone is born into fortunate situations. When g-g-given a chance to flee from the unfortunate and rise t-t-toward fortune, of course not always financial, one sh-sh-should carpe diem," she said remembering the beautiful man's words at the club.

Ms. Jewell's brow wrinkled yet again. "Carpe...diem?"

"Yes. Seize the day. A beautiful man in a grocery store once told me those words. It resonated w-w-with me."

"Did you marry this beautiful man?" Ms. Jewell asked with a wistful smile.

So that was it. Ms. Jewell was a romantic. Had to be for her to ask the type of questions she did. How disappointed she would be to learn her true story. "No. Unfortunately, I met him after I was married. In fact, I met the man in the grocery store just the other day."

"You met him under unfortunate circumstances?"

"I did. However unfortunate, it led me here. I believe here is where I will find fortune."

"Where you will be able to seize the day as your fortune?" Ms. Jewell smiled.

"Yes, very much so," Trinity answered feeling more at ease.

Ms. Jewell bit the end of her pen, leaning back into her chair. Her eyes looked thoughtful as she assessed Trinity's fidgeting form. After a couple of awkward minutes, she tossed her pen down and pushed up from her chair.

"You're very well spoken, Mrs. Fallon. I have a good feeling about you. And, I'm guessing so does Eugenia since she tried to get you directly into Mr. Venturi's office," Ms. Jewell chuckled.

Trinity's eyes widened at the mention of Eugenia's name and the transformation to Ms. Jewell's face when she laughed. She was indeed a pretty woman. But, wait. She had a good feeling? Did that mean there was hope?!

Ms. Jewell waved her hand, "That's neither here nor there, my dear. I'm hiring you. Yes. Yes, I am. This is going to workout wonderfully."

Chapter 4

She scored...a job! She scored a job and it felt amazing. Her hours would be from eight in the morning until three in the afternoon. Perfect for getting home in time to clean and fix dinner.

In two days, her life was going to change. Hopefully, for the better. Hopefully, David would be pleased with her announcement. Today was beyond successful. She couldn't erase her smile if she wanted to.

Trinity stirred the Spanish rice and finished the taco meat. All she needed to do was arrange the rest of the fixings and set everything onto the table. He would be home soon.

Deciding against changing out of the pink dress saved her time to be able to finish a few more items on her chore list and be ready at the door when David came home.

For some reason, her heart was beating a little faster than it normally did. Please be happy. Please be in a good mood. The sound of the car door slamming shut and the jiggle of the door knob seemed louder than normal. David came in not sparing her a glance, swinging the front door shut with a bang. Oh no. He was in a bad mood.

"Welcome home," she smiled wider if that was even possible.

With a grunt, he threw his keys into the dish then unlaced his boots tossing them toward the door.

"I have great news." Trinity followed him into the kitchen.

David sat down at the table not bothering to wash his hands or remove his gun. Why didn't he remove his gun? That wasn't like him. Her throat instantly dry, she tried to swallow against it to no avail.

Quietly, she sat down across from him and arranged her skirts while she waited for him to pile his plate with food. Once he was done, she filled hers. Not too much, not too little.

"I found a job like you asked me to," she said soft.

"Where?"

"An office."

David looked up, his fork mid-way to his mouth. Trinity watched a few grains of rice, perched at the end of his fork tines, fall to the table. His hand looked a little shaky. Was he high again?

"No shit, Sherlock. I fucking asked you where."

"Oh. I-I-I'm s-s-sorry."

David rolled his eyes. "Jesus fucking christ, Trinity. S-s-spit it out."

"V-v-venturi Transportation," she rushed.

"Venturi Transportation," he thought a moment before his eyes widened. "Transportation?" he slammed his fork down. "I fucking told you to get a job in an office. How can you tell me that's an office? Transportation?

How 'bout trucking? I know that company. You're not fooling me. It's a fucking trucking company."

What? No it wasn't. Why couldn't he just look it up? Why was he doing this? Why did he ever do this? Should she tell him it wasn't? Should she show him?

"N-n-no, David. It really is an office. I can show you on my phone," Trinity slid out of her seat.

"Sit the fuck down. The fuck you think you're doing? This is the dinner table. This is dinner time. We're eating dinner. What is wrong with you?!"

Drops of sweat gathered at his temples. His eyes strained wild in no particular direction. Then he did what she expected him to do. What he's done before. With one fell swoop of his arm, he cleared the table of all the hard work she had put into the meal. All of it. Food was scattered everywhere over the floor. It would be her responsibility to clean the mess he just made. Hopefully, he wouldn't overturn the table again.

"I'm sorry," she bowed her head.

"I should shoot you. Yeah. I should kill you right here and now," he laughed short while her head snapped up. "Do you know how easy it would be to get rid of you? Everyone on the department loves me. No one would question a thing. I could say it was an accident. We were sitting here," he gestured over the table, "while I was cleaning my gun and boom. Gun went off. Your brains splattered against the wall there behind you. Horrible, horrible accident," he said shaking his head, his fingers stroking the butt of the gun sticking out from his holster.

"I love you, David," she swallowed, tears welling in her eyes as her body shook.

"No. No, you don't. You hate me. You resent me. That's what this is. You think you're gonna work for some company where there's other men around so you can leave me? I don't think so."

"It really is an office." What did she have to lose? May as well speak her mind if she were going to die anyway.

David's breath was sucking in and out in a heavy way. It looked like he wasn't sure what he was going to do. His hair was plastered against his forehead. Was he okay? The obvious answer was no, but he looked a little stranger than normal. He was never this sweaty or looked as confused as he did right now. Was he on something?

"David? Are...are you alright?"

Her concern caused him to pause. Interesting. Maybe this was a new tactic she could use. Hopefully.

"What do you mean?" he barked. "I'm alright. It's you who's not, remember?"

"You look ill, David. Are you...are you sick?"

Abruptly, David stood throwing his chair across the room. Nope, that angle was not the right one to play. It was worth the try. Maybe. Looking at the broken chair, she wondered if she was going to be expected to fix it. It was beyond repair. One of the legs was splintered into what reminded her of a stake.

A wooden stake. Those were used to kill vampires. If she could get to it, could she use it? Would she be strong enough to run him through? Would it be hard or easy? Was flesh that vulnerable?

When she cut herself with the knife, it didn't feel like anything at the time it happened. It sliced through like butter. Soft and smooth. Would stabbing a chest feel the same? Then what?

Would she be in trouble? She asked this question before and reasoned out that she probably wouldn't under normal circumstances. But this wasn't normal circumstances.

Pacing the small kitchen like a caged animal, he looked more out of his mind than any other time before. For some reason, a strange calm blanketed her earlier panic. Maybe it was the calm before the storm. Maybe it was the realization of defeat. Was she defeated?

It was so quiet. This space. This tiny square of land they stood on could be the last surface she'd ever feel under her feet. The last chair. Her hand gripped the hard edge of the square, and she palmed the smooth surface. It was opposite to the sumptuous leather she had the pleasure of stroking earlier today.

Either way, whether she were defeated or just getting started, she would try to get to the stake. She would try to kill him. Enough was enough.

Slowly, she gained her feet. He didn't seem to notice too busy with pulling at the ends of his hair and mumbling while he paced the kitchen. If he weren't on drugs, then he was definitely having a mental breakdown of some sort.

One step, then another til she reached the broken chair. Kneeling down, making sure to face him, she gripped the leg only to find it still attached to the other legs by a wooden dowel at the base. She wouldn't be using this weapon today. So it was defeat then. David's narrowed eyes finally met hers.

"What're you doing?"

Trinity shook her head. "N-n-nothing."

"What? What the fuck are you doing?"

His approach was faster than what she could register, his hand even more so. His palm connecting and following through with her cheek, caused her neck to whip. Her raw face snapped to the side. Her jaw felt unhinged. Again.

A dull ringing deafened her hearing, but she ignored it testing to see if her jaw was intact. Too distracted by her ministrations, Trinity didn't notice David discover the weapon of choice. She didn't see him tear it from the chair. She didn't see him lunge for her. She only felt. Felt the pull, then burning pop of the rough wood penetrate and grate against the bone in her arm. Instant nausea rolled through while dots of black danced in her vision. All oxygen stole away from her lungs, leaving her gasping in shocked pain.

This pain wasn't like the cut to her palm. This was much worse. It was chaotic and everywhere. Twisting and searing. Tears blurred her vision, but she managed to look down, in disbelief, at the piece of wood sticking out of her arm. David staggered back seemingly surprised by what he had done, yet not jumping to help her.

Would he stab her again? Would he shoot her now? Was this it? Gulping and swallowing air, Trinity brought her arm up til she gripped her opposite shoulder. The wood hung in a painful pull. She couldn't yank it out. What if it started a blood flow she couldn't stop? She needed to call 911 somehow, but she was stuck. Her back was now braced by the wall where she stood unsteady. David was breathing heavy, standing in the middle of the room staring at her.

She had to get out of there. She had to take a chance and will her body to move.

"I'm going to get cleaning supplies, David. The kitchen is a bit messy. I'll be right back," she managed to make her voice smile as if nothing was wrong.

His nod was barely perceptible, but she saw it. His fingers rubbed at the back of his neck, his face confused. He was so strung out, he didn't see the chaos around them. Her next move might get her killed in the future, but it didn't matter. It was a move that needed to be taken.

"nine-one-one, what's your emergency?"

"I need an ambulance and the police. I'm at Fifty Euclid Manor. I've been stabbed," Trinity whispered into the phone while she locked the bathroom door.

"Who stabbed you ma'am?"

"My husband."

"Your name?"

"Trinity Fallon. My husband is D-d-david Fallon," her eyes squeezed. "He works for the city police department."

"Is he still in the house with you?"

"Yes."

"We have paramedics on the way, and the police have been dispatched. Is your front door locked, ma'am?"

"Yes."

"Are you able to unlock it?"

"No. My husband has his gun on him still. I-I-I think he's on drugs."

"Okay, ma'am. Stay on the phone with me until they arrive. Where are you in the house?"

"In the upstairs bathroom. It's connected to the master bedroom. First door on the right."

"Okay. Where were you stabbed, Mrs. Fallon?"

"My right forearm. He stabbed me with a broken piece of our kitchen chair."

"Are you bleeding?"

"Not really. I have my arm up. It's numb," Trinity whispered unable to control the shake to her voice.

"Alright. That's good. Keep it elevated and do not pull the object out of it."

"I won't."

"Do you have a hospital preference?"

"The closest one."

"Okay. They should be there soon, Mrs. Fallon."

"I-I t-t-think I hear the sirens."

"Yes. They should be there any minute now, Mrs. Fallon."

"Do, do they have to announce they're the police? Can't they just ring the doorbell? He'll open the door if they just ring the bell."

"Okay. Hold on for a moment while I update the units. Please don't hang up."

"I'm s-s-so scared."

"Just breathe, Mrs. Fallon. I'm here with you. Can you take a deep breath in?"

"Mhm."

"Okay. That's good. Take a nice deep breath and just stay in the bathroom. There's going to be a bunch of people there in a few seconds that will take care of you."

"Oh my God. The doorbell is ringing," Trinity whimpered.

"Okay, Mrs. Fallon. I'm going to be quiet so you can listen, but I'm going to stay on the phone until the paramedics find you."

"Okay," Trinity whispered.

Trinity placed her ear by the door. The doorbell rang a second time. Why wasn't David answering the door? Wait! She could hear his heavy footsteps, then the door opening. The rumble of deep voices could be heard along with beeps from the police radios.

Then the shouting began. A scuffle had to be happening. David was screaming over the voices of the police officers. It was clear he knew them as first names were being thrown around. What would happen? Would they let him go? Was he going to get away with what he did?

It was quiet then. What did that mean? Trinity's heart started to race as the minutes stretched on and on. One, two, three, four, five. What was happening?

"Mrs. Fallon?"

She had forgotten about the dispatcher on the line.

"Yes?"

"The paramedics are going to be sent upstairs now. You can unlock the bathroom door. I am now going to end the call."

"Okay. Thank you."

"Of course."

Just as the dispatcher said, the paramedics appeared immediately after she hung up the phone. There were two men who had a stretcher. She didn't need that. Did she?

"Mrs. Fallon?"

She nodded.

"Everything is going to be okay, Mrs. Fallon. Let's stabilize your arm and get you downstairs. A police officer is waiting to speak with you as well."

"Do I have to go on the stretcher? I think I can walk down."

"We'll get your arm wrapped and vitals before we make that decision."

Trinity did as told while the paramedics worked on her arm then took her blood pressure, pulse and temperature. Once they were finished, they deemed her fit to walk and allowed her to go downstairs where she was then ushered into the living room and to the couch. One of the paramedics added more protection to her arm for purposes of traveling to the hospital.

"Mrs. Fallon, can we speak with you while the paramedics are working?"

Trinity looked up and bristled. The officer was a man she recognized from the night at the club. He was the one who commented on how she looked. Was he a good friend of David's?

"A-a-are you D-d-david's friend?"

The officer cleared his throat. "Can I ask you some questions?"

"Sure," she whispered. Of course the man was his friend.

"What happened here tonight?"

"We had an argument and...it got out of hand."

Her plan crumbled right before her eyes. Her bravery was for nothing. Her opportunity to have him arrested, gone. The cop standing in front of her was David's friend. Anything she had to say wouldn't be taken seriously. David wasn't going to be arrested for this. And, if he was, he definitely would kill her once he was released.

He would kill her for embarrassing him in front of his friends. This was going to backfire on her. She needed to fix this.

"So, tell me how this happened? David did this?"

"Oh, not on purpose. I-I-I know I told the nine-one-one operator my husband stabbed me, but that's not how I meant it. See, we were arguing and it kind of morphed into a food fight as you probably saw. I slipped on the food and landed on the chair he had tossed aside and the leg went through my arm. I'm sorry if it sounded like an attack. It w-w-wasn't." There. That should be a good enough excuse. It didn't need to make sense.

"So you don't want to press charges?"

"Of course not," she smiled.

"He's been placed in our squad car, Mrs. Fallon. Do you want to speak with him?"

No. She didn't, but would have to. She had to let him see she was protecting him. That she wasn't having him arrested. But what if he asked how the paramedics arrived? Maybe he was too out of it to realize she had.

"Yes, please."

When the officer left, one of the paramedics placed his hand gently onto her shoulder. "Ma'am, are you sure you don't want to press charges?"

Trinity nodded her head without saying a word and the paramedic shook his. She knew he didn't understand. No one did, and no one ever would.

David came through the door looking a bit more composed than he had earlier. It was as if he instantly sobered. His eyes were focused and trained on first her arm and then on her. He knew she had called. There would be no getting out of this. This was a mistake. She should have pressed charges. Why was she always making wrong decisions?

"Trinity! Thank God you're alright. See, guys, my wife is strong. She was able to call the paramedics even before I could," he laughed.

The police officers laughed along with him. They were on his side as predicted. How was she going to get through the night if the hospital released her back home? Maybe there was a way to stay overnight. Maybe.

"There's no need to transport her. No need to incur a bill when I can just take her myself."

"We're already here and the cost has been incurred, plus she'll be much more comfortable."

David's challenging glare didn't deter the paramedic who knew better. Trinity thanked God for the small favor. There was no way she wanted to ride with David. Especially with him being high right now, no matter the fact his high was wearing off.

"Fine. I'll meet you there," he grated.

Once loaded into the ambulance and on the road, she could see David's headlights shining behind through the tinted glass. Luckily, he couldn't see her.

It was a queer feeling riding in the ambulance as she was facing backwards and looking out the back windows. It felt like she was on an amusement ride. She wasn't partial to amusement rides and closed her eyes, resting her head against the gurney. It was hard to believe she wouldn't have been more comfortable in David's truck now that she was being transported.

She felt every bump radiate to her numb arm. Guess it wasn't as numb as she thought it to be.

This would be the second time to the emergency department in less than a week. Hopefully, the same doctor wouldn't be working. How would she explain a wooden stake sticking out of her arm? And would he recognize the redness of her face as burns? Would he be obligated to press charges on her behalf? The last time the doctor mentioned he could. Crap. She wished she knew the law.

After she was triaged, the nurse ushered her into a room which was a miracle. A miracle, because this was the second time where she didn't have to wait in the waiting room.

David joined her shortly afterwards and sat down on one of the hard plastic chairs provided for visitors. He kept silent while the nurse started Trinity's iv line and took blood. What was the blood sample for, Trinity wondered.

Once alone, Trinity couldn't help but glance up at David. He was staring straight at her. She felt like they were in a staring contest. First to blink was the loser. Her eyes were drying out.

"So I stabbed you, huh?"

Trinity shook her head. Even though it wasn't, it felt like a betrayal. Why did the operator have to tell on her? The operator was just doing their job, she knew. But, still, why? When was this nightmare going to end?

"My boys are liars? Is that what you're telling me?"

"I t-t-told them you didn't."

"Good evening, Mrs. Fallon."

Trinity wanted to groan when Dr. Logan entered the small room, but David did it for her.

"Get someone else. My wife doesn't need to be treated by you," he snapped.

"Well, sir, I hate to disappoint, but I'm the only attending physician tonight. There's no other choice unless you go to a different hospital. Judging by the looks of this nasty wound, treatment shouldn't be delayed. Mrs. Fallon, do you mind if I take a look?"

Trinity shook her head. Dr. Logan approached, ignoring David's mumbling. His fingers were cool to the touch as he gently inspected her wound the best he could with the wood hanging from it.

"I don't want to yank it out without a scan to ensure your basilic or cephalic veins weren't punctured or severed."

"Basilic or cephalic veins?" Trinity asked.

"They're the larger veins in your arm. I'll type in the order and transport will come to get you. In the meantime, what's your pain scale?"

"I feel kinda numb right now."

"Alright. Let me know if you need anything before surgery."

"Surgery?" Trinity and David both chimed.

"Yes. If nothing was damaged, it will be a simple outpatient procedure to remove the wood. If, on the other hand, the x-ray shows concern, it will be a much more involved process. Either way, it most likely will need to be removed surgically." The doctor turned back to Trinity. "Now, what happened to your face?" He tilted her chin up while pulling the overhead light down. "It almost looks like you sustained second degree burns in some areas and first in others. What happened?" he demanded.

Trinity remained silent. Why was she so surprised he noticed? Her face looked a mess. It would be a miracle if the painful makeup she had worn out to the club and on her job hunt wouldn't cause an infection.

"Are you wearing makeup to cover this?!"

Trinity nodded.

The doctor sighed frustrated. "I'll have my nurse come in to take care of your face. I'm going to prescribe antibiotics. I can tell you blistered in a few areas. I don't want an infection to settle. Actually...," he tapped his lip, "I'm going to have an iv dose of antibiotics hung while you're here and then send you home with a prescription for oral pills. I'll be back after the scan."

It was nearly two hours later before Dr. Logan returned with good news. Then another two hours waiting for transport to take her to surgery. Then another three hours from the time she was in the operating room, til the time she came to from the twilight sedative she was given.

Finally, after nine hours at the emergency department and travel, she was home. The kitchen was still in shambles, and she knew she would have to clean it regardless of her injuries. Thank goodness she didn't start her new job tomorrow. That would have been impossible.

Trudging up the stairs, Trinity was surprised David didn't yell at her. He hadn't said a word all the way home in fact. Maybe he would kill her in her sleep and end her suffering. One could always hope.

Not bothering to change, she laid down. Her eyes drifted shut. Maybe David would think she was asleep by the time he came into the room.

"Trinity, you can't sleep in your clothes. You need to put on pajamas."

Why? Why did he hate her so much? What had she ever done to him?

"Let me help you. Get up."

"Why do you hate me?" It must be the drugs talking. She cringed the moment the question left her lips.

"Hate you? I don't hate you, Trinity. I love you. Come on now. Get up."

He was surprisingly gentle as he undressed her being mindful of her arm. Once he was finished, he even twisted her hair into a bun so that it wouldn't get into her way while she slept.

"I'm going to sleep in the guest bedroom so that I don't bump into your arm or wake you in the morning."

"Wake me? What about your breakfast and lunch? I have to make them for you. I also have to clean the kitchen."

"No. I'm going to take care of all of that now. Tomorrow, you need to rest. I expect you to stay in bed all day. I will pick up your prescription and bring home a pizza for dinner. Sleep now." David bent over and kissed Trinity's head.

"Thank you, David. I love you."

"Love you too."

David flicked the light switch off and closed the door softly behind him leaving her in the dark, alone. Blissfully alone. Finally.

Savoring the dark coolness of the room, Trinity's mind couldn't help but wonder over David's words. She had been granted a day off. She never had a day off before. She worked all seven days out of the week, year round, cooking and cleaning just for him.

What did it mean? What would happen once she were fully healed? Was that when he was going to kill her? Maybe worse. Maybe he would torture her instead.

Closing her eyes, she tried to put it out of her mind the best she could and stay in the moment. In the moment where cool, dark and calm existed. She needed to savor them. Savor them as if they were a comet flying through space to be admired for only a short time before it flew out of sight or shattered into a million pieces.

Funny how she felt like a comet. Only question was, would she get away or crumble into oblivion?

Chapter 5

Today was the big day. A nervous energy coursed through Trinity. While there was a modicum of sadness that yesterday, her day off, was over with, it was easily swept away with the happiness for something new.

Answering the phone was part of her new job. She wondered what the other tasks might be. It would be hard to work with only one arm, but it was doable. Trinity had managed to make breakfast and lunch for David, waking extra early to stay on schedule. Her day off afforded her enough rest to be able to rise at four and do all of the morning chores without feeling too drained. Plus, her pain medication helped. All in all, the day could be labeled so far so good. It was the impending night that had her bothered.

Pushing the worry far into the recess of her mind, she tilted her head at her reflection in the mirror. Did she look professional enough? Hopefully, David wouldn't think she was trying to attract attention.

Her navy dress seemed appropriate. The fit and flare cut showed capped sleeves with a modest square neckline and hem below the knee. It was perfect with black ballet flats. She kept her wavy hair loose. It was too hard to style with one arm, and she doubted David would help her. To finish off her demure look, she curled and swept mascara over her lashes and glazed her lips with a clear lip gloss. She also decided to add foundation despite the doctor's order. She was on antibiotics, so any chance of infection was now lower. Right? Didn't matter. She couldn't show up to her first day looking like a zombie. Satisfied with her face, she headed back to the kitchen.

Today would be her first work day outside of a restaurant. Hopefully, she wouldn't stutter answering the phone. She practiced in the mirror a bunch of times yesterday and didn't stutter once. For some reason, she didn't feel too nervous about it.

Becky had texted her with good luck wishes this morning. Trinity didn't have the heart to tell her best friend what happened. She didn't want to hear what Becky had to say about it. She already knew.

"First day, huh?"

David startled her out of her head, and she immediately filled his plate with food setting it down onto the table.

"Mhm."

"Are you excited to be working in an office?"

Why was he being so nice? "I am. I think it was a wonderful idea of yours to suggest I apply. I'm anxious to contribute."

"My ideas are always wonderful, babe. By the way, I want lasagna tonight. I gotta go. Be good." He kissed her on the head before leaving her alone.

Trinity looked at his plate. He hadn't touched it. He made her cook his breakfast, and didn't eat it. What was more, he hadn't taken his lunch either. He also wanted lasagna for dinner. How was she supposed to fill the pot up with water and haul it to the stove to make the noodles? Even if she found the kind of noodles you didn't have to pre-cook, how was she supposed to get a heavy pan filled with food into the oven? Guess she'd have to put the pan on the oven rack first and then put the recipe together.

Tears started to well, but she blinked them away. She had to leave if she were going to be on time. Grabbing her keys, she left the house with her mind on her schedule. After work, she would need to go to the store and get right home to clean the kitchen up. She could clean while the lasagna was in the oven...somehow.

Needless to say, today would need to be planned perfectly. Work ended at three in the afternoon. Once three hit, she would jet to the store. If traffic was nice to her, it would take ten minutes to get there. So, arrival time would be quarter after three since she would have to account for time to punch out and walk to her car. Once in the store, she would allow ten minutes to shop. That would put her at twenty-five after. From the store to home would be another ten minutes give or take. No matter what, her arrival home couldn't be later than quarter to four.

From that point, she would immediately start her oven to preheat and allow fifteen minutes of prep time for the lasagna provided she found the noodles she didn't have to boil first. Fingers crossed. Once the lasagna was put together, it would be about four o'clock. The lasagna would only take about thirty minutes to bake. During the thirty minutes, she would clean the kitchen. It would be half past four when the lasagna finished baking. At that point, she would have an additional thirty minutes to vacuum, set the table and freshen up before David arrived home, or make up for lost time if anything went wrong with her plans.

This would all work out. Things would be okay. David would have no reason to hurt her tonight. She wouldn't given him a reason. If he didn't want to eat her food out of spite or as a form of punishment, so be it. It was better than sustaining physical harm to her body.

Lost in thought, Trinity arrived at work faster than she anticipated. The lights must have been in her favor, or she just teleported. Either way, she didn't remember the ride which was a dangerous thing. Distraction caused accidents. If she ended up in the emergency department one more time, she was pretty sure Dr. Logan was going to lose his shit. He looked just about ready to kill David when he saw her arm and face.

"Morning, Trinity! Woah! What happened to your arm?!"

"Good morning, Eugenia. It was a freak accident. But I'm fine," Trinity reassured with a weak smile.

"I'm so glad you're okay! Ready to get started? You'll be taking over my position once I train you. I'm movin' on up, girlfriend!" Eugenia snapped her fingers.

"That's great. What position will you be filling?"

"I'm going to be an assistant to one of the managers. I'm super hyped," she giggled.

"That's awesome."

Eugenia beamed from behind her desk. She started to wave Trinity closer to her but was distracted, plastering on a megawatt smile. Trinity frowned following Eugenia's glowing eyes. She couldn't quite believe her own when she found the source of Eugenia's delight. What was the beautiful man doing here? Was he a customer? Did he work here? What the heck?!

The man smiled pleasantly and nodded, "Good morning, Eugenia."

"Morning!" she chirped.

Trinity watched, fascinated, their exchange. The beautiful man's eyes widened a fraction when he saw her, before they returned to normal.

"Mrs. Fallon," his voice rose. "What a nice surprise. What brings you here?"

"Mr....,"

The beautiful man held up his hand to silence Eugenia.

"I...I work here now," Trinity looked to her feet.

"You work here?" he asked surprised.

"Duh. Didn't you just interview her two days ago?"

"Hush, Eugenia," the beautiful man said softly, waving at the receptionist annoyed.

"Ms. Jewell interviewed me."

"Ms. Jewell? Funny, I never saw an email," he said more so to himself. "For what position, Mrs. Fallon?"

"My position," Eugenia dared to interrupt again.

The beautiful man darted Eugenia a look before he promptly ignored her. "Follow me, Mrs. Fallon."

"Is...is there a problem? Ms. Jewell said she was going to tell the owner she hired me despite my experience."

"There's no problem. I simply have a few questions to ask you."

The beautiful man showed her into the conference room where she had filled out the application. Was he going to fire her before she even started? Did he even have the power to fire her? What was his position here?

"I...I really need this job. Perhaps if I spoke with the owner, I can clear up any misunderstanding?"

"There's no misunderstanding, Mrs. Fallon," he crossed his arms and looked down at her.

"Oh," Trinity bowed her head for a moment with a frown. "But if he hasn't been informed as you say he hasn't, then he might not allow me to work here. Please, sir, couldn't I have a minute of his time?"

The beautiful man uncrossed his arms then sat across from Trinity. "You have my attention, Mrs. Fallon. I simply want to ask you a few questions," he smiled.

Trinity's eyes snapped up, "W-w-what did you say your name was?"

"I never did. Dante Venturi. Pleased to make your acquaintance."

Dante Venturi's hand dwarfed hers and was soft and rough at the same time. His handshake was firm. It felt warm and protective, sending jolts of electricity through her body.

"Likewise," she swallowed against her dry throat.

"What happened to your arm?"

The question was firm. He stared straight at her, daring her to lie. Lying about her injuries was second nature. He would know if she did, undoubtedly. Still, she wasn't about to tell him the truth.

"I fell," she supplied. The lie didn't roll off her tongue as easily as it usually did. It was also the lamest excuse in the book. Although, people fell all of the time and broke their arms. Maybe he would believe her.

"You fell." It was a statement rather than a question.

"Y-y-yes?" she asked, hating herself for not forming a sentence.

"Where?"

"Oh. Um, in my kit...down my stairs," Trinity cleared her throat.

"Excuse me?" he leaned in. "I didn't quite get that. You fell in your kitchen or down your stairs? Which one?"

"Stairs."

"I see. And how did you fall?"

"My dog tripped me." There. That was a good, clear sentence.

"Ah. You own a dog. What kind?" his lips pressed together in a smile that failed to reach his eyes.

"A coon...hound," she smiled. Ha! There was no way he would know what a coonhound was. Maybe. Hell, who was she kidding? She didn't even know what it was. She only remembered the name of the dog from the dog show she watched on Thanksgiving. The breed stuck with her because it reminded her of a tall beagle.

"Coonhound?" his brows shot up. "I love them," his smile turned genuine. "I had one growing up. A treeing walker coonhound, to be exact."

Of course he did.

"Amazing how quiet she is, no?" he asked.

"Very quiet. You know how that breed is," she waved her hand no-non-sense. "Quiet like a mouse," Trinity laughed nervous. Maybe she was pulling this off. She leaned back in her chair with a confident smile.

Dante itched the back of his neck, closing his eyes for a second. "Trinity, you don't mind if I call you by your first name?" he nodded when she shook her head. "If you're going to lie to someone, know your lie. Know it inside and out. Know it...like you lived it. Coonhounds are some of the loudest dogs on the planet. So, now I'll ask again. How...did you sustain the injury to your arm?" he finished his question with a whisper.

Crap. How stupid could she be? She closed her eyes embarrassed. Should she tell him? He was staring at her, waiting expectantly. Something in his expression told her he didn't tolerate liars. His eyes were so black, she couldn't see his pupils. Hell, he looked to be seeing straight into her damn soul. So what did she have to lose? The worst that would happen would be her termination. If it came down to that, she'd figure it out.

The bigger question wasn't what she had to lose or what if she lost her job. The bigger, perhaps biggest, question was...did she have enough courage to tell the truth? Looking at this man, for some reason, gave her a feeling of empowerment. Courage. Without further thought, her eyes met his and she spilled.

"I didn't fall."

"Of course you didn't. Your idiot husband did that to you."

There was no need to confirm. Her courage hadn't mattered. He had her figured out. Was she fired now? Should she save herself the humiliation and leave. Yes. That was probably the best bet. Dragging in a defeated breath, Trinity gained her feet and started for the door.

Dante beat her to it. "Where are you going?"

"Home?"

"Why?"

"You don't want me here. I understand. I didn't know you owned this place. Becky found the ad on the internet. It was a coincidence."

"Trinity, you're not going anywhere. And if you think I'm going to allow you to go home to that, excuse my language, fucking piece of shit, you've got another thing coming."

If her mouth could separate from her face, it would be on the floor. She heard the gasp escape, but she couldn't seem to close her lips.

"I'm sending Eugenia to help you this afternoon and tomorrow. I own several properties in the area, one being a townhouse twenty minutes from here. You'll stay there. Eugenia will help you shop for clothes and stock the fridge. I do not want you in any store other than boutiques for your clothing. If you need anything from your home, let Eugenia know. Is that understood?"

"Why?" she breathed.

"Why what?"

"Why are you helping me?"

"I should have helped you the day we met in the grocery store. I failed you, Trinity. That won't happen again," Dante leaned over and pressed a button on the phone panel. "Eugenia, get in here."

After a few seconds, Eugenia popped her head in. "Yes, boss?"

After digging in his wallet, he handed over a shiny black card.

"Here. Take this and these," he said producing a set of keys. "Trinity is going to stay in the Dawson townhouse from here on out. Take her shopping for a new wardrobe. Once you're finished, she'll give you a grocery list. Under no circumstances is she to accompany you to the grocery store. She's only allowed to shop for her wardrobe. Understood?"

"Yes, sir," Eugenia happily agreed and quickly turned to leave the room.

"Oh, and get her a new phone. Mrs. Fallon, may I please have your phone?"

"My husband is a police officer, Mr. Venturi."

"Dante. I don't care if he's a police officer. Phone please," he held out his hand and waved his fingers.

"He'll find me."

"No. He won't. Trust me on that."

"I can't repay you."

"I'm not asking for repayment, Trinity."

"Nothing in life is free."

Dante smiled, "I see why Ms. Jewell hired you. You'll do well here."

"I might not, Dante. I don't know what I'm doing."

"You're smart. You'll learn. Case closed. Phone please," Dante smiled when she finally put her device in his hand. "Thank you. Now, if you'll excuse me, I have an unexpected meeting to attend. I'm glad you're here, Trinity. More than glad."

Trinity was left standing alone and utterly confused. What the hell just happened? How did she go from worrying if David was going to kill her tonight to having been rescued? Seemingly rescued. Wait. Had she just been rescued? By the beautiful man no less? The beautiful man who now had a name. Dante Venturi who owned Venturi Transportation, a club and properties. Was she dreaming? Her heart started to race.

"Hey girlfriend. You ready?"

Trinity nodded absently.

"Oh, Mr. Venturi said to leave your vehicle here. He's giving you a company car. He said your's is a piece of shit. What do you drive?"

"It...it's a two thousand sedan. Nothing special."

"Yeah, you can't drive something like that working here. Glad you're getting a new one and new digs. He's into you for sure. Chicks are gonna be jelly," she sang with a snicker.

"What?" Trinity gave herself whiplash.

"Come on, Trin. I saw how he looked at you. He's into you."

"No. He's just trying to help me. We ran into each other two times before this."

"Oh yeah?" Eugenia elbowed Trinity with a wiggle of her eyebrows.

"Not like that. Once was in a grocery store and another time was at his club. And I was with my husband at the club."

"Ha! The grocery store. I can't picture that. My car is over there. So, your husband did that to you?"

"Yeah."

"You could have told me, hun."

"I'm sorry."

"Nah. Don't be. What did he do?"

"He stabbed me with a chair."

Eugenia's nose wrinkled up. "Say what?"

Never in her life had she ever told another living soul the details of what happened to her behind closed doors. Sure, Becky knew David was abusive but Trinity never volunteered the gory details. Mainly because the thought of opening up was too terrifying and traumatic. Why she just spilled to Eugenia and not Becky was beyond her, except to say there was a weird feeling in her gut of late whenever she thought of Becky. Either way, she couldn't stop her tongue.

"We got in a big fight the other day. He threw the kitchen chair against the wall and it broke just right. He stabbed me with the just right piece of it," Trinity's voice trailed off.

"Holy shit. Are you serious? I would have killed the bastard. Please tell me that's all he's done to you."

"No," Trinity whispered, looking out the window as they drove.

"I'm sorry. You don't have to tell me shit. I didn't mean to get so personal and in your business."

"It's okay. I've never told anyone. It feels kind of good to get it off my chest."

"What about your friend? Becky was it? She doesn't know?"

"She does, but not the details."

"I'm being, like, way too forward but your friend didn't make the greatest impression on me."

"No?"

"Not at all. There's something about her that rubbed me wrong."

Trinity nodded. So it wasn't just her gut. Eugenia felt it too. Eugenia was an outsider looking in. There would be no reason for her to lie about Becky. They didn't even know each other. A strange pit in her stomach formed.

"Was that the worst?"

Trinity shook her head refocusing on the conversation. "I think the absolute worst was when he dunked my head over and over in a tub of hot water. I thought I was going to die that night. I prayed to die." Trinity ran her finger tips over her lips as she told the story.

"Trin," Eugenia whispered, her hand automatically finding Trinity's leg and giving it a squeeze. "God must have brought you to Dante. I really believe in divine intervention."

"Maybe. I did pray a lot."

"Don't you worry. If anyone can help you, it's Dante. Trust me."

"Why him?"

Eugenia shrugged her shoulders, "Just is. Look. Third house in. Cute or what?"

Cute was a good word for the townhouse. Three stories high and constructed of redbrick, it was perfectly nestled among others in a neat line forming the block. The small lawns were perfectly manicured, hedges pruned with full pink and white impatiens potted in low ceramics decorating the stoops.

This looked to be a quiet neighborhood, much to Trinity's relief. Her home she shared with David was mediocre at best with the loud rumble of motorcycles or teenagers drag racing up and down the street. It wasn't the best place to raise a family. But here, would be. Not that she would ever have the luxury of having her own family one day. She needed to count her blessings. Living a quiet life here while she regained her feet was perfect. Too good to be true really. The only thing to do was live it up til she woke up from the dream.

If it weren't a dream, then she needed to add a notebook to her grocery list and come up with ideas to hide from David. There was no doubt in her mind he would find her. Hell, he knew where she worked. If she was expected to sit out front, then she was a literal sitting duck. And what was up with Eugenia thinking Dante was interested in her? No way.

Dante was just a businessman who had a means to help her out. Nothing more than that, which was fine with her.

"Come on."

Eugenia nearly skipped up the stairs and unlocked the door opening it wide for Trinity to cross the threshold. Once inside, she smiled. The narrow entry gave way to a small hallway, with a little table for placing keys and what not. There was a living room, kitchen and another sitting area.

"How big is this place?"

"I think this one is around twenty-five hundred square feet. It's pretty big. You even have a fireplace. Did you see it? I remember Dante remodeling this place. The floor where we walked in is Italian marble, and the floor in the living room and kitchen is some sort of expensive wood. The cabinets are all oak, Viking appliances and upstairs is some more expensive stuff. Come on, I'll show you."

Trinity followed her up to reveal three bedrooms, all with their own bathrooms. The master bedroom had an en suite that boasted a walk in shower and separate tub area. The other bedrooms had walk in showers. Still, everything sure looked expensive like Eugenia had promised. The third floor had what looked like another living room or bonus room, with two more bedrooms which could be made into an office and exercise room, or anything for that matter.

The house was way too big for her. What if David found her and tried to break in? How was she supposed to stay here by herself?

"Eugenia? Is there a security system in place?"

"Hell yeah. I'll show it to you. Don't worry. If you get broken into, Dante has a security team that comes. It's not the police. But all that doesn't matter, because you won't get broken into. Never have in this area. I don't live far away either. You're safe."

Not the police? What the hell? Who was Dante and exactly how rich was he? Did it matter? Not really. As long as no police were involved, it would be okay. Hopefully.

Trinity didn't have any more time to think about it. After Eugenia showed her everything she needed, she pulled her out the door and back into the car. She quickly learned Eugenia loved to shop. She also learned Eugenia was an expert when it came to the task.

They bought several different outfits for work, everyday and lounge wear, workout gear, pajamas and outerwear. Trinity tried to stop Eugenia telling her it was too much, but Eugenia shooed her away. If Mr. Venturi gave her a job to do, she was going to do it whether Trinity liked it or not.

Dead on their feet, Trinity thanked the lord Eugenia declared it lunchtime. Her feet felt swollen and sore from all of the walking they did. She definitely needed sustenance.

"This café is my absolute favorite. I usually come here every Saturday. They know me," Eugenia whispered.

"What do you usually get?"

"Their French Onion soup is to die for. You gotta try it. It comes in a big bowl, so it's like a meal. Oh, and I love, love, love their brie on french bread. I'm gonna order it as an appetizer."

"I've never had it," Trinity bit her lip looking over the menu.

"Ugh. Girl, you don't know what you're missing. They spread brie on French bread, drizzle it with honey and top it with cracked peppercorn and bake it. Sounds gross, but it is out of this world."

"Eugenia, does Mr. Venturi own more than our work and the club?"

Eugenia glanced up at Trinity, but then back down at her menu and shrugged, "I don't know. Probably. Why?"

"I was just curious. I don't know anything about the business world."

"You're gonna love it."

Trinity gave an inconspicuous glance around herself. The table they were sitting at was a tiny square of wood resting on a pedestal with a crisp, white linen tablecloth. A sprig of bluebells and baby's breath were cut low to fill an eight ounce tin can as the table's adornment. Rolled white cloth napkins were set upon blue appetizer plates. The chairs they sat on were of uncomfortable wood but complemented the rustic aesthetic of the place.

A cube of ice in Trinity's water shifted, making a nearly inaudible clinking noise. Their table was sandwiched between two others and everyone around them competed to be heard. Laughter and storytelling voices boomed throughout the room without a care.

That was it, wasn't it? These people were carefree. And if they did have a care, they were good at masking it. There wasn't a serious table in the place. Everyone was enjoying themselves whether they were on a lunch break or a day off. She was like them now. She was at a work lunch. Except, this didn't feel like a work lunch.

This felt like a dream. Dreams were dangerous. They were dangerous because they ended with a wake-up call. What kind of wake-up call was she going to get? She wasn't dumb. Nothing good ever happened to her. Sooner or later, this dream was going to end.

Only then would she know if she had a sweet dream or a nightmare.

Chapter 6

Dante paced his office, occasionally looking out the window to watch the afternoon bustle. This was his city. His family's city. They kept the streets safe and businesses running for over one hundred years, and now it was his turn to serve. He was don. Capo dei capi. Boss of all bosses.

It wasn't something he asked for. It was assumed. A position he was born into. To turn it down or walk away was to be traitor. There was no getting out. No need to try, no need to even think about it. Why would he anyway? The world was his oyster.

Money, power, women, vacations, homes, the list went on and on. He had it all. Most importantly, he had respect. He couldn't remember the last time he was disrespected. Although, that wasn't true. The last time he had been disrespected was a few days ago in his very own club by one, David Fallon.

When someone gets invited by the most powerful mob boss in the nation, let alone the world, you don't fucking turn him down. But, that's what Mr. Fallon had done. Peckerhead was too stupid to know who he was dealing with which was hard to wrap his own head around. How, the fuck, did the cop not recognize him? He owned the goddamn police. The man needed to be taught a lesson for his disrespect. The man needed to die for hurting Trinity.

It was nearly four in the afternoon. Eugenia was scheduled to be back to the office soon. Hopefully, she had some information to give. He wanted every detail. Something told him, Trinity would be less likely to spill her guts which was just fine. He had ways of getting the information he needed.

For now, he would wait. Wait and think. Trinity was never far from his thoughts. Ever since he had seen her in the grocery store and again at his club, he couldn't stop. She was, hands down, the most gorgeous woman he had ever seen.

Petite and curvy in all of the right places. And her hair? Don't get him started on her hair. It was so pale and looked silk soft, she could easily pass for an angel. What he wouldn't give to run his fingers through that platinum.

Her eyes were a dark blue reminding him of sapphires, wide and deep set. High cheekbones complimented a slim, pert nose and full pink lips begging to be bitten. Every inch of her was perfect. She was made for him.

The only obstacle standing in his way was her husband, which really wasn't an obstacle at all. The guy was a schmuck. Easily dealt with. A phone call was all it would take. But he'd wait. He wanted to know every detail before he wrote his prescription for Mr. Fallon.

A soft knock broke Dante from his thoughts. It had to be Eugenia. He quickly bade her entry.

"Expecting someone else?"

Dante frowned at his vice president. "I was. What do you want, Gio?"

"Is that anyway to treat your right hand man? Your capo in training? Your nephew?" Giovanni smirked.

"As your boss and uncle? Of course it is."

"Fair enough. Anyway, order number nine is scheduled for shipping tomorrow morning."

"And where's the shipper's export declaration? Didn't Jewell type it up for me? I haven't seen it."

"Woah, uncle. Relax. I've got it right here."

"I want the ocean bill of lading too," Dante mumbled.

"Mhm. It's there."

Dante quickly read over the documents, making corrections in red pen before handing it back to his nephew.

"You realize how important this shit is, Gio? Someday, you'll be in my shoes."

"Unlikely. Especially if you have a son. Then I'll be off the hook," Gio grinned.

"I'm not having any kids. It'll be you next."

"Right. Anyway, nine isn't a worry for me. I've got it handled."

"What else?"

"Took a call from Mexico this morning. Sanchez wants to form an alliance."

"No."

"No?" Gio rubbed his eyebrow confused before taking back the paperwork from Dante. "Why not?"

"Why not?" Dante narrowed his gaze. "Since when do we operate like some biker gang, Gio? Our family didn't build this business to have it tainted by some wanna be. If he calls again, I'll handle it. Other than that, brief me tomorrow. Go," Dante waved him off.

Jesus fucking Christ. Was it so hard to follow instructions? Gio shouldn't have even entertained a phone call from Sanchez. Anyone with balls big enough to call his organization was bad news and needed to be castrated. One more thing he didn't have time to deal with. Add it to the fucking list.

Shipment nine was scheduled to set sail tomorrow and it was something he'd monitor very closely. The deal would finish off the month ahead of projections. After all was said and done, there would be a total of eighty million spotty dollars to wash.

Yeah. Eighty million was a bit more than what Sanchez could ever bring to the table on one deal. He could hear it now. Some peon gang offering to split amounts in the thousands. The last time he dealt with anything in the thousands was when he was a teenager. What a joke. If a deal didn't contain seven figures, it was an easy no. He was the earner, and there were far too many people on the payroll to fuck around with a small-time gang.

Not to mention the fact, his family had given their blood, sweat and tears to make Venturi Transportation the flawless machine it was today. It wasn't gummed up and corroded. It was kept pristine. At least in the government's eyes it was. And, it would stay that way. Everyone else could stay the fuck out. Gio was going to have to learn before he became don.

Dante's jaw ticked. Gio wasn't a good choice to become head of the family. The kid didn't think. But what was he to do? He wasn't planning on having kids of his own. He would definitely need to keep training the kid. Maybe he was the one fucking up. Maybe he needed to have Gio move in with him. That way, he'd be able to keep a closer eye on him.

A knock on the door sounded. Before Dante could say anything, Eugenia poked her head in. This bitch was fucking daring. She had balls bigger than some of his employees. Hell, bigger than some of his friends. Then again, he had no friends.

She closed the door and sat down without an invitation. He'd give her a pass this one time. The woman looked exhausted.

"Hi boss."

"Eugenia. I trust Trinity is settled. How does she like it?"

"She's very overwhelmed," Eugenia picked at her nail. "Scared is probably the better word."

"Understandable. What did she tell you?"

"Tell me?"

"Don't fucking play coy with me, Eugenia. I want to know what she told you about her husband. Don't leave out any details."

He had Eugenia's attention until he said to not leave out any details. That's when she looked down. Jesus. Anytime anyone ever looked away usually meant bad news.

"He's hurt her. Really bad."

"Tell me."

"He...he dunked her in a tub of hot water. Over and over...," Eugenia's voice broke.

Maybe his anger problem stemmed from a family history of issues. He didn't know. All he knew was that the familiar heat which usually started in the pit of his stomach was starting to coil and spread...rapidly. He knew his face was turning red.

"He...he broke a chair and...," Eugenia swallowed closing her eyes, "and took the leg and rammed...," she raised her fist, thrusting the air, "rammed it into her arm."

Eugenia's sobs were a bit loud. Her words jumbled up with tears. It was hard to hear what she was saying. It didn't matter. He didn't need to hear the rest. He would get the rest from Trinity herself. Tonight. He needed to be certain what Eugenia just told him was correct. Because, if it was, David Fallon's corpse wasn't going to be viewable at his funeral.

"Thank you, Eugenia. Here. Dinner's on me. Go home and relax," he pulled out a couple hundred dollar bills and handed them to her.

Happy she didn't argue, Dante moved to grab his suit jacket and keys. He really wanted to wait until Trinity was settled before paying her a visit, but it couldn't be helped. Not after the information he just received.

It really was hard to digest how any piece of shit could cause any degree of harm on a woman and be fine with it. Women were to be cherished, not fucking abused. Especially Trinity.

Dante drove the short distance to Trinity's new home without thought of the drive. Street lights, cars and pedestrians were all a blur for how much he was in his own head. The drive came and went seemingly without the passage of time. He pulled up outside her door and parked.

The block was quiet. Everyone was probably eating dinner having been after six. Hopefully, she was home. Fuck. He didn't think of that. What if she didn't stay put? What if she went back to that motherfucker? He hastened his steps til he was at the front door, ringing the doorbell. He leaned his head near the door.

He was trained to listen. Trained to pick up on sounds not everyone would hear. Why? Well, when someone drops a fork, puts down a glass, closes a cabinet door or even drops a newspaper onto a table, it's never heard. It's never heard because it's an everyday sound. A sound that the brain doesn't care about. Yeah, it's heard but it's also filtered out or pushed aside to make room for a more important thought process.

That's where training comes in. His training, to be more exact. His brain didn't filter. His brain juggled. One can't really multitask. There's no such thing. Instead, the brain kind of does a juggling act when it's doing more than one thing at once. Everyone can usually juggle two items. Dante's brain, could juggle far more.

If he were to bet, he'd say she was in the kitchen and just dropped a magazine down onto the quartz countertop. He'd further venture to guess she probably had been writing in the magazine or book because two taps of a pen dropped down pricking his ears. Crossword puzzle? Weird that she would be so relaxed this soon. Also disturbing was the fact that he could in fact hear all of those telling sounds. The front door would need to be replaced with something thicker.

The unmistakable clicking of heels approached until it stopped. She was at the door checking him out through the peephole and, undoubtedly, trying to figure out her next move. If she were wise, she would open the fucking door before he took out his own key and used it.

With a swoosh, the door opened to a wide-eyed Trinity. Her face was flushed a pretty pink, but her expression was all wrong. How would it be to have her actually happy to see him? Instead, she looked terrified and unsure. This was David Fallon's work. How many years had it taken the schmuck to create this expression?

"M-mr. Venturi?" Trinity bit down onto her lip and glanced past him to the street.

Dante turned slightly to see what Trinity was looking at. The street was empty save a bird who landed to pick at an unfortunate dead squirrel.

"It's Dante. May I come in?"

"O-of course," she opened the door and stood back a few steps for him to enter the small foyer.

What the hell? The living room needed furniture. Did Eugenia tell her to order some? Was the bedroom even furnished? He couldn't have Trinity sleeping on the floor. Forgetting Trinity, Dante went into the kitchen taking in a thick magazine and pen laying on the countertop along with a glass of water. The kitchen was fully stocked. Why didn't the living room have furniture? He better check on his other properties.

"Do you have a bed?"

"I-I do. T-t-thank you," Trinity cringed out.

"No need to thank me twice. I'm just going to see for myself. You may stay down here if you'd like."

And she did. Quickly, he took the stairs by two and ducked his head into each bedroom until he came to the one obviously occupied by her. It was also the only one with a bed. He'd talk with Jewell tomorrow about his other properties. It wouldn't do to not have them fully furnished. How would it look to potential renters to tour a home which advertised fully furnished only to find it not? Fucking irritating.

He didn't intrude on Trinity's privacy by going into the bedroom but rather went back downstairs instead. He wasn't surprised to see her in the kitchen. It did, however, surprise him to see she was standing shifting her weight from side to side. She was definitely nervous. Rightfully so.

"Did Eugenia tell you to order living room furniture?"

"I-I don't remember."

Dante smirked. So Eugenia made quite the impression on his new little employee. Already friends it seems. There was a definite level of courage in Trinity to have no problem covering for Eugenia. Of course she was courageous. She endured her husband's beatings.

"Please see to it that you order whatever you feel you need for the place, Trinity. Spare no expense. I'm having Ms. Jewell order items for my other properties as well tomorrow."

"Oh. Okay. Thank you."

"Can we sit?"

Trinity gestured to a chair while taking one herself.

"Is this to your liking?"

"Yes. Very much so. Th...,"

Dante held up his hand. "One thank you is enough. Anyway, aside from checking on you, I had another motive for stopping by."

"Y-you did?" Trinity's forehead wrinkled in worry, her teeth abused her lip once again.

She needed to stop doing that. Her mouth was a major distraction. Her lips were extremely plump. Were they natural? He needed to taste them. Lingering on her mouth too long, he tore his attention away feeling like an asshole.

"Yeah. Trinity, we're going to have to talk about some things you're not going to want to talk about."

"Oh," she looked away.

"I'm going to need to know everything he did. And I'm going to need details."

Trinity was quiet for a long time. Her fingers took to twisting the hem of the dress she still wore from earlier today. The worry for having to divulge her most private secrets to him commingled with the undoubted worry for what her husband must be thinking in this moment was weighing heavy. Maybe too heavy. Maybe he shouldn't have come here. Maybe he should have waited for another day. It wasn't like her husband could find her. She was safe. Question was, did she feel safe?

"Do you feel safe here, Trinity? Do you think your husband will find you tonight?"

Her eyes snapped up, "Do you?"

"No. Even if he did, he's powerless. Trinity, I own every property on this block. And, every property has home security."

"That's linked to the police. Mr. Venturi, my husband is the police."

"I'm well aware who he is. Trinity, I assure you, no harm will come to you living here."

"C-can you guarantee that one hundred percent?"

"Absolutely. Now, tell me. I need to hear everything."

His tone was commanding. Despite it, she didn't owe him anything. She could easily tell him it was none of his business, but somehow he knew she would cave and spill her guts. After some coaxing, it was exactly what she did. A glaze settled over her eyes, and she let loose all the demons clinging to her shoulders. He was sick.

Countless beatings, rapes and near death experiences all on one person nearly every day for the past year. She was living in a hellhole. Was being the keyword. Had they not crossed paths again, her death would be imminent. It would have been a waste of a gorgeous woman. His woman, he decided.

She was broken, but he would fix her. Starting tomorrow.

Chapter 7

Back and forth. Back and forth. David Fallon paced his kitchen. The weight of his steps were enough to crush bone. His thumbs slipped over his index fingers and pressed down causing a loud pop of his knuckles. He repeated the action for each digit.

She was late. Where was she? Five o'clock and no dinner. Didn't he tell her he wanted lasagna? That new job was making her late. His teeth ground together.

Why did he ever listen to his mother? He shouldn't have complained about the money problems he was having. It was just that he thought she'd lend him some. Instead, she suggested Trinity start pulling her weight and get a job. It was a good idea in theory. But in reality? Not. He was fucking hungry, and she wasn't home yet.

To make matters worse, she wasn't answering her goddamn phone. Maybe she was driving. Yeah. That had to be it. He scratched his head pulling it to the side until his neck cracked. She was a pretty careful driver. Paid attention to detail. David nodded with a smile. Of course she paid attention to detail. He trained her. He had to. She never went to college. How else would she have learned if he hadn't taught her?

But this was inexcusable. If this job was making her late, she'd just have to find a different one. As soon as she got home, he'd tell her. Well, first she'd take her punishment and then he'd tell her.

The digital clock flashed quarter after five. Fifteen minutes passed. He went to the living room and stared out the window. A random car zoomed by, but it wasn't her. Then another and another. A bead of sweat gathered on his upper lip. He dragged it away with a swipe of his sleeve and a loud sniff of his nose. A fourth car. Not her. Not her, not her, not...her! Pulling at his hair, he let loose a frustrated shout. A small nicknack of a fairy picking flowers sailed across the room smashing into tiny pieces against the wall.

David's chest heaved up and down as he stared at the now broken ceramic he gave to Trinity for her birthday the first year they met. A small cut on his hand welled with fresh blood, and trickled down his hand unnoticed. His mumbling lips twitched as fast as his mind raced. The rhythmic ticking of a wall clock counted his disjointed thoughts until a moment of clarity provided a realization to settle inside his brain. His eyes grew wide.

"She...left me," he whispered in an astonished hush, eyes wild. "She fucking left me."

There was no other explanation. Had to be. She would have been home on time if not. Dinner would have been on the table. But it wasn't. Was there ever even a job? He'd ask Becky. Becky would know. Becky would tell him.

In the meantime, he would find her. He was a cop after all. This sort of thing was his job. He did it everyday. Sure he was only a beat cop, but he had friends who would help him.

"Yeah," David nodded satisfied. A maniacal smile spread over his face.

He would find her. And when he did...she better pray.

Chapter 8

Yesterday had been cathartic. It was a purge. It felt great to unload. When it was over, it felt horrible. How could she have divulged all the gory details of her marriage to the beautiful man? Correction. Her boss, of all people. Shame and embarrassment filled her.

How was she supposed to look him in the eye today? Oh yeah, she had the day off. The day was meant for furniture shopping. On line of course. Mr. Venturi told her to stay home and call Eugenia or Ms. Jewell if she needed any help.

Why was he helping her? Better yet, could she trust him? Trinity cupped a warm coffee mug in between her hands and stared out the sliding glass door of her new bedroom. The room faced the back of the building which overlooked a flower garden. It was probably lovely in the summertime. Would she be there that long?

The bigger question she kept pushing to the back of her mind was David. Would he find her? What did he think when he discovered she didn't make it home? He probably tried to call. She wouldn't know. She was provided with a brand new cell phone to use instead. It was a bit overwhelming trying to figure everything out. Eugenia showed her a few things, but she promptly forgot what she said.

Eugenia went on and on at lunch about how sure she was Dante was interested in her. Too bad it wasn't under different circumstances. There was no way she'd entertain the idea of a relationship with anyone ever again. How could she? There'd never be trust. It was bad enough she couldn't even trust him as her boss.

Well, that wasn't entirely true. If she hadn't trusted at least a little, she wouldn't have stayed the night. But, her gut told her to stay despite the fear she had for David finding her. The truth was, he hadn't. He hadn't found her last night. Nor did he discover her new phone number. Shit! She forgot to call Becky. How could she have forgotten? Becky was her best friend for crying out loud.

Trinity put her coffee cup down and grabbed her phone. No missed calls. Of course there weren't any. No one aside from Eugenia, Dante and probably Ms. Jewell had her number. What if David went to Becky's house last night? What if he hurt her? Her fingers flew over the numbers, but she paused midway and hung up only to redial.

"Hello?"

Relief. Becky's sweet voice answered after the first ring. An inquisitive tone reflected in her greeting.

"Becky!"

"Where the heck are you? What number is this?"

"Oh, I...has David been to see you?" Trinity frowned. Didn't Becky care if she was alright? She was glad she dialed star sixty-seven first.

"He called and asked if I've seen you. I told him I didn't."

"Oh, thank God."

"It's wasn't a lie. Where exactly are you?"

"I'm safe."

"That's good. So, are you gonna tell me what's going on and where you are?"

"I...I can't tell you," Trinity cringed.

"What? Why not?"

"I got away, Becky. I'm safe," Trinity breathed.

"What? How?"

"I can't...,"

"Tell me. I get it. So you're someplace safe?"

"Very."

"Okay, but when will I see you?"

"I don't know."

"You don't know? Are you talking a few days, weeks?"

Something in the pit of Trinity's stomach told her it was going to be a hell of a lot longer than days or weeks. So long as David was looking for her, she would need to stay away from her best friend. Even if it took months. Might as well be straight with her.

"Becky, it could be months. I don't know. Maybe...maybe even longer."

"You have to start over, don't you?"

"I don't know. All I know is I have to stay away for awhile. I'll try to call you again when the dust settles. If you really need to reach me for anything, call Eugenia at Venturi Transportation. She knows how to contact me."

"Got it."

"Becky, thank you for everything you've ever done for me. If it weren't for you, I wouldn't have been saved. I love you."

"This sound like you're saying goodbye to me."

"I guess, for now, I am."

"Take care of yourself."

The line went dead before Trinity could say anything else. She sniffed. Becky didn't tell her she loved her back. She hadn't even asked if she was alright. She was so...cold.

Brushing her tears away, Trinity decided to distract herself from the weird feeling she got after talking to Becky and looked up a local furniture store. She needed a sofa, maybe a recliner and coffee table. Oh, and an end table. A lamp would also be nice. The living room wasn't very bright with its few canister lights. She liked to read, so a lamp was a definite. Also, a nice area rug for under the coffee table would look pretty. Grays and blues were a favorite combination of hers. She'd try to stick with that pallette.

After she finished her order, she clicked the checkout button. The grand total staring back at her was way more than what she felt comfortable spending. Fifteen thousand dollars? Seriously?! Her teeth clamped down onto her bottom lip. How? Scrolling through her list, she counted six items. Six measly items! A couch, recliner, coffee table, end table, rug and lamp. Jeeze. Remove, remove, remove, remove, remove, remove. Shopping cart is now empty. Hmm. Did Walmart sell furniture?

The doorbell chime startled Trinity. The sound was foreign. A crisp, single ding. Was it David? Her heart galloping in her chest, tightened her diaphragm making it hard to breathe. She needed to calm down. David didn't know where she was. There was no way to find her. Dante assured her.

Taking in a deep breath, she made her way down the stairs and jumped when the bell sounded again. It was Dante. Crap. He would expect her to answer, but she was still in her bathrobe and her hair was in a messy bun! She looked terrible. Wait. Why did she care what she looked like? Screw it.

"G-good morning, Mr. Venturi."

"Dante. Good morning. I brought doughnuts and coffee," he smiled.

"Oh."

"Can I come in?"

"Oh, yes. I'm sorry," Trinity smiled shy, letting him in.

His warm scent of citrus and sandalwood caused her eyes to drift closed before she caught herself, quickly blinking away the intoxicating effect of his cologne.

"I only have a few minutes. I'm doing doughnut runs this morning and since you won't be in today, I didn't want you to miss out," he held up a small box.

Wow. That was...super sweet. Could Eugenia be right? Was he interested in her? If so, why? She was damaged goods. She wasn't worth the time, that was for sure.

"Thank you so much. I'm sorry, I'm not dressed yet." Trinity tightened the belt on her robe wishing she put slippers on. Not that her feet were bad. She had just done a pedicure on herself before she ran away from home. Still, there was something intimate about bare feet. The very bare feet Dante was staring at. Why was he staring at her feet?! Stop staring!

"No, forgive me. I should have called you first," Dante smiled up at her. "How's your shopping going? Did you find furniture?"

"Oh. Um...yes and no." Trinity took the box of doughnuts and placed them onto the kitchen table.

"What do you mean?" he followed her.

There was no way she could tell him she almost spent fifteen thousand dollars on only six items. It was an obscene amount. How embarrassing.

"I just haven't found the right store. But, I saw Walmart sells furniture. So, I'm sure I'll find something reasonable."

Dante choked on his coffee causing him to cough for a few seconds.

"Oh my. Are you alright? Do you need water?"

He held up his hand, then adjusted his tie. "Trinity. Please don't fill this home up with furniture from that repulsive store."

"Oh...b-b-but I...,"

"Shop at either Finn's or Table Leaf here in town, please. I'm having Ms. Jewell use those stores for my other properties. And, that's my fault. I should have told you where to go. I wasn't thinking. There's no budget, so buy whatever. I don't care."

"N-n-no b-b-budget?"

"No."

Trinity was in full panic mode. How the hell was she supposed to spend someone else's money without knowing what was and wasn't okay? Sure he said no budget, but was that true? What if she did accidentally spend too much, and he got mad at her? No way. There was no way she would risk it.

"P-p-please, Mr. Ven...Dante, can you please set a budget?"

Dante stared at Trinity for a long while. He was assessing her. It was obvious. She started to fidget under his appraisal. Why couldn't he just give her a number and leave? She couldn't make the decision herself. Couldn't he see that?

"I suppose I could give you Ms. Jewell's budget if that will help."

Trinity brightened. "Oh, yes, thank you so much."

"Fifty thousand per room."

Her jaw was on the floor. It had to be. She couldn't even answer him. Perhaps she made a sound, but it definitely didn't form words. Fifty thousand? Per room? No way. That was ridiculous. Who spent that kind of money on living room furniture? There was no way she was going to take advantage and spend that. No way.

"I trust your first night went well?"

She nodded.

"I've been thinking, I'd like you to work from home the rest of the week."

"Work from home? What will I do?" Trinity blinked out of her stupor.

"Settle in. Also, I have a business dinner tomorrow evening I would like for you to attend with me."

"What about your wife? Can't she do it?" Why was panic mode setting in again? She knew he wasn't married. If he was, Trinity wouldn't have said he was interested in her or how everyone was trying to nab him as their boyfriend.

"My wife? Hmm. I suppose she could."

What?! He was married?! What the hell. And, just why she felt disappointment was beyond her. Who the hell was she kidding? This was the beautiful man standing right in front of her. Of course she was disappointed. Trinity found herself nodding.

"But she can't."

She can't? Trinity's brows rose. "Why not?"

Dante leaned over and whispered, "I don't have a wife," he chuckled.

Relief and heat flared across Trinity's face. Her cheeks must look as red as apples. How embarrassing. Could her embarrassment grow any bigger? Maybe.

"What about your girlfriend?" Now she just looked thirsty. Little did anyone know, she was the farthest thing from thirsty. So, yes, it was possible to be further embarrassed.

"Again, if I had one. Thank goodness I don't."

"Why?"

"I wouldn't have the pleasure of your company tomorrow night."

What was she supposed to say to that? She wasn't used to compliments, of any sort. She wasn't used to compliments nor was she comfortable with them. Maybe if she diffused the situation.

"What will be expected of me?"

"The dinner is one I'm hosting for a long-term client of mine. It's a thank you dinner so to speak. I would simply like you to be my date. I expect you to enjoy yourself. Nothing more."

A thank you dinner so to speak? How was a thank you dinner so to speak? A thank you dinner was a thank you dinner, unless there was an ulterior motive. Should she ask him? Maybe not. Something told her, not many people questioned him.

"Then I accept. Thank you. What time should I come down to the office?"

"I'll be picking you up. Never show up to the office unless I tell you it's alright to do so."

"Okay. Should I wear one of the suits Eugenia picked out for me?"

"No. Actually, the dinner will be at my club. In the VIP room you never got to see," Dante smiled. "Wear a dress."

The slight smile Trinity held melted from her face. She had to go back to his club? Would she be expected to wear a dress like the one from that night? She felt like a whore. Please don't let it be the case, she mused.

"A-a-a dress?"

"Sure. Whatever you like. Only, don't bother with a suit. You might feel out of place. Although, I'll be wearing a suit. I guess I always wear a suit come to think of it. Screw it. If you want to wear a suit, go right ahead. Who am I to tell you how to dress? Forgive me."

It was then she heard it. His laugh. A genuine, full-bodied laugh at himself. It lit his face, erasing years. He looked so...young. How old was he? She didn't think longer on it and joined him in his amusement.

Wow, that felt nice. When was the last time she laughed with a man? Never. The thought was sobering. She swallowed hard.

"I'll be sure to dress appropriately. What time will you pick me up?"

"Nine."

"At night?" What the heck?! Why so late? Ugh! She was usually getting ready for bed at nine. Great.

"Yes, at night," Dante laughed again.

"Sorry. I've never been much of a night owl. Also, I'm not old enough to even be in your club, Mr. Venturi."

"Dante. And, oh?" His brows rose, a wry smile on his lips. "And how, pray tell, did you gain entrance to my club?"

"My husband's a cop."

"Yes. You needn't remind me," Dante's voice hardened for a fraction of a second before clearing his throat. "How old are you?"

"Twenty. How old are you?" She couldn't stop the question from flying out of her mouth. Curse and rot her damn tongue! How could a person make one feel so comfortable and uncomfortable at the same stupid time?!

"I'll be thirty this year. I should get going."

"I'm sorry. I didn't mean to ask you that question. It was too personal," she rushed.

"I asked you the same question. There's no need to apologize, Trinity. I have a meeting in ten minutes, and I'm running very late."

"Oh. I'm sorry."

Dante walked to the front door and swung it open. "Trinity, I actually do have an assignment I'd like for you to work on today aside from ordering furniture."

"Absolutely. You name it."

"Erase the word sorry from your vocabulary, please. Don't use it around me ever again."

"I...okay. Thank you, Mr....Dante."

"Til tomorrow," He smiled.

Trinity leaned against the door and closed her eyes. He asked her to dinner. He asked her to dinner, and she accepted. Was it a date? No. It was for work. He was hosting a thank you dinner for one of his clients, and he needed a date. It was that simple. Plus, had it been a real date, she would have had to decline. There was no way she would ever date. Dating led to relationships, even if it were a friendship. No one from the opposite sex would ever get close to her again. It wasn't feasible.

If it were, then the relationship would crumble. Eventually. Deep down, she knew she would be the cause. Her distrust, her fear, her lack of confidence were all deal breakers. But what was she worried over? He wasn't interested in her like that. He was simply helping out his employee because he cared a lot about people, and tomorrow's dinner was work related.

There. Case. Closed.

Chapter 9

Dante was ten minutes late for his next appointment. Something out of character for him. He was never late. But, he couldn't resist stopping by to check on Trinity and invite her to the dinner he was hosting.

Dante smirked recalling how she pressed him on his marital status. She was genuinely embarrassed when he teased her, but then dismissive. Eager to change the nature of the conversation to a more professional tone.

He was an ass for making her blush, and an ass for inviting her to La Notte. The very club where her husband exploited her for bragging rights. What was wrong with him?

Nodding at a few people, Dante was happy when he finally reached his office. He wasn't surprised to find his appointment waiting inside. Samuel. The man was pacing. He never seemed the impatient type. Yeah, he was ten minutes late. So what? Samuel knew his place. He knew better than to question him. Why the fuck he was pacing was beyond him.

"Samuel. Thanks for waiting."

"No problem. Just getting my steps in."

"That so?" Interesting.

"Wife has me on a diet. Says I gotta gut. I don't know what the hell she's talkin' 'bout," Samuel's mustache stretched over his lip.

Dante gestured to a chair before taking his own seat. "What do you have for me?"

"Straight to business today, huh? Aren't ya gonna offer me a drink?"

"It's nine in the morning, Samuel."

"Heh. Forgot. My old mind thinks I'm halfway across the world some-times," Samuel scratched his head.

Dante rolled his eyes.

"Where was I? Oh yeah. Mr. David Fallon. Boy, did he go crazy last night. Paced 'round his kitchen for 'bout an hour. Then tore the place up before making some phone calls."

Dante laced his fingers leaning forward over the desk. Samuel was one of the best investigators he ever employed, but the man was a little scatter brained at times from all the drinking he did. He could hardly blame him. Samuel had been witness to some gruesome shit. Still, he seemed to be a bit shaky today. Hopefully he was sober while he worked last night. He didn't need any slip ups.

"Were you drinking last night, Sam?"

"No. I can give you my word on that, boss."

The stone-cold expression was either very practiced or genuine. Dante chose the latter. The man better be genuine. He didn't care how long he'd been in his employ or how good he was. There was no room for error in his line of business.

"Go on."

"He called Becky Reynolds who, judging from the call, is a friend of Mrs. Fallon. Becky told him she hadn't seen Trinity. She tried to ask him a question, but he hung up on her. Then he called a guy by the name of Stephen Lauren. He works with Mr. Fallon. He told Stephen to put out an all-points bulletin on Mrs. Fallon. Stephen was reluctant to do it, but told Mr. Fallon he would address it today. After that call, he drank till he passed out."

"Did he go to work this morning?"

"Yup."

"Thank you, Samuel. See Ms. Jewell before you leave. I'll be in touch."

Samuel saluted Dante on his way out the door.

Interesting Mr. Fallon hadn't yet paid a visit to Venturi Transportation. He was certain he would. Dante drummed his fingers on his desk, biting the thumb of his other hand. It was only nine. And even though Fallon was already at work, he was sure to be hung over. He might just be moving a little slow. Time would tell.

In the meantime, he'd stick around the office in the event the cocksucker did decide to show his face. He pressed the intercom.

"Ms. Jewell?"

"Yes, sir?"

"Cancel my ten o'clock meeting. Reschedule it for sometime tomorrow morning. Send Gio in."

"Very good, sir."

His nephew was surprisingly quick to enter. That was a first. Maybe he was learning after all.

"That was fast."

"Ms. Jewell has fresh doughnuts."

Of course she did. He was the one who brought them. Christ. So much for the hope in his nephew.

"I'm hosting a dinner party tomorrow night at the club."

"Which club?"

"What do you mean, which club? The club. La Notte."

"You have two other clubs, Uncle Dante. How was I supposed to know?"

"I don't serve food at the strip clubs, Gio. Jesus Christ. Focus. Listen, I want you to circulate an appreciation night flyer for the first precinct. Schedule it for ten tomorrow night. Open bar, free food."

"You don't think ten is a little late?"

"I don't care. Open bar and free food on the flyer will have them there. That's all I care about."

"Any VIP invitations?"

"No. I'll be occupying the VIP lounge. I have the men from Creedy Company coming for dinner a little before then. I don't want to be disturbed."

"I don't get it? Why have the cops then? They're always rowdy."

"Forget about it. Just get it done before noon. How's my ship?"

"Sailing."

"Good. Tell Andrew and Michael to get in here."

Gio wasn't the right person for this job. He wasn't the right person for any of the jobs which would make him a terrible capo dei capi. He'd have to worry about it later. For now, he needed to assemble a decent crew. He didn't need too many. Maybe two guys at most. The fewer the better. That's how it always went.

Andrew and Michael. Any time he needed a messy job done right, he called them. They were his buttons. Except, this execution was going to be done by himself exclusively.

"Boss?" Andrew walked in without knocking.

"Where's Michael?"

"I don't know."

"I'm here." Michael wiped his mouth, then his tie.

Doughnut day was getting out of hand. How the hell was a piece of dough making everyone late?

"I'm having some cops at La Notte tomorrow night. Keep your eye on David Fallon."

"He a cop?"

"Yeah. I want him to see me. I'll be with his wife. Her name's Trinity Fallon. She's been recently employed with us. Under no circumstances do I want him near us. I only want him to see," Dante stroked his tie. "He's going to try to get close. Don't let him cause a scene and don't kill him. We'll be in the VIP room hosting a dinner party for the Creedy Company boys."

Andrew clicked his tongue. "And we can't kill him? Why not?"

"Because. After he sees his wife with me, it'll be safe to bet he'll show up here the next day. That's when I'll kill him."

"You want us to prep for it?" Andrew asked.

"Yeah."

"Ooo. We should use shed two. It has all the blacksmith tools," Michael rubbed his hands together.

"I don't give a shit which shed. Just be sure it has some sort of tub with access to running water...and a wooden chair."

"That'll be shed ten then. It has plumbing," Andrew interrupted.

"Hot water?" Dante asked.

"Mhm."

"Good. Get it set up."

This would be easy. Probably easier than most hits. Hmm. Was he rushing this? Trinity suffered an entire year at Fallon's hands only to be snuffed out in one night. He should suffer longer. Be made to experience the same terror he put his wife through. Three hundred and sixty-five days of pure hell. God knew he was capable of it. He could easily sustain a person for a year whilst torturing them. Something told him, Trinity would hate him for it if she ever found out.

It would be better to kill the fucker right away. Get him off the planet as soon as possible. After that, he'd clean house in the first precinct. He didn't need wife beaters on his payroll.

He would also need to convince Trinity her husband was dead, and she was out of danger. The best way would be to have a police officer tell her, but they were apparently all fucking corrupt. But, maybe Fallon's buddy would be a good candidate. After the asshole breaks the news, he'd off him too. Easy.

"Mr. Venturi," Ms. Jewell knocked once before poking her head in the doorway.

"Come in."

"Eugenia buzzed me and said there's a police officer asking for you."

Ah. What took him so long? Really, he didn't need to go through the dramatics of hosting an appreciation night for the cops now. He could just take him to shed ten and kill him today. But where was the fun in that? Nah. He liked to play with his food.

"Did he give a name?" Dante swivelled his chair back and forth, his fingers steepled.

"David Fallon, I believe Eugenia said. Is he any re...,"

"Perfect," Dante interrupted. "Send him up. See that we're not disturbed."

This was going to be fun. David would demand to know where his wife was, and he'd tell him he hadn't seen her. Then, when he sees them together tomorrow night, he'll really lose his shit. He couldn't wait to see his face.

Ms. Jewell opened the door for David, then quickly disappeared. Well, Samuel was definitely right. The man looked frazzled, hung over and straight up pissed. Yeah, there was no way he was going to touch a hair on Trinity's head ever again.

"Where the fuck is she?" David's chest puffed in and out.

"Excuse me?" Dante stayed in his seat, expression blank.

"Don't play games with me. I remember you. You're that asshole who claimed to own that club."

"I do own that club. How can I help you, deputy?"

"Where. Is. My. Wife?!" David spat.

"I honestly do not know. Why do you think she would be here of all places?" Dante tilted his head, his brow wrinkled in feigned confusion.

David pulled at his hair letting out a frustrated cry. "Because!" he erupted. "Because! Because! Because! She told me she got a job here working for you! Are you fucking her?"

"Sir, I'm going to have to ask you to calm down. I'd hate to call security."

"Oh, that's rich. Do you not see the badge?" David jabbed his chest.

"I see it just fine. Now if I'm to understand you correctly, your wife informed you she is employed here. May I ask her name?"

"You fucking know her name. It's Trinity Fallon."

Dante gave David a look that silenced him for the time being, then turned to his computer. "Surely you must know with a company this big, I would never know all of my employees as I don't do the hiring personally." He knew all of his employees. Every single one of them. He also frequently sat in or conducted interviews himself. David didn't need to know that. "But, I have a database of everyone at my disposal. I'll be more than happy to see if she's a registered employee."

Luckily, Trinity's paperwork wasn't fully processed. She wouldn't yet appear on the employee list, which was perfect. He could show Mr. Fallon. Normally he would never do such a thing, but the man wasn't long for the world.

Dante shook his head with a grimace. "I don't see your wife's name, sir. Take a look." He turned the computer screen so David could see.

David's eyes were blown and red from either too much drink or drugs, probably both. He was out of his mind. Perhaps his plan wouldn't go too well. Would the guy put two and two together? He hoped not. Would he even show up tomorrow night? He hoped so. It would ruin his fun, if the plan fell through.

David licked his lips nervous, seemingly at a loss for what to do or say. Aww. How sweet.

"I'm sorry I couldn't help you, sir."

"I don't get it this. She told me she worked here. She got a job here," David pounded his fist into his palm.

"I don't even have a record of an application from your wife, Mr. Fallon. Are you certain she told you it was my business she interviewed with?"

"Yeah. Ya know something ain't right," David sniffed, looking around. "You, of all people, own this joint along with that club. You saw my wife at the club," he planted his hands onto his hips. "You liked her. I saw the way you looked at her," David laughed, jabbing his finger toward Dante. "I'm not dumb."

"Mr. Fallon, if your wife walked into my office today, I wouldn't recognize her. I'm a businessman. I mingle with all of my guests to ensure they're having a good time. Once I move onto the next guest, the last is forgotten. I don't have time to play games," Dante laced his fingers over his stomach. "And, not for anything, but don't you think I could have any woman I want? If you knew anything about me, like most do, they know I'm only seen with supermodels. No offense, but I highly doubt your wife is a supermodel. You wouldn't be a cop if she were."

David was getting on his nerves. This guy had to believe Trinity didn't work here. He had to believe Dante didn't know her. Otherwise, this wouldn't be as fun. Fucker was ruining the game for him.

"You're an insulting prick. You know you're talking to a cop, right?"

"I'm speaking with a man frantic to find his wife. I hardly blame you, sir. I would be the same way. But how fortunate you are to be an officer of the law with many resources at your fingertips. If anyone can find her, I'm sure you can. I'm sorry I couldn't help you. I wish I could have."

David's demeanor shifted. "Here's my card. If she happens to come in to interview with you, please call me."

Dante stood up. "Absolutely."

"Oh, and don't tell her I'm looking for her. I'd like our reunion to be a surprise."

Oh, it will be. Not to worry, David Fallon. It's gonna be a big fucking surprise you piece of shit, Dante mused. "I wish you all the luck, Mr. Fallon."

No amount of luck was going to help David Fallon. No amount of luck, no amount of resources. Had David been a smart man, he would have known just who he was dealing with. He'd known Dante owned his ass. But, not everyone could be so smart. That was just fine with him. Tomorrow night was going to be perfect. He couldn't wait to see the fucker's expression.

-#-

Unlike his other employees from the day before, Trinity was on time. When he rang the bell, it took her only a few seconds to open the door and his breath caught. So this was what the gates of heaven looked like. Trinity stood in a modest, ankle length cocktail dress. It was like something out of the thirties with its black chiffon design. Dante stared at the vintage Hollywood vision before him. Even her hair was fashioned in large waves framing her face much like the era.

"Beautiful," he breathed.

She blushed, allowing him in.

How could anyone lay a finger of harm on this woman? She was so young, so gorgeous. He was going to mutilate David Fallon. Then, he was going to make her his. No one would ever touch her again. Not so long as he drew breath. He would protect her til he died.

"I know this isn't something women normally wear to a club, but I really fell in love with it," she quietly remarked, skimming her hand over the fabric.

"It's perfect. You match my attire well. I'm pretty certain not many will be in a three piece suit," he smiled.

Trinity giggled soft. Not that it was a laugh. It was a one syllable giggle. Still. It was nice.

"I-is there anything I should know going into tonight? Should I know about the company or the people you're entertaining?"

"We're entertaining. And, no, you don't need to. I'm not going to allow any shop talk. It's simply a dinner. Their wives will be along. It won't be awkward. But, uh, Trinity, I do have one request."

"Okay?"

"We're going to be in the VIP lounge. I'd like it if you would stay in the lounge at all times. The lounge has everything you'll need for the evening. Restrooms, bar, even a terrace if you need air. I was made aware I have a rowdy group coming in tonight, and I really would prefer you stay by my side."

"Of course. Thank you for telling me."

"Good. Shall we go?"

"We shall," Trinity smiled brightly.

That's what he liked to see. There was a slight strain to her smile, but there was also a glimmer of hope. She wanted this night, needed it. She had taken care when she styled her hair and applied her makeup.

It didn't take a genius to know David Fuckhead didn't take her out ever. Oh, wait. That wasn't correct. He had taken her to the club, but it wasn't for her benefit. No. It had been for his benefit. She was a showpiece.

While Dante couldn't ignore the fact she was the hottest woman in his club, he would never make her dress like she had been for his sake. Nor would he want her to. Her assets were on full display, with many eyes ogling her. Never would he want others seeing what belonged to him. David Fallon was a sick fuck. A sick fuck who was going to pay. Dearly.

It was a little after nine when they arrived. Dante's guests would either be there or arriving soon. This was good. He needed time to assess the place. Glancing around, things seemed to be in order for tonight. Soon, the place would be full of officers of the law. Once he saw David in the building, he would make certain the man stayed around until at least midnight.

At that point, Dante's dinner would be wrapping up. Even if his guests weren't ready to leave, he would announce his departure. That's when he'd also cue his men to force David into position, using a distraction, and gain his attention on the VIP staircase. He'd see Dante and Trinity leaving together, yet be unable to get anywhere near them. It was an easy plan. He had every confidence it would go smoothly. It had to.

David Fallon needed to see Trinity moved on without his ass. That she was brave enough to do it. Then, tomorrow, David would undoubtedly barge into his office. It would be a fatal and final mistake. Dante had to stop himself from rubbing his hands together like some mad scientist.

Dante escorted Trinity up the staircase to the VIP lounge where the two couples he invited were already waiting. The Creedy Company was a legitimate company who used Venturi Transportation to ship medical equipment overseas. The two men were older, in their fifties, and their wives looked overly excited to be there.

"Mr. Creedy, Mr. Gimbel, ladies, I hope you haven't been waiting too long."

"Dante! Not at all. Nice to see you."

"Likewise. Trinity, I'd like you to meet Edward Creedy and his wife, Gladys, and Jake Gimbel and his wife, Olivia. This is my new assistant, Trinity Fallon."

"Nice to meet you," Trinity whispered with a soft smile and shook everyone's hands.

"Assistant? That's a shame," Edward said.

Trinity looked nervous at Dante making him smile. "Not at all. All my employees have every opportunity to move up the ladder."

"That's not what I meant. She looks prettier on your arm, son," Edward nudged Dante.

"Oh, yes. You two are a handsome couple. Aren't they, Olivia?"

"Mhm. They remind me how the old mafia gangsters used to dress. You know, the ones from the forties?"

Dante stiffened, but forced himself to relax. "Fashion does have a way of circling around every so many decades. Shall we have a drink?"

Relieved to be off the topic of mafia, he waved over his waitress and settled down at the dining table. It was interesting to see where everyone chose to sit. It reminded him of how every family gathering ended up. At least in his family. All the women in the kitchen, all the men around the television. The women tonight decided to sit next to each other, and the men the same. Looking at Trinity, she seemed very relaxed. He smiled. She needed this.

"Is your gown chiffon, dear?" Olivia asked, gently touching the fabric on Trinity's arm.

"It is. I found it at a boutique near my h-home," Trinity looked at Dante worried.

Dante sent a reassuring smile. "Trinity just moved to town. I was delighted she chose to apply at my company."

"Ha! I bet you were, you sly dog," Jake laughed.

Dante chuckled with a shake of his head, then thanked the waitress who distracted everyone by serving the drinks.

"Is that mother of pearl sewn into the fabric," Olivia continued to ask about Trinity's gown.

"Oh, um, I believe it's freshwater pearl. B-b-but I don't believe they're real." Trinity swallowed hard, obviously embarrassed of her stammer.

"Gorgeous. You have wonderful taste. Not like the women downstairs."

"I didn't mind the view," Edward nudged Jake.

"Yes, well, it's a bit difficult to impose a dress code. I'd have no customers if I did," Dante remarked amused.

"Oh, I know it's the way young people dress nowadays. But, there's no fashion in it. It's just seems to be about how much skin someone can show. Tacky if you ask me."

"It is not. I think it's revolutionary," Jake pounded his fist on the table.

"Shut it, Jake," Olivia complained.

"Yes, dear. So, Dante, how is business lately?"

"Nah uh ah. No shop talk tonight, boys. This night is purely for relaxation. However, it's very good," Dante winked opening the menu.

"So what's good, son?" Edward sniffed looking over his choices.

"Everything, not that I'm biased or anything," Dante joked.

"I want a big, juicy steak."

"Your cholesterol, dear," Gladys reminded.

"I don't care. I'm havin' it. Plus, it's free."

Gladys gasped embarrassed causing everyone to laugh. Dante's eyes roamed over to Trinity. She seemed relaxed among his older guests, and genuinely laughed at the banter the couples had going. God, she was beautiful. What he wouldn't give to taste that lip she kept biting. It wasn't something that would be happening any time soon, but daydreams were meant to be fun.

"So, dear, do you have a boyfriend?" Olivia asked curious. "You must. You're so gorgeous."

Trinity's face fell. Fuck. He didn't want Trinity to ever have to talk about her stupid fuck of a husband. Perhaps he would let her handle this on her own. He wasn't Trinity's father. It would be interesting to hear what she would choose to disclose.

"I-I'm married."

The two women stared at her, blinking a few times surprised.

"Married? My goodness, child. How old are you? You couldn't be a day over eighteen, nineteen?"

"I'm twenty. I was married last year."

"Ah. So you and your husband decided to move to a new city to start your lives. How romantic," Gladys assumed.

"Actually, I'm getting divorced. I moved here on my own," Trinity bit her lip.

Interesting. It was a surprise hearing Trinity lie. Dante didn't know she was capable of it. Also interesting was the fact she bit her lip when she told the lie. Come to think of it, she bit her lip when he told everyone she was his assistant. A telltale sign for whenever she lied. Good to know.

"I'm so sorry. I didn't mean to bring up a sore subject, dear."

"It's alright," Trinity smiled kind. "I've definitely had fun exploring all of the boutiques in my new town. The townhouse I'm in is beautiful, so I'm having fun decorating it," Trinity breathed sinking her teeth into that plump flesh of hers.

Lying to make another feel good, or better in this case. She was selfless. No surprise there. However, what part had she been lying about? Probably the part about decorating the townhouse. She was straight up uncomfortable spending his money.

"Isn't it fun? I loved doing that when we first moved into our new home. Remember Jake?"

"Nope. I'm having the steak too."

Olivia rolled her eyes.

"Trinity, what do you think you're going to have?"

Trinity hadn't looked at her menu. She picked it up and quickly perused the choices, then closed it not more than a minute later surprising Dante.

"The Portobello ravioli dish."

"You don't want a steak? They're the best here," Dante coaxed.

"Tempting, buuut steak doesn't trump my love for Portobello anything," Trinity giggled placing her fingertips to her lips.

Sweet. This girl was going to be his undoing. He could feel it. Yup. David Fallon was going to pay for hurting his future wife. Fucker. He needed to get the douche out of his head. For now.

The rest of the dinner went off without a hitch. It was beyond pleasant. The women chatted about whatever women talked about, and Dante spoke with the men about sports and hunting.

It was nearing midnight. He needed to make excuses or maybe he wouldn't have to. Gladys hid a yawn that quickly became contagious. Perfect.

"This was a wonderful evening, Dante. Thank you so much for inviting us."

"It was my pleasure. We should do it again soon."

"Only if Trinity will be there," Gladys smiled giving Trinity a friendly squeeze of her hand.

"Oh, yes! In fact, let's exchange numbers. I'd love to go to lunch with you girls." Olivia held up her phone.

Trinity was quick to agree, partaking in the exchange of phone numbers. Aside from Eugenia and this so called Becky friend, she now had two new ones. True they weren't in her age group, but that hardly mattered when it came to friendship.

Everyone stood up, shook hands and soon departed.

"Trinity, I need to use the restroom. Please wait for me here, yeah?"

"Sure."

Dante quickly entered the bathroom and pulled out his phone.

"Andrew. Please tell me he's here. Good. Get him into position. Trinity and I are leaving in exactly one minute."

Showtime. Dante's heart beat fast with excitement. He couldn't wait to see the fucker's face. Couldn't wait to see the astonishment, the anger, the resolve. Yes, the resolve. That resolve was what would bring him to the office tomorrow morning. It would be then he'd learn what a fatal error he made. Time couldn't pass fast enough.

"Did you have a nice evening, Trinity?"

"I did. Thank you, Dante."

"You are very welcome. Perhaps next time you could try my chef's steak?"

Trinity blushed and looked away with a slight nod.

"Let's be on our way."

Dante opened the door and gestured for Trinity to leave, a hand on the small of her back. But it was a mistake to let Trinity out of the room first. She spotted him right away. The small intake of air from the breath catching in her throat, and she was frozen on the first step. This was bad. If David looked up to see them too soon, it would make Andrew and Michael's job harder than what it had to be. It would be better if David caught a glimpse of them when they were near the foot of the stairs. Fuck. Dante leaned in til his breath fanned Trinity's ear.

"Walk. He won't touch you. He'll never touch you again, Trinity. You have my word."

A shiver went down her spine, but she listened. Thank God, she listened and started down the stairs. He wasn't going to lie, it swelled his pride a bit to know she trusted him. It didn't matter how much, but it had to be a great deal. If David got his hands on her, it would most certainly be game over. Her life was in his hands. There was no way, he'd drop her.

As if there was some sort of radar between them, David's eyes fell onto Trinity as they were mid-way down the staircase. This was okay. Andrew and Michael were on it. A smirk automatically lifted Dante's lips.

David's face fell, his eyes grew large, and all color drained from his skin. He had gone from pink to paste in a matter of seconds. All the while, Trinity was stoic. Dante even wagered to say, her chin lifted and her shoulders squared as she continued her descent.

Then it happened. David's eyes tore themselves away from Trinity and settled onto him. Dante's smirk in place, he saluted David and ushered Trinity safely out the door. Mission accomplished.

Dante wanted to let out a whoop of triumph. The moment was too perfect. David's ghostly parlor had quickly changed to red, unmitigated fury. He would bet his fortune the fucker would pay him a visit tomorrow morning. That's when the real fun would begin.

Till then, David Fallon.

Chapter 10

Trinity unzipped her gown, let it fall to the floor and stepped out of it. Instead of her customary shower, she decided a hot bath would be better. The jets in the tub were too enticing to pass up. Especially after the night she had. At least that's what a normal thought process looked like. If she did have a bath, it would be the first since the dunking incident. To say she wasn't nervous about submerging her body in a vat of water would be a lie.

The truth was, her old self would have loved a bath. She needed to push her new self aside so that she could hang onto at least one thread of who she used to be, no matter how scary. She couldn't lose sight of who she once was. If she did, she would never remember her truth. Never remember her strength. And she used to be strong way back when. Now...maybe not so much.

With a great sigh, Trinity thought on it no more deciding to fill the tub and her mind with the fresh memories of the night. Dante paid her a compliment. Her first outside of David. Only, David's compliments were never heart felt. Dante's compliment was. He had a look in his eyes that, she'd wager to say, was almost one of reverence. It had to have been her imagination. She didn't do anything to earn his respect or awe. However, he sure seemed to truly mean it when he said she looked beautiful.

Trinity sucked in a breath, gingerly stepping inside the tub. She sunk in with a loud sigh. The water seeped into her pores down to her bones, cradling her entire body in warmth. While the water wasn't hot, it was far from cold triggering flashbacks of David's cruelty. Trinity bit her lip as her breath turned shallow and her chest tightened. The logical part of her brain fought the quiet panic. She needed to breathe. In for a five count out for an eight. But, it was no use.

The familiar sensations of panic started their waves. Tight chest, tight throat, unable to take a satisfying breath. She tried again to fill her lungs only to be stopped by the grip. If she could only take a large breath, she would feel much better. Again and again, she gulped air to no avail. It didn't take long to hyperventilate. She knew her erratic breathing was to blame. Lightheadedness caused a queer sensation, making her nauseated. Finally, the buzz happened.

How she hated the buzz. Tiny tingles started in her fingertips and toes, slowly moving upwards. Soon, the odd sensation would find its way across her diaphragm and into her face, working into a full, paralyzing numb.

"This isn't new. I've had this before. I'm okay." Trinity grabbed her knees pulling them up to her chest and started to rock. "I'm okay. I'm okay. I'm okay," she whispered the mantra.

Attempting to swallow against her parched throat, she grabbed the sides of the tub in a panic when she couldn't, sloshing water over the floor. Her heart thrummed wild in her chest, and the room spun for a brief moment.

"Stop. It's just a panic attack. I can do this. He's not here. I'm safe," she whimpered. "I'm safe. I'm safe. I'm...safe!" she screamed with tears running down her face.

Out of breath, Trinity flexed her hands, shooing the numb away. While her chest heaved, she worked to transition her breathing from chest to belly. If she put her hand against her stomach, she could feel the soothing rise and fall. Again. In for a five count, out for an eight count. Over and over she did this until she found a comforting rhythm.

Then, she remembered another grounding technique. Glancing around the bathroom, she found different colors. White tile, blue towel, green plant, pink pajamas.

"White, blue, green, pink. White, blue, green, pink. White, blue, green... pink," she yawned squeezing her eyes shut. At last a large breath.

Finally. It was passing. How long was that? Five minutes? Ten? Had to be at the very least. Trinity dared to drag her hands from her stomach to run them along the porcelain tub rails. Smooth and cool. Comforting. The numbness in her arms and legs started to ebb despite her still tight chest. It was to be expected. That was always the last to loosen up after a panic attack.

Laying her head back exhausted, she refused to get out of the tub. She used to love baths, and she deserved to love them again. Truth was, David wasn't there. She was safe. And...this moment was under her control. She would not, could not, allow her emotions to get the best of her. The realization for it caused her toes to wiggle and bubbles to swish in lazy circles. Her lips curled upward. Yes, she had a panic attack. Yes, she survived it. Instead of feeling ashamed, she allowed herself to feel proud. It felt good to be able to regain control as quickly as she did.

Trinity rewarded herself by reflecting on the new memories, and only the new. Her smile widened. She never felt more beautiful in the chiffon gown with its freshwater pearl details. It was something she never owned before. Eugenia insisted she buy it, promising it was necessary she look her best for Dante's dinner. She promised to pay Dante back with her first check.

Eugenia promised the check wouldn't cover the dress and told her to forget paying Dante anything.

It felt strange handing over a credit card that didn't belong to her, then handing the receipt to Eugenia who claimed it was a business expense. Was this how the rest of the world worked? Something told her it wasn't. But it was at Venturi Transportation.

Trinity owed everything to Becky who talked her going into the business. How she longed to call and tell her all about this night. About shopping with Eugenia and meeting new people. Especially Gladys and Olivia. Sure they were older than her, but were so much fun to talk with. They treated her as an equal and seemed genuinely interested in what she had to say.

Olivia even patted her hand to tell her she was glad she was divorcing and starting her life anew. How strong she was for doing it. Gladys agreed and kept alluding to how much Dante was looking at her. Trinity never blushed so much in her life. Even in the present moment, Trinity could feel the heat climbing into her cheeks. She pressed her knuckles against her dewy skin.

Another thing Trinity wished to tell Becky was how, with each minute passing, her stammering lessened til she didn't do it at all. She felt so relaxed with the women, there was no need to stammer. But, she couldn't call Becky. She wouldn't. Though she owed much to her friend, she had to keep her safe. That and there was something in her gut which told her something wasn't right. She remembered how unconcerned Becky sounded on the phone when she called her. It didn't settle well with her.

Dismissing further thought of Becky, Trinity ran a loofah over her arms and legs. It felt so good to luxuriate over the feel of the natural coral against her skin comingeled with the creamy soap.

Oh! And, yet, another thing was how amazed she felt to be able to choose what she wanted to eat for dinner. Sure, Dante mentioned the steak but it was to be expected. According to Dante and the men in their party, the club was known for its steak dinner. Dante didn't make anything of the fact she wanted the ravioli dish. It wasn't a big deal whatsoever. It was an amazing feeling.

She felt on cloud nine when he suggested she try the steak another time. Another time! God, to think he actually suggested they'd go to dinner again. It was unthinkable! Sure, Dante probably didn't mean it and was just being nice. Still. It felt so wonderful to be treated normally.

But that wasn't the best part. One of the best parts was when he covered for her telling the women she had moved to town. He didn't embarrass her and tell them she lived in his townhouse. He could have, but didn't. To not be belittled but, rather, lifted was truly a foreign feeling.

The grand finale was when he dropped her at the doorstep. He told her what a wonderful evening it was, then kissed her hand. Kissed. Her. Hand! In that moment, fireworks might as well have shot up into the sky exploding in a spectacular show. Their imagined, thunderous ramparts pressing against her chest with heavy excitement. This was what his one simple gesture caused throughout her being.

Never in her entire life did she ever feel like that. Not even in the very beginning with David. Not ever. Yet, this man, her boss, made her feel so much with the smallest, briefest kiss to her palm. A gesture considered gentlemanly and timeless. That's what he was. Timeless.

Olivia compared him to a nineteen forties gangster. Actually, that wasn't entirely true. She compared their outfits to the nineteen forties mafia gangsters. Trinity giggled. Dante really did look the part too. He was also smooth, put together, classy, smart and kind. He was probably much more, but those traits were what she gathered so far.

Her memories then skimmed over the worst part of the night, and she shifted uncomfortable in the tub. She would never forget David's face when he saw her on that staircase. He looked like he had seen a ghost. She would also never forget the surge of courage coursing through her in that moment. Somehow she managed to square her shoulders and lift her chin, continuing her way out the door. But she knew why. She knew how she managed. It was Dante. He was strong for her, telling her to walk. Assuring her David wouldn't harm her.

Letting go and trusting felt amazing. Letting go, trusting and having someone uphold that trust was even better. Was this too good to be true? Was she walking into another controlling situation? Maybe. She would keep her guard up.

Thinking further of David made the water feel tepid. Trinity's stomach started to tighten with old memories worming their way and darkening the bigger, pleasant thoughts. It was time to get out of the tub.

Dressing in her new teacup printed pajamas, Trinity brushed the curls out of her hair, replacing the style with a loose messy bun, then quickly brushed her teeth. The sooner she could crawl into bed, the sooner she could return to her fantasies.

It was well after one in the morning. Thank goodness she had the rest of the week off from work. She would need to sleep in. She wasn't used to staying up late. Early to bed and early to rise was her usual routine, one she didn't think she would ever stray from. Tonight was an exception because of the dinner. In reality, she doubted she would have any more late nights. That was okay.

The memory of this night would keep her just fine for awhile. And, once she started her receptionist duties, she would eventually fall into a peaceful routine. Dante would probably forget about her at that point.

Just how would a new routine feel? Would she be able to do the job? She told Dante and Ms. Jewell she didn't have any experience for the position. They didn't seem to mind. Eugenia would train her.

That was another thing she wanted to tell Becky. Eugenia was a fast friend. It was too bad the three of them couldn't spend time together. But, it was for Becky's own good. David knew Trinity and Becky were friends, but he didn't know how close they really were. Kind of. In any event, she had done that on purpose. She wouldn't be able to bare it if anything ever happened to Becky at David's hands because of her. Even if Becky was acting a bit strange lately. So, the extent of their friendship was a definite secret.

Becky never seemed to mind. Did she mind now? She didn't seem angry with her, only distant and...cold? Still. It felt uncomfortable spending time with Eugenia over Becky. A part of her felt guilty for it, but it couldn't be helped. Becky needed to stay alive and well. If she continued a friendship with her, Becky would be in danger.

Trinity shivered under the heavy covers of her new bed. It was odd sleeping alone. Usually David's snoring filled the room. While she wasn't quite used to its absence, she didn't miss it either. He never lulled her to sleep. Sometimes, when his breathing would stop for a few seconds, she felt disappointed when he would breathe again. It was a bad thought, she knew. She often prayed for forgiveness.

Did God set her on this new path or was it dumb luck? Did it really matter? For now, she was on a new path. She had a new job, new clothes, new home and new people to befriend. This was her second chance. She would work hard and save her paychecks and then maybe leave the entire state behind. She could change her name, even her hair and eye color. David would never find her.

It was probably a wise plan to make. If David ever remembered where she worked, he could easily go there and hurt her. It was a concern she needed to speak to Ms. Jewell about. Although, if she did that, would Dante fire her? No. He promised David wouldn't hurt her again. But how? How could he ensure her safety at the front desk?

Yawning, Trinity decided to let the worry go. Morning was soon, and she needed sleep. She needed to call Eugenia and find out if she needed to do anything from home. If she wasn't mistaken, Eugenia told her she should expect a laptop delivery. Maybe setting it up would be her assignment for the day. That would be good. She had computer classes in high school, and would occasionally use David's computer whenever he wanted her to look things up for him. So even though it was limited experience, it was still experience she could put to good use.

A second yawn over took her rambling thoughts until the darkness of the night swept her away into sleep.

-#-

Morning was cruel. It forced its way into everything. Into the air, into and between the curtains and filled the room with annoying brightness.

Trinity groaned pulling the covers over her head. What time was it? She peaked at the nightstand clock to see it was already seven. Wow. She never slept that late. She should get up, eat breakfast and get her body moving. Even though it was going to be a quiet day, she didn't want to get lazy.

Pulling on her robe, she felt around her head for the hair tie clinging to a lopsided bun and pulled it out letting her hair fall in a tumble of waves. Ah! That felt much better. How the heck did she sleep like that all night? Shaking her head with a laugh, she went into the bathroom to pop in her lenses and assess her face. Mascara was smeared under her eyes.

Great. She forgot to remove her makeup despite her bath. Splashing water onto her face, she cleansed then moisturized herself back to normal. Much better. Now for breakfast. For a brief moment, she contemplated going for a run. Food was definitely more appealing.

What she wouldn't give for one of the doughnuts Dante brought the other day. Those things were to die for. She could easily eat them on the daily. A moment on the lips, a lifetime on the stupid hips. A lifetime was so short, she whimpered.

At least she had a Keurig. A nice cup of coffee was the ticket. Yawning wide, Trinity tapped her nails on the counter waiting for the machine to gurgle to life. She jumped a mile when her doorbell rang. Was it the laptop already? Nervous, she silently made her way to the door and peeked out the peephole. A large breath of relief let loose. It was Dante. Did he have a doughnut bag in his hand? She peeked again. Nope. Dang it.

"Good morning, Dante," she smiled bright then remembered she still had her robe on and tightened the sash.

"Morning. Can I come in for a minute?"

He looked serious. Oh no. Was he going to kick her out? Was she fired? Did she do something wrong? Why was he here? She swallowed hard against her quickening pulse.

"I-is t-t-there something wrong?"

Dante whirled around nearly knocking into her. Instinctively, he reached out and steadied her shoulder.

"I'm sorry. No, no. There's nothing wrong. Uh, Eugenia told me your computer is arriving today."

"Y-yes."

"Good. I would like for you to set it up and spend today getting familiar with it. Eugenia will give you a network code to enter and it will then link our accounts. You'll keep the laptop here because you'll have a desktop in your office."

"My office?" her brow creased confused.

"Yes. I told you. Ms. Jewell is going to train you for the assistant position. Have you forgotten?"

"I-I don't remember. I-I-I t-t-thought I was hired for the receptionist position."

"No. I don't want you out front. You'll work on my floor in an office next to Ms. Jewell's. She'll be retiring soon, and will train you to take her place."

Trinity wasn't sure she heard correctly. Was she still sleeping? What the heck? Not that she had any experience working in an office, but she did remember Eugenia telling her how excited she was to have received a promotion into an assistant position. Why would someone like herself be given a position usually earned like Eugenia had to do? How was that fair? And wouldn't other employees be envious and angry with her?

"With all due respect, Dante, I don't see how I can accept that position."

"Why not?" he frowned.

"I haven't earned it. Won't other people be upset with me?"

"I don't care about other people, Trinity. It's my company," he shrugged. "People know not to question my actions. If you have a problem, you come to me. Besides, no one aside from Eugenia, Ms. Jewell and I know your work history. Eugenia and Ms. Jewell aren't going to say anything to anyone. They're trusted employees. Plus, they owe me. Anyway, you'll take the position and that's final."

"Oh. Okay," Trinity's voice shrunk.

Dante took an instinctive step closer and hooked his finger under her chin lifting her face. "Trinity, don't ever feel small. Last night you displayed courage. I'm proud of you. I've known men who could never do what you did last night."

Trinity's eyes watered, "Thank you."

"I should go. I have a meeting." Dante turned to leave but stopped at the front door. "Oh, one more thing. Don't go anywhere today. Stay home."

"Oh. Okay. Is there any reason?"

"Your husband saw you last night. I want you to stay home. Check in with Eugenia before work ends. If you need dinner, have it delivered."

Trinity stared into Dante's eyes for a full minute. An uneasy feeling scaled her spine causing the hairs to raise on the back of her neck.

"Wh-wh-who are you, Dante?" she whispered.

Dante held her gaze for a measure, "Your boss."

The door closed soft with a click.

Chapter 11

Why did he go to her house again? It was as if he couldn't stay away. In doing so, he raised her suspicion. He didn't need that. If she were very curious, she could easily do an internet search and find numerous articles linking him to his famous family. Actually, he was surprised she hadn't already. Perhaps the attraction was one sided. God, he hoped not.

Either way, he couldn't stop thinking about last night. It kept him awake. She was so perfect. Especially when they were leaving. Never had he seen such bravado in such tiny packaging. Some of his toughest men would never be so bold. It was as if she were daring David. It was truly impressive.

Trinity was the one for him. No doubt about it. She complimented him perfectly. Even Gladys and Olivia noticed going so far as to comment on them as a couple. It felt damn good. But, Trinity was damaged. For him to establish a relationship, even with attraction, would take a very long time. It would require finesse.

Not that he particularly relished the thought of manipulating Trinity's feelings, but it had to be done. He needed to win her trust. Once he established that, he could move forward with suggesting therapy if she wanted it. Hopefully she did. She didn't deserve to live with the demons she carried.

If only he had met her before David Fallon. But for any real chance of that, he would have needed to be ten years younger. Perhaps attending the same school. If his nephew, Gio, wouldn't have had private schooling, he could have met her a few years ago himself. No matter what, Dante's age was against him. Nothing could be done for it. Well, that wasn't particularly true. One thing could be done. One thing would be done. Eradicating David Fallon's age all together. Today was the day.

If the cocksucker didn't show up, he'd hunt him down. He wasn't about to play any more games. Then, after today, he'd have someone tell Trinity David was dead and go from there. Dante dragged in a deep breath. Today was Trinity's independence day. She just didn't know it yet.

What time was it? Seven thirty. He needed to get to the office. He'd go in through the private entrance in the back rather than the front. For all he knew, David could be waiting for him when the damn building opened. He didn't need that. Hopefully, the idiot didn't go in with guns blazing. Of course, even if he did, he'd be gunned down immediately. There was no way he'd let any of his employees suffer any harm by the fuck.

Dante stepped on the gas and made it to the office in record time. The scrape guard on his vehicle hit the ramp causing him to cringe. Too fast. Slowing his speed, he parked into his designated spot and went inside.

Everything seemed normal. People were heading to their offices nodding their hellos, some more enthusiastic than others. A woman, who took care of some of the data entry, ran up and offered him a coffee. Was that her coffee? He politely declined. He wasn't about to drink someone else's coffee.

Another employee, one of his accountants, offered his newspaper. What was wrong with people? He'd bet a finger the man had that thing in the bathroom with him. No thank you. Dante shook his head. He couldn't get to his office fast enough. Christ!

"Mr. Venturi! Oh! Mr. Venturi!"

Great. Margaret. She tried nearly everyday to gain a word with him. He didn't have time for this. He needed to brief Andrew and Michael. When David arrived, which he would, his men needed to be with him. From his office they would transport David to shed two, or was it ten? Yes, ten. Ten had plumbing. He would definitely need running water.

"Good morning, Margaret. Have a nice day," Dante smiled but kept walking. If he stopped now, he'd be doomed.

"Oh, Mr. Venturi, can I have a moment of your time?"

"Uh...I have a meeting. I'm sorry, I can't sit down."

"I see. Perhaps lunch?"

"I'm not free today, Margaret. My calendar is quite full. Whatever it is, I'm sure you can ask Ms. Jewell."

"Ms. Jewell is so busy, Mr. Venturi. I'd hate to bother her. I was hoping to speak to you directly. It's about my position."

"Mmm." Sure it was. Dante picked up his pace.

He didn't want to hear about how she should have Jewell's position when she retired. Of course, it wasn't one hundred percent about the position. It was about trying to get him alone. No way. Margaret was nasty. One couldn't necessarily see she was nasty by the looks of her. She was too put together with manicured nails, styled hair and tailored clothing. It was her actions which gave it away. She never hesitated to throw someone under the bus if it suited her. She was the direct opposite to Trinity.

"I was curious to know when interviews were going to be held."

"There will be no interviews, Margaret," he answered exasperated.

"No interviews? Why not?"

Dante stopped short, causing her to stumble. He waited till she righted herself. "The position has been filled."

Margaret's face dropped. "Filled? I don't understand? By whom?"

"No one you know. Now, if you'll excuse me. Have a wonderful day."

Fuck, but she was a harpy. He'd have to tell Jewell to steer clear of the woman and to remind her not to speak about Trinity with anyone other than himself or Eugenia. Something told him Ms. Jewell already knew as much. Still, he would remind her. He didn't want to take any chances.

When Dante reached his office, he set his briefcase down, shrugged off his jacket and loosened his tie a tad. He needed to breathe. Pressing the intercom he called for Andrew and Michael. As boring as it would be, his crew would have to hang out with him for the day. Hopefully, they wouldn't have to wait around too long.

In the meantime, Gio should also be stopping by to update him on things. He pressed the intercom.

"Ms. Jewell, tell Gio I have a meeting this morning and not to report. If he has an issue, tell him to call me. Also, tell Eugenia if David Fallon comes in to send him straight to my office. And I want this floor cleared in the next ten minutes, including yourself. Move everyone to the second floor, please. Just for today." Chances were if David decided on shooting him, he would hold his bullets for his floor alone. He didn't need anyone injured.

"What about Eugenia? Shall we have security next to her desk?"

"No. I don't want them visible. Eugenia will be alright."

"With all due respect, Mr. Venturi, are you certain?"

"Quite. Now get to it. I don't want any delays."

"Yes, sir."

Good. Now there would be no interruptions. He should have thought of moving people ahead of time. Hopefully, everyone would move faster than he instructed. They usually did when he gave orders without question. He sat down and turned on his computer.

"Hey, boss. All clear on this floor," Andrew strolled in a few minutes later and sat down on a couch Dante had against a wall. Michael soon followed and closed the door behind him joining Andrew.

"Thank you. Hopefully, this asshole shows up sooner rather than later."

"It's fine. I have plenty of games to play on my phone," Michael held up his device with a grin.

"Same," Andrew chimed.

A pendulum clock sitting on the credenza behind Dante's desk ticked the seconds. The cadence was soothing and nerve wracking at the same time. Surely, he didn't misjudge this guy.

Time passed into the eight o'clock hour. Where was he? It was probably too early for David Fallon. The guy probably got piss drunk last night. Dante ground his teeth. He wanted to get this show on the road. He wanted David Fallon dead already.

"Do you want me to put some feelers out?"

Dante looked up at Andrew who was correctly judging his mood. "No. Let's give it some time. If it gets close to noon, we'll order lunch and then find out his location. We'll take him if we have to. This gets done today."

Another hour passed before his desk phone rang. The three men exchanged knowing looks. It had to be Eugenia. Dante picked up the receiver.

"Yes?"

"David Fallon is here to see you. He's disgruntled."

Of course he is. Perfect. Dante smirked, "Send him up unescorted, please."

Instinctively, Michael stood and positioned himself, to where it would soon be, behind the door. He drew his gun and held it at his side. Andrew stayed on the couch. Dante pulled his gun and held it under his desk.

Seconds felt like long minutes. The excitement was overwhelming. The room felt charged with energy from the anticipation of all three men. It would be surprising if David didn't feel it when he walked into the room.

Suddenly, the door burst open but stopped short of the wall. David didn't notice Michael stationed behind it.

Ah, yes. This was the face Dante expected to see. He couldn't help his smirk. A very hung over David, eyes red from the previous night's festivities, stumbled into his office. It was clear the only effort he had put into getting ready this morning was getting dressed, and haphazardly at that.

David's shirt was untucked, the buttons didn't line up, one of his shoes were untied, his belt had missed some loops, his hair was sticking up all over the place from obvious pulling and his five o'clock shadow was more like an eclipse. The man was a mess and out of his mind. Perfect.

"You fucking bastard!" David screamed, lunging at Dante's desk and slapping his hands down onto the shiny surface.

Dante swivelled slightly in his chair, his mouth downturned. "What ever do you mean?"

"Shut up!" Spittal sprayed from David's mouth.

Dante craned his neck back to avoid the shower.

"You, shut up! You fucking told me you didn't know her. That she didn't work for you. You goddamn liar! Where is she? I'll search every fucking room here, you prick!"

"That won't be necessary. She's not here."

David pushed himself away from Dante's desk, tripping over the chairs he apparently didn't see. He stumbled backward, but caught himself.

"Seems as though you're still in the bag from last night. Tell me, have you been to the precinct yet? Has your boss seen you today?"

"Are you stupid? I can arrest you for talking to me that way. Do you know who I am?"

"Why, yes, I do. You're David Fallon. Wife beater," Dante smiled, his eyes challenging.

David hesitated. "What the fuck you saying? You know I'm a cop right? I asked if you're stupid?"

"Are you? You must be. Stupid that is. Because, if you were smart, you'd know exactly who I am. And, you'd know exactly who your boss listens to."

It was the first time David took a second to look around himself, finally noticing Michael and Andrew. His step faltered. "What is this? Who are you?"

"I'm Dante Venturi, head of the Venturi Family, Mr. Fallon. You're boss takes order from me. I own his ass just as much as I own yours."

Dante gestured to David with a nod of his head, and Michael quickly disarmed him. David didn't have time to protest.

"Oh, Mr. Fallon, how unlucky you are. I have to tell you, when I first saw your wife in the grocery store not too long ago, I should have stepped in. Really, that is my one regret in life. But, God was smiling down upon me. What were the odds of your gorgeous wife setting foot in my club? Then again, when she came to fill out an application," Dante laughed holding his hands out wide. "I mean, truly, what are the odds? It had to have been meant to be. Wouldn't you say?"

"No," David whispered.

"Oh yes. I've crossed paths with your wife on more than one occasion."

"Where is she?" David's teeth were clenched so tightly, they could have broken a tooth. The vein in his forehead bulged.

"Safe. That was your last question by the way. It's my turn to do the questioning, if you don't mind."

"I'm not answering a goddamn thing."

"That's fine. But, if you don't, Andrew over there will break a finger for each question that goes unanswered. That's twenty-eight questions, may I remind you."

"I only got ten fingers, dickhead."

"Yes. Ten fingers. Three knuckles for each digit with the exception of the thumb which has two. Three multiplied by eight is twenty-four, plus four for the thumbs equals twenty-eight. I don't have twenty-eight questions for you but if I wanted to have some fun now, rather than in a little while, I can come up with them. Your choice. Now shall we begin?" Dante rubbed his hands together before lacing his fingers together.

David swallowed hard, his jaw ticking.

"Great. First question. How is it that you find it so easy to hurt your wife?"

"I never fucking hurt her."

Dante shook his head in regret. "See, I thought this would happen. I thought you might lie to me. Andrew, can we see to it Mr. Fallon is truthful from here on out please?"

Andrew nodded, and stood from the couch cracking his knuckles. He shoved David down onto the chair he had tripped over and took a seat opposite, waving David to give him his hand.

"W-what do you want? I'm not giving you my hand. I answered your question," David said panicked.

Andrew didn't wait grabbing David's hand and slamming it down onto the desk. Holding David's hand down, Andrew picked up Dante's marble paperweight and smashed it down onto the base of David's thumb. David screamed in pain, but Andrew didn't wait for him to finish with his cries quickly smashing every knuckle in all five fingers.

"What the fuck?!" David screamed. "I thought you said twenty-eight questions, god dammit!" he cried. Tears instantly streaked down David's face, erasing all natural coloring till there was only a gray tone left.

"That's for lying. I hate liars. Good job, Andrew. You know me so well."

David cradled his hand against his chest with a shaky grip. His entire body trembled, a cold sweat breaking loose. Oh dear. A vagal response. He didn't need the man passing out on him.

"Michael. Get the man some water, if you would be so kind." Dante continued to swivel observing David with curiosity. "You alright, Mr. Fallon? You look a little pale. I really don't need you passing out on me. There, take the water and drink it. You're probably dehydrated."

"I-I need a doctor," David whimpered.

"A doctor? For what? Did you get Trinity a doctor for each time you beat her?"

"I-I did. I did!"

"Really? Hmm. I did see her hand bandaged when I first met her and then again her arm the other day. You could be telling me the truth, but somehow I doubt it. Andrew, can you do the honors? You're so good at it."

"No! Wait! Wait, wait, wait! I'm sorry! I swear to God I took her."

Andrew hesitated looking to Dante who nodded slightly to go ahead. David's grip was weaker than expected when Andrew stood to grab his other hand, but his lungs still worked. Dante was pretty certain everyone could hear David's screams and pleas as Andrew bashed his other hand to pieces. This time, David did pass out.

Dante itched the back of his neck, then checked his watch. This was to be expected. In fact, he predicted David would be doing a lot of passing out today.

"What a pussy," Andrew remarked.

"Yes, well, not everyone is cut out for pain. We all can't be tough as nails, now, Andrew. Don't judge and help the man stay in his chair," Dante smiled.

After several minutes, David regained consciousness.

"Welcome back, Mr. Fallon. Now, where were we? Ah, yes...,"

"P-p-please n-n-no more," David gagged.

"Well, now," Dante's brows rose surprised. "You know, there's something so interesting. Do you know what it is?" Dante asked waiting for David to answer.

David's head hung low, his arms cradled across themselves. He shook his head.

"I'll tell you. Your stuttering is interesting. I find it so only because your wife stutters. Amazing what fear causes. You did that to her. She can't control the motor movements of her tongue because of you. I find your tongue useless, Mr. Fallon."

Panic filled David's eyes, and he shot up from his chair. "No! Wh-what is this?!" He tried to leave not waiting for an answer, but it was Michael's turn to spin him around sending him back into his seat.

"Haven't you figured it out, Mr. Fallon?"

"N-no," David rasped.

Dante's eyes narrowed, "It's revenge. You see, for Trinity, today is independence day and, for you, today is execution day. You're a dead man walking, Mr. Fallon. Well...sitting," Dante chuckled.

Chapter 12

A hazy resolve settled over David's eyes. Finally, the man sobered and understood. The pain from his broken hands must have numbed or dulled as well because he was no longer screaming and crying. The tears had dried, and he was now silent.

It came at no surprise to Dante. Anyone he ever tortured always experienced what he liked to call the awakening. It was the realization for what was happening...was in fact happening. It was the realization that nothing would save them. No one would come, no one would look for them and no one would miss them once they were discovered gone.

Dante was actually somewhat impressed the awakening happened pretty fast for David. With all the hysterics, he thought it would take longer. The next stage would probably be the bargaining. Surely, David would think of some fantastic argument meant to sway him. Surely. Dante chuckled. As if. Nothing would or could save David Fallon at this point short of a bomb being dropped on the city. And that, most definitely, wouldn't happen.

"Before we leave, I'll let you have a last meal. What would you like?" he asked rubbing his hands together.

"I-I want my wife's chili!" David abruptly shouted, his eyes expectant.

Of course David would take this as a chance. He really had nothing to lose. But, did David truly believe he would ever grant such a wish? If Dante wasn't mistaken, he thought he actually saw a real glimmer of hope in the man's eyes. This hope, yet false, was still hope indeed.

"You wife's chili?" Dante feigned surprised. "And would you like for her to bring it in herself?"

"Yes...please." David dared to glance up.

Hmm. Was it hope in his eyes or was it calculation? Hilarious. Dante nodded and turned to his keyboard to type a few keystrokes, then rubbed his chin. "Let me see here. Ah," he clicked his tongue. "That's a real shame. She is not on the schedule today. Mmm. Mmm. Mmm. That's too bad, Mr. Fallon. I truly was hoping to get you that last meal. I guess it's not gonna work out." Dante slapped his hands down onto his armrests. "Well, boys. Shall we get going? Phase two?"

Michael held the door open while Andrew took David by the elbow.

"What are you doing? Where are we going?" David panicked, darting his glance between Andrew and Dante. "I-I-I'm not going anywhere!"

"Yes, you are, Mr. Fallon. My guess is that you're going straight to hell," Dante answered.

"You're no better!" David screamed. "You're no better!"

"I don't beat or kill women, Mr. Fallon. I suspect if God had to choose between the two of us, he'd definitely pick me thereby making me the better man. Of course, I don't really consider you a man. Anyway, I have a special treat in store for you."

"What?" David stumbled while Andrew push and pulled him along keeping him somewhat upright.

"Oh, you'll see. Once we're on the road, it'll only take us a few minutes to arrive at our destination. I don't know about you, but I am excited."

"I'm not excited at all! Help! Help!" David screamed at the top of his lungs as the men navigated their way through the building's back hallways.

David's voice reverberated off the walls creating an echo. Not all rooms and hallways were soundproof. However, the hallway they were currently in was. A good thing at that. David was extremely loud.

"No one can hear you, Mr. Fallon," Dante explained bored.

Bright sunlight and a black limousine greeted them as soon as they stepped out of the building. Andrew shoved David inside the vehicle while Michael pulled him through the other side, righting him in his seat. Dante followed, sitting opposite David, with a smile and a taunting raise of his brows before a thoughtful expression settled over his face.

"You know," Dante crossed his legs and laced his hands together settling in his seat, "back during the crusades when men fought with shields and swords, they were not afraid of death. Their only concern was fighting for their king and dying with honor. Going out in a blaze hot enough to denote how hard and valiant they fought was sacred. Of course, you're no knight so I can understand your cowardice. But, what a fine coward you make. Tell me, how could beating such a small and defenseless woman make you feel so big? I'm truly curious."

"It didn't. I never meant to hurt her. I never wanted to. I-I love her."

Dante uncrossed his legs and leaned forward. "No, you don't. Don't ever say that again. I'll slap your teeth right out of your fucking mouth," he reclined back, fixing his cuff.

"How are you better?" David glared.

Dante looked up. "How am I better? Truly you jest? That means you've gotta be kidding me. Killing you is going to give me the greatest satisfaction that will undoubtedly last the entirety of my life. I'm better than you because I'm eradicating a monster who tortured a woman. You, by the way, are the monster."

"Murdering wop," David sneered.

Dante chuckled, "You've got some balls talking to me like that, son. Don't you know it's not polite to use ethnic slurs? Hasn't your mother taught you anything? Of course she hasn't."

David spat at Dante, missing him and hitting the floorboard instead. Dante rolled his eyes. Honestly. This guy was going to be a pleasure to kill.

Finally, the sheds came into view and they quickly pulled up outside of shed ten. Dante rubbed his hands together with a loud clap.

"We're here. Excellent," Dante exclaimed brightly.

Andrew and Michael worked on taking David out of the car. He squirmed and kicked uselessly as they pulled him into the shed.

Dante looked around with interest. The unit was mostly empty save a few vehicles that were being stored. What caught his eye was the wooden chair and large metal tub. The tub resembled a horse trough. Upon closer inspection, Dante could see it was. Good enough for his purposes. A long hose, connected to a water source with two spigots, was set down near the trough.

Dante walked over to it, spinning the hot spigot. The sound of running water worked its way through the hose till it spilled out onto the floor. He picked it up and tossed it into the trough, then leisurely worked on shrugging off his suit jacket and rolling his sleeves.

After he was finished righting his clothes, Dante took the wooden chair and dragged it across the floor setting it near the tub. Standing back, he took in the scene before him but shook his head.

"This isn't going to work. I think we'll need to work...backwards," he hissed drawing out the s.

David narrowed his eyes, "W-w-what are you doing?"

David's question had Dante tilting his head bewildered. "Haven't you figured it out? I might be a wop, as you say, but you are truly dense." Without further hesitation, Dante grabbed the wooden chair and whipped it against the concrete wall effectively shattering it to pieces. Running a hand through his hair to smooth it back into place, he strolled over to assess the remains. He found a particularly sharp piece, and held up with a satisfied smile. "First try. Perfect."

David's expression dropped. Ah ha! Did this piece of shit finally understand? About time. He squirmed under Andrew's heavy grip.

"No!"

"Yes." Not wasting time, Dante grabbed David's arm and ran him through with the sharp piece of wood in one swift move.

David howled as his skin gave way with a loud pop. If it weren't for Andrew holding him steady, he would have collapsed. It took a good deal of effort for Andrew to hold the shaking man on his feet.

"Set him down, Andrew. No need to waste your energy."

When Andrew complied, Dante crouched next to David. "You're wife had to endure this. How does it feel?"

"Fuck you!"

"No, thank you. I asked you a question and you will answer. Judging from experience, you know that if you do not answer me the consequences will be severe. So, I'll ask you again. How. Does. It. Feel?" Dante's voice rose higher with each word.

"It burns! Alright! It f-f-fucking burns and p-pain. Y-you hit my b-bone!" he sputtered with a cracked voice.

"Ho! What a coincidence," Dante rang out. "Your wife told me you hit her bone too. You finally have something in common. Too bad you'll never exchange stories," Dante's jaw ticked watching David rock back and forth. Droplets of blood oozed from the fresh wound.

A cold sweat broke out over David's body, his arm pressed against his stomach. After a few seconds, David vomited what was probably his breakfast. He would pass out soon. Stupid vagus nerve. Always in the way.

Dante gestured to the passed out man with a shake of his head, then picked up the hose to wash the vomit down a drain situated in the center of the room. At this point, the tub was filled. Hopefully, David would wake soon. He needed the water nice and hot.

Prodding David with his foot, Dante smiled when his eyes fluttered open. "Welcome back...again. Glad you could join us, Mr. Fallon. Thought you quit on us for a second."

"Fuck you!" David spat. Long, thin strings of saliva hung from his stubbled chin.

"You keep offering, but I must decline. Now it's time for a trip down memory lane, if you will. Michael, Andrew, bring a chair for our guest. Let's see if he can sit up in it," Dante started to pace back and forth waiting for his men to do their job.

Once Michael and Andrew had David in the chair, Dante applauded. "You are good, Mr. Fallon. Very strong indeed. Weaker men wouldn't have been able to sit like you. Anyway, where were we? Ah, yes, memory lane. Do you remember the night your wife made you chicken noodle soup?"

David's expression could be called murderous, but he didn't say a word. Wise.

"Was it good? The soup, I mean?"

David grunted, a slight nod of his head.

"It was store bought. A little detail she enjoyed sharing," Dante smiled.

"Bitch," David spat.

"Tut tut, Mr. Fallon. Do that one more time, and you'll make execution day far better than it already is. That was your final warning."

David's jaw clamped shut, the muscle flaring in and out. The dots must have connected for him. His eyes traveled to the trough much to Dante's delight.

"Anyway, I'm glad you do remember. That was the night your beautiful wife sliced her hand open with a kitchen knife only to be punished for it later. Tell me, what punishment did you prescribe for her?"

A bob of an Adam's Apple, the drip of sweat from the sheen of heavy perspiration and the tremble of skin. All indicators of stress. In David's case, extreme stress. If he didn't think he was in hell already, he soon would.

"I-I don't remember."

Dante's brows rose, "You don't remember? Well, I can't have that. It's okay though, truly it is. I have a story to tell you that will definitely jog your memory."

Dante pulled David to his feet. "Walk with me, won't you?" He took his healthy arm and guided him over to the trough. David whimpered and stumbled, but Dante ignored him.

"Once upon a time there lived a family of four. They were farmers, the husband and wife. They had two children. Well, one afternoon, the wife decided to bake a very special treat. Do you know what special treat it was, David?"

When David didn't answer, Dante shoved him down slamming his knees against the concrete floor. "No? It was a gingerbread man. The wife had cut out a large gingerbread man and outfitted him with candied eyes, licorice lips and striped buttons. A handsome devil."

Dante checked the temperature of the water and decided to top it off with fresh heat. "She popped him into the oven to bake and thought about how much her family was going to enjoy this delicious treat. She pondered it for so long and filled her thoughts with so much love, that love transferred right into her baking. So much so that when she opened the door to the hot, hot oven, the gingerbread man winked at her. Then he jumped out of the oven and took off running. Can you imagine what happened next?"

Dante grabbed hold of David's hair, yanking his head back to peer down at his exhausted face. It didn't surprise him to see fresh tears streaming from the man's eyes.

"The wife took off running after him, David. And soon her husband and two children joined the race. The gingerbread man thought it so funny telling them to run as fast as they could because they would never catch him. He was, after all, the gingerbread man. The family tried despite how fast this piece of bread was moving."

Dante drummed his fingers on David's head, shaking his own. "Amazing how people's fortitudes are. I mean, these people never stopped running.

They had to be in such discomfort. But, you know how people are. They always try to persevere. Much like your wife. But, I digress. Back to the story. So this gingerbread man ran and ran till suddenly, he reached a river bank." Without warning, Dante's hands clamped down onto David's shoulders and pulled him to the edge of the trough. He fisted David's hair in a brutally tight grip, holding his head above the hot water until his nose nearly touched.

Dante brought his mouth close to David's ear. "Does this look familiar, David? Your wife would say so. She would remember this well. Do you feel the heat of the water washing your face? Soaking in? The steam gets everywhere, doesn't it? Dries out your eyes, fills your mouth, burns the hairs in your nose. Not the most comfortable, I would wager. Is it?"

"No! No! Please, I'm sorry. I'm so fucking sorry!" David sobbed.

"Too late to apologize. Hmm. I think that's a song lyric. I'm not sure. I'm a bit old school if you haven't noticed. Anyway, back to the story. As luck would have it, a very nice fox spotted the gingerbread man's plight. He decided to help and coaxed the gingerbread man onto his tail." Dante's fist still held firm onto David's hair while his other hand encircled the back of his neck. Water sloshed over the tip of David's nose causing him to squirm.

"As the fox traipsed further into the river, he noticed the river water threatening to cover the gingerbread man. He urged him to move further up his body until the little bread straddled his back," Dante stopped. "Excuse me for a moment, David. Andrew, please top us off. Thank you."

The sound of the spigot turning along with a whooshing thrum worked its way through the hose, elicited a gurgled cry from David as a fresh wave of scalding water bobbed around his nostrils.

Dante continued, "The water rose higher and higher. Much like this. And, the gingerbread man was in a position much like you are right now. Much like your wife was, in case you forgot. The poor fox was concerned for his new friend. Truly, he didn't want him to get wet. So, what was there left to do but to offer the gingerbread man a seat atop his head."

"Seeing the threat of the water, the gingerbread hopped onto the fox's head. But, you see, the poor gingerbread man never landed on that bad fox's head because...snip swallow!" Dante roared, quoting Little Golden Book's, Gingerbread Man, thrusting David's head into the water. He did it so fast he would bet that, despite the story, David wasn't anticipating the precise moment. His arms flailed and his legs kicked. The man was strong, Dante would give him that. It took a great deal of strength to hold him under for thirty seconds. He ignored the burning of his own flesh as he held David under.

Satisfied, Dante dragged him up. David choked and gasped for air until he finally settled into a fit of coughs.

"The innocent gingerbread man had been eaten by the foxy fox, David!" Dante yelled over David's coughing fit. "But that wasn't enough for you was it? No. You had to dunk her over and over and over again. So that is what you will get, my friend."

Dante dunked David far more than what David had done to Trinity and for longer stints of time. But, he deserved it. He wanted his skin to blister. It should blister.

The struggle, flailing of limbs and straining lungs, was music to Dante's ears. It was the gavel in the judge's hand, the clink of jail cell bars. Music indeed. If only he could hear the flames of hell open up to this piece of shit. That would be the cherry on top. Dante threw David's body down. The man was out again.

"Are you gonna end it soon, boss? I'm getting hungry." Michael dared to ask.

Dante looked between his two men. They had been a very nice help to his mission. He supposed he should get on with it. There was no way he could ever fully repay David the kindness he extended to Trinity over the years without keeping him in a cell and torturing him on the daily. For one, Trinity hadn't really enlightened him to anything other than the most recent events. And, secondly, she would be mortified if she ever found out.

The bastard was getting off easy. It wasn't satisfying. He wanted this guy shitting his pants before he died. Perhaps one more act of kindness.

"Once he wakes up, we'll give him one more lesson before sending him on his journey."

"Sounds good, boss."

What to do, what to do? Dante sat down, dragging his arm over his wet forehead. That fucking steam from the tub was causing him to sweat. He couldn't imagine the horror Trinity endured that night. The idea of it riled him. He needed to make the grand finale...grand.

Looking around, Dante spotted something perfect. Shed ten housed a couple of vehicles and the horse trough, Dante thought was strange. But then he saw why. There were farrier instruments stored here. A rasp caught his attention. It reminded him of a cheese grater. A very coarse cheese grater with a very sharp tang. Dante walked over to it and brushed his thumb over the surface of the instrument. Still sharp. Perfect.

He held it up to Michael and Andrew, and they nodded their approval. David would be waking soon. He stood over the collapsed man, then knelt down and slapped his face. He didn't get a response.

"Give me the hose. Turn on the cold."

Dante sprayed David down until he came to with a sharp intake of breath. His eyes were wild, taking in his surroundings. Dante knew the moment he realized where he was, as the look of doom crossed his expression.

"Yes, Mr. Fallon, we are still here. You are still alive. Now, since you are not going to be alive tomorrow, there's no way you'll ever know how Trinity's skin must have felt. You burned her pretty good. Her skin was tender and blistered. I would like to do you a huge favor and recreate what that may have felt like before you leave here today despite your own fucked face. Fair?"

"Kill me. Please...kill me," David whispered.

"Oh, not to worry. I most definitely will kill you. But you have to fulfill the requirements of death before you are entitled to it. Shall we carry on?"

David nodded.

"Excellent. This tool I have here in my hand is called a rasp. It's used by farriers in the changing of horse shoes. It's very very sharp. I don't know about you, but it reminds me of a cheese grater. At least this one does. Anyway, I figure it to be the perfect tool to create a raw surface on delicate skin thus emulating your wife's injury quite nicely.

"No. She wasn't blistered! She wasn't anything but a little red! Please, Mr. Venturi, I'm begging you," David cried.

"You know, Mr. Fallon," Dante looked down at the rasp in his hand, "I may not be better than you after all. God forgive me, but I can't find it in me to care."

Dante lunged forward connecting the rasp with David's face in a grating motion reminiscent of a brick of cheese. David's screams filled the large storage shed. Unlike the hallways of his office building, this unit was not soundproof. Luckily, Dante owned the property and no one would be bothering them. David could scream as loud as he wanted.

Craning David's neck to the side, Dante took a look at David's bloodied face and cringed. He may have been a bit aggressive. It was highly doubtful Trinity's face felt like David's at the moment. It certainly never looked it. Oh well. Dante threw down the rasp in exchange for his forty-five.

"Had enough?"

David's broken hand trembled violently as it hovered near his skinned face. His breathing was labored. Dante figured the end was probably near. His heart was probably working double time to keep him alive.

"I'm s-s-sorry. Tell her I'm s-s-sorry," David gasped.

"No. I won't be delivering your message. I don't care if you're sorry, and I don't care if it's your dying wish. Today was an eye for an eye, Mr. Fallon. It was vengeance for what was done by your hand to an innocent woman. Michael, open the windows then place Mr. Fallon under them please."

Dante watched on while his bidding was done. David's body was so wrecked, he hadn't made a sound when he was being dragged. From where he stood, he could feel the crisp air reaching into the room to steal the warmth.

"You left Trinity in a cold bathtub, severely injured, with the window open overnight. She could have died. Today, you will either bleed or freeze to death. Whichever comes first."

Dante took aim and shot David in each of his limbs. Blood immediately found its exits, quickly creating small pools around his battered body.

"Till we meet in hell, Mr. Fallon. I bid you a goodnight."

Chapter 13

What to have for dinner? Trinity couldn't decide. It was definitely a takeout and movie kind of night. She hadn't been in her new place long, but already loved curling up to watch a good movie. Preferably romance. Smiling satisfied with her plan, she searched restaurants nearby on her phone.

How would it feel to have a romance of her own? Was it like the movies or books she enjoyed reading? Maybe. The thought surprised her. Never had she really thought about romance or love outside of trying to survive David.

When his face popped into her mind, it instantly killed her mood. She tossed her phone down with a sigh. It was already seven o'clock and getting late. She should be busy ordering, but couldn't. Instead, she allowed her thoughts to go to the dark place she created just for David. So far, she had done a pretty good job of blocking herself from thinking of him. But she wasn't always successful.

Either way, it was kind of weird how he came into her mind just now. More so, it was weird how she couldn't shake his image. Nor could she shake the flashbacks. Perhaps she wasn't so good at blocking her memories afterall.

Shivering, she pulled a blanket over her lap and rubbed her arms. It was seventy degrees inside her place. Comfortable. Still, she felt cold. She felt strange.

It would be awesome if she could call Becky. Anytime she ever felt like she needed a friend, Becky was there for her. But why she even kept thinking about Becky was beyond her. She already settled with her decision to cut ties. Her only other friend now was Eugenia. She knew more than Becky any way. Should she call her? She would have to if she wanted to talk. Grabbing her phone, she dialed.

"Hey girl," Eugenia answered on the second ring.

"Oh, hi, Eugenia. A-are you busy?"

"Nope. Just making a late dinner. I got so caught up in my reality show, I lost track of the dang time. I sah-wear to the lord. What's up?"

"Um, I was just trying to think of what to have for dinner. Any suggestions?" Trinity cringed.

Eugenia laughed, "Hmm. Let's see. Have you tried Rochester Beets yet? They have super yummy sandwiches and they deliver. My favorite is their grilled cheese with tomato soup combo. To die for. Dang it. I should've had that," she whispered under her breath regretful.

"I think I will. Thanks for the suggestion. I was really stumped."

"Mhm. Sooo, why did you really call?"

Eugenia was smart. No wonder she earned a promotion. Better not beat around the bush and come clean.

"I'm s-s-sorry. I was doing okay and then David popped into my head for some weird reason, and I don't know. I feel...off."

The line was quiet for an extended amount of time. So much so, Trinity thought Eugenia hung up.

"H-hello? Eugenia, are you still there?" She looked at her phone display still counting the seconds.

"Y-yeah. Sorry 'bout that. I was stirring my noodles. Um...you know he's always gonna be part of your memories, Trinity. You just gotta distract yourself the best you can. You're safe now. He can't hurt you anymore," she cleared her throat.

"Yeah," Trinity whispered.

"Order your food, put on a good movie, then take a warm bath before bed. You'll feel so much better. And, if you don't, call me up again and we'll talk."

"Thank you, Eugenia. You've been so good to me. I'm not sure I can ever repay you."

"Girl, what are friends for? No need for repayment. I'll talk to ya later, okay?"

"Talk to you later."

Trinity hung up the phone feeling a little better. Not much, but a little. A little was enough for her. Eugenia was right. She needed to push David out of her mind with distraction. What better way than with food? She wondered what David was eating. Had he been cooking for himself or did he impose upon his mother for his dinners? Ugh! Stop thinking about him!

Making the call to the deli, she placed her order then set to picking out a movie. What was a good romance to watch? Something where opposites attract or something with similarities? Scrolling through the options, she paused on Cinderella starring Drew Barrymore. It was an older movie, but it looked good.

If she thought about Cinderella, she actually had a lot in common with her having been worked to the bone and abused. Would she ever have a prince come rescue her? In a sense, she had. Dante rescued her. But he did so out of the kindness of his heart. He looked out for his employees. It was nothing more than that.

Even if it were more, she doubted she would be capable of returning any feelings of affection from anyone. David ruined the idea of sex for her with each time having been filled with pain. She knew that couldn't be how everyone experienced sex because too many people liked it. But, she highly doubted she would want to try it ever again. It was too risky.

The idea that pain was even the slightest possibility turned her off. She was tired of pain. Tired of enduring. Tired of fear. The best thing was to avoid.

Once Dante allowed her to start working at the office, she would need to work on those avoidance skills. If men tried to talk to her or ask her out, she would just tell them she was married. No one needed to know she was separated. Trinity spun the simple gold band around her finger. Despite everything she went through, the ring was like a fixture. Still in its place.

She recalled coming across the receipt for the ring when she had been cleaning one day. It was from a popular jewelry store near their house. The small circle of gold was pricey at two thousand dollars. She felt special when she saw the receipt. He didn't have to buy something so expensive. He could have gotten a ring from any department store, and she would have been satisfied. Why did he spend so much at the time? Was it because he really did love her back then? How had his love changed so much to the point she was running for her life...away from him? How?

Now that she was separated from him, physically, should she file for divorce? Or, would he? And if either one of them filed, would she need to go to court? And if she went to court, would she have to see him? Could she ask the court to be excused? Should she file a restraining order?

If she filed a restraining order, would his police officer friends find her? Did she have to list her address? She didn't know the answer to any of her rambling questions. Maybe she should go to an attorney. It might help to form a solid plan rather than wonder about everything. Her wandering mind would surely drive herself nuts otherwise.

There really seemed to be no turn off button. While she managed to shift away from thoughts of David, her attention went to Dante. It was hard to believe how kind people could be towards one another. Eugenia was so warm and accepting from the very beginning and quickly befriended her. Ms. Jewell seemed eager to mentor her. And Dante, well, he literally saved her. Her life went from an impending doom to hope, in a blink of an eye.

But, as nice as it was for Dante to provide for her, she couldn't keep taking forever. She needed to be able to save enough money so she could start fresh in a different state far, far away. She would cut her hair, maybe change her eye color and gain some weight.

The doorbell rang startling Trinity out of her head. Wow. The deli sure delivered quick. She'd make sure to keep their name handy if the service was this great. Forgetting to check the peephole, she swung the door open. Trinity's wide smile melted into fear. A police officer.

"Mrs. Fallon?"

"Y-yes?" Trinity closed the door a bit, keeping herself mostly behind it. How did the police department find her? A cold sweat broke out all over. Dante told her she would be safe here. That David would never find her. Wait. If David found her, wouldn't it be himself standing on her doorstep?

And, she was pretty sure she didn't recognize this man. Not only that, he didn't seem to recognize her either. He assumed. He didn't directly address her. She forced herself to calm down enough to listen despite her fear and confusion.

"My name is Officer Lee. I'm from the third precinct. Ma'am, do you mind if I come in?"

"Yes. I-I'm sorry, but I do mind. What's this about? How did you find me?" her brows knitted.

"You may need to sit down, ma'am," he warned ignoring her last question.

Trinity's heart was thrumming in her chest. Officer Lee. Officer Lee. Third precinct. Her mind raced for recollection. There was nothing. David never spoke about that precinct. She was certain. Something was wrong. She'd been feeling off all evening.

"What is it?"

The officer took off his hat and fingered the brim while he looked her in the eye. "Ma'am there's been an accident. Your husband was involved."

"What?" An accident? She watched the news earlier and didn't see any reports of an accident.

"Your husband didn't make it, Mrs. Fallon. He passed away on the scene."

Trinity's field of vision started to narrow and dim. What did Officer Lee just tell her? David was...gone? Dead? The officer's lips were moving, but she couldn't hear him. What was he saying to her? She couldn't hear him over the loud ringing in her ears. Her head was so light it felt like she could hear the dizzy. Concerned eyes came close, then far, then black.

-#-

Trinity woke to soft murmurs. Who was talking? Becky? No. Eugenia. It was Eugenia who was speaking. Was she on the phone? Why was Eugenia here? Trinity looked to the window, but the heavy drapes were drawn. Was it morning?

Sitting up, she put her hand to her spinning head not feeling so great. It was too hot. Pushing the big comforter aside, she realized she was overheated. Had Eugenia stayed over last night? She couldn't remember? Better find out. Looking down at herself, she frowned. She was still in her clothes from yesterday. Was it still yesterday or was it tomorrow?

Trinity pushed the drapes aside to see the dark sky. It was night. Why was she in bed with Eugenia here? How strange. Trinity padded to the living room where she could hear Eugenia talking. She shook her head confused.

"Hey."

Eugenia hung up the phone and jumped up from the couch. "Hey you. How're you feeling?"

"Like I'm hungover. What's going on? Why are you here?"

"Sit down, hun." Eugenia reached her hands up and clasped Trinity's. "What's the last thing you remember?"

"I ordered from that place you recommended and then the doorbell rang a nd...," Trinity trailed off realization dawning. "I remember," she whispered. "H-he's...dead," Trinity looked to Eugenia with watery eyes.

"Are you alright?"

Trinity nodded. She didn't know why she was crying. Maybe it was for the memories she had from when she first met David. Those were fun times. Sort of. So many thoughts were running through her mind, and all at once. David died. He was dead. The mere idea of it was surreal.

"Thank you for coming, Eugenia. T-thank you for helping me, but I think I really need to be alone right now."

"Are you sure that's a good idea, Trinity? I could stay in the guest bedroom. You'll never know I'm here."

"I need to be alone," she brushed a tear away.

Trinity felt relieved when Eugenia finally agreed to leave and then actually left. She closed the door with a soft click and put the locks into place. Those locks were meant to keep her safe from David. Now, David was no longer a threat. He was...nothing.

"David's...dead." Trinity sunk down onto the couch and rubbed her hands together. "David died. My husband died," Trinity tested the phrase on her tongue, rocking back and forth. "I'm a widow. My husband died. David Fallon died," she swallowed. "How did he die?" she whispered. "An accident," she answered herself. "What kind of accident? I don't know." Tears welled, but she blinked them away covering her mouth and nose with her hands. Her index fingers pressed into the corners of her closed eyes.

Breathing in and out, she let the heat of her breath warm her cold nose. "I can't believe you're gone. What were your last words to me?"

She searched her memories. "Be good. He told me to be good." In a twisted way, she was doing exactly as he instructed her to do. She fled away from him. Anyone would tell her it was good what she did. So, in essence, she was being and doing good. It just wasn't exactly what he meant.

Her rambling thoughts jumped back to the officer from earlier. He told her David died in an accident. What type of accident? Was it a car accident? Should she call the precinct and find out? Which one did he say? Why couldn't she remember? Without further thought, she dialed David's work number.

"First precinct."

Trinity knew that voice. It was a policewoman who seemed to always be on phone duty. Her nasally tone reminded her of the receptionist from Ghostbusters.

"H-hello. This is Mrs. Fallon...,"

"I'm so so sorry for your loss, dear. David was a good man. A great officer."

"Ye-yes. Um, I was wondering if you could tell me what type of accident my husband was involved in. An officer stopped by my home earlier, but I'm afraid I m-m...,"

"It's alright, dear. I was told your husband perished in a drug raid in a neighboring ward."

"I want to see him. C-c-can I see him?" she blurted.

"Oh, I don't know about that. I'll have to ask. One moment please."

Trinity was on hold for what felt like forever. Checking the clock, it was nine. Would they let her see him this late? They should. She was David's widow. They wouldn't deny her. Would they?

"Mrs. Fallon?"

"Yes?"

"Thank you for holding. Mrs. Fallon, I'm told his body has already been positively identified. There's no need for you to do that job, sweetie."

"I-I need to," Trinity whispered. Her hands shook as they squeezed the phone.

"Mrs. Fallon," the policewoman soothed, "you may come down if you insist, but I don't feel it would be wise for you to do so. Don't you have anyone staying with you right now?"

"Let them know I'm coming."

Trinity hung up the phone before she could be talked out of it. She needed to see him with her own eyes. To confirm he was actually gone. She needed to see she wasn't in danger anymore. She needed to know this nightmare was officially over with. Perhaps seeing him would give her closure than simply living with the idea of his death.

Quickly, she dressed in jeans and a sweatshirt. She grabbed a pair of socks and her sneakers. Finally, she put on a jacket and stuffed her phone into the pocket along with her wallet then took her keys before heading out the door.

The first precinct wasn't far. Convenient for the station, the morgue was one building over. Someone should be willing to escort her. Hopefully, the people at the morgue would let her see him.

She felt like she was on autopilot. The city was alive around her while she floated inside a bubble. Looking out, everything seemed to be a blur. She didn't remember the lights changing from green to red. Didn't remember stopping. She just pushed the pedal to the floor and drove while images of David flashed through her mind.

No wonder she thought of him. Was he trying to tell her? Was he hoping to gain her forgiveness? Had he changed in the last moments of his life? Did he have a chance to ask for forgiveness from God? Did he receive his last rights?

Sooner than what was reasonable, she arrived outside of the police station. Her hands gripped the wheel until her knuckles turned white. Was she strong enough for this? Would she be okay once she saw him? One way to find out.

Unbuckling her seatbelt, she got out of the car on wobbly legs and forced herself inside. Trinity could tell the same woman she spoke to on the phone was the same one currently staring at her with pity-filled eyes.

"Mrs. Fallon."

"I need to see him."

"The morgue is closed, sweetie."

"I said I need to see him. Someone can take me. Anyone," Trinity's trembling voice hitched.

"What's going on?" An officer came from around his desk and approached the front. His eyes grew wide a moment too long. "Mrs. Fallon. I'm so sorry for your loss."

"I. Need. To see him. Please. Please," Trinity voice caught on the last note.

"Okay. Wait here a moment."

Ignoring the woman staring at her, she waited for the officer she didn't recognize to return. When he did, he had a set of keys in his hand.

"We can take the skywalk over."

"When did he die?"

"Your husband was brought in, I believe, a little after five this afternoon."

What was she doing at five? She searched her memory, but it was lost. The rest of the way to the morgue was made in silence much to Trinity's relief. She didn't want to talk. She just wanted to see David and leave.

After walking for five minutes, they arrived before a heavy steel door where the officer waved his name tag in front of an electronic keypad. The red light flipped to green and the door unlocked to a long hallway. They stopped in front of a plain door the officer had to ring a buzzer for. Once they were buzzed in, he spoke with another officer and they waited some more.

Finally, an older man in a lab coat came out. His expression was severe not softening when his eyes landed on Trinity.

"Can I help you?"

"This is Mrs. David Fallon. She would like to view her husband's body."

The man's eyes flicked to Trinity, his jaw ticked. "Mrs. Fallon, I'm very sorry for your loss, but your husband's body has been identified. While it's your right to view the body, we don't usually allow people into the morgue. I strongly urge you to wait until he's been prepared by the funeral home you choose to make arrangements with."

"I need to s-s-see him. Please...let me see him," she begged.

The lab-coated man seemed to vacillate before relenting. "Very well," he sighed defeated.

The officer told Trinity he would wait for her, and she proceeded to follow the man in the lab coat down another hallway and into a stark looking room. Drawers similar to a file cabinet lined an entire wall. Were they all filled with bodies? Trinity pushed the morbid thought away.

The man located the proper drawer and pulled. It was like a scene from a movie. A metal tray with a body bag laid on top. The bag was black and had a shiny metal zipper. When the man pulled the zipper down a short way, Trinity averted her eyes.

"I'll leave you alone for a few minutes. When you're done, just come on out. I'll take care of the rest."

Trinity didn't say anything, but waited until he left the room. Suddenly, she was alone. Alone with her husband, once again. Without looking at the corpse, she found her way up to him.

Slowly, bravely, she lifted her gaze to David's face and immediately gagged. Pressing one of her hands hard against her stomach with the other to her lips, she dragged in a deep breath through her nose and let it out through her mouth and repeated two more times. She was okay. She was okay. She had to be.

Again, she tried. This time, she didn't look away. Instead, her eyes narrowed as she took him in. His head was slightly turned and his mouth hung agape. His face was mottled red and gray with deflated blisters on one side. Most, if not all, of his skin was missing on the other. Was it...road rash? His eyes, the people didn't have the decency to close, were glazed over with a milky white film. Was this him? It barely looked like him. The more she stared, the more she couldn't tell.

Feeling bold, Trinity unzipped the bag further until she could see his hands. David had a large birthmark on his thumb. If she could see that, then she'd know it was him for sure. Moving the plastic over a bit, revealed injuries to his arms. Were those...bullet holes? She ignored them finding exactly what she was looking for. His fingers appeared to be mangled, but she could see the birthmark. It was him. Breathless, she quickly zipped the bag to his neck where it snagged to a stop. She ran her hands over her face and through her hair.

Trinity's foot nervously tapped the floor. She closed her eyes, breathing puffs of air through her nose. "You're gone. You really are," she whispered. "I'm sorry you were so miserable, David. I forgive you." Bravely, Trinity looked into his haunting eyes for the last time. Squaring her shoulders, she steeled herself while a feeling of resolve wove through her. "Be good."

She turned on her heel and quickly left the room not bothering to thank the lab-coated man. Through some miracle, she remembered her way back to the officer kind enough to bring her here but walked passed him as well. There was no need to say one word to any of these people. At least not tonight.

The officer must have felt the same way. He didn't prod her for information or answers. He didn't even bid her goodnight. Trinity found herself back into her own vehicle and turning the key. She drove straight home. She parked, got out, went inside, locked and deadbolted the door, and set her home alarm system.

David's grotesque image would stay with her forever. It would haunt her, she knew. Yet, she felt closure. There was no need to have a funeral. David wished to be cremated, and she would contact the funeral home to have that accomplished. She would then contact the cemetery and have him buried in the plot he bought next to his father. All of this would be handled without her presence.

If his mother wished to have a funeral, that was fine with her. She simply wouldn't be attending. As far as the house was concerned, she'd contact a realtor and have them stage it for showings. Again, no need for her to be there.

It was strange. Everything felt so clear all of a sudden. As if all of the answers dropped right in front of her face. Maybe it was because, for once in her life, she felt calm. So this is what serenity feels like.

Untroubled and quiet...at last.

Chapter 14

A week passed since David died. During that time, Trinity was busy arranging his cremation and burial while his mother held a celebration of life ceremony. Trinity chose not to attend.

Her next project was selecting a real estate agent to take care of the house. Perhaps she would have them do an auction for all the furniture and items too. She didn't really keep anything of any sentimental value to worry about. Her clothes and shoes weren't that great either, and so wouldn't be missed. To sell everything would be so much easier.

Although, on second thought, she did have a few picture albums. Maybe if she gave Becky a list, she could grab some things for her. If not, she'd let it go. Maybe she'd call Becky after work.

There were a bunch of financial things she had to take care of as well. Contact the Social Security Administration, let her banks know and talk to someone about David's pension. Eugenia suggested she hire an attorney. She agreed. All the things needed to be done when someone died was surprising and extremely overwhelming.

Pushing everything out of her mind, she started to get moving. Slipping into her buff-colored heels, she checked her appearance in the full-length mirror mounted to the back of her bedroom door. She chose a navy Pointelle skirt that dropped just below the knee and matching short-sleeved top with a cute ruffled hem. She decided to pull her hair back into a curled ponytail for a clean look. Her makeup was kept simple, mascara and a very light pink lip gloss.

Trinity turned a little to see the back of the outfit, then faced front again. Did she look like a widow? No. She looked put together. Smart. She looked like a business woman even though she was far from it. It didn't matter. Everyone at Venturi Transportation looked important. She would fit in well.

The finishing touch to her professional ensemble was her handbag. Eugenia insisted she buy an expensive Prada bag. At the time, she had no idea what Prada was. Then she saw the tag. Twenty-four hundred dollars later, she knew. Eugenia waved off her mortification telling her accounting wouldn't blink an eye at the receipt. She also told her to get used to it. It must be normal for Dante to shower his employees then? Shrugging, she headed out.

After a short drive, she entered the building noticing a new girl at the front desk. Originally, she was supposed to be sitting there but Dante told her she was going to be working on his floor. May as well head up. Trinity wondered what floor Eugenia worked on. With everything going on, she never asked her. She was a bad friend.

Luckily, they worked in the same building. She would make it up to her. Maybe after she received her first paycheck, she could take Eugenia out to dinner and spend more time with her. It was the very least she could do after everything the woman had done for her. Eugenia was a great friend. Not many people would bend over backwards like Eugenia did. So it was a plan. She had Becky and Eugenia to call after work.

Stepping onto the elevator, Trinity was happy to be alone. The small hot box wasn't exactly her most favorite place to be. Visions of being stuck in one with strangers always danced in her mind. Suddenly, the elevator stopped. She glanced up to see it was the second floor. The doors opened to reveal an attractive man a little taller than herself with a stocky build. He looked to be in his mid-thirties.

"Hello," he greeted with a happy smile.

"Hello." Thank goodness she didn't stutter. She hated when she did that.

"I've never seen you before. You new?"

"I am," Trinity smiled back. Hurry up elevator. Why did she have to work on the top floor?

The man looked at the button panel. "You work for Ms. Jewell?"

"U-um, yes."

"Nice. Name's Roger. Good to meet ya," he held out a meaty hand.

Trinity didn't want to take his hand. She didn't want to touch another man's skin. Was it because David was dead? She extended her hand despite it. His closed around hers in a firm, sweaty grip. She quickly pulled away resisting the urge to wipe off the moisture against her skirt.

"My name's Trinity. Nice to meet you as well."

"Maybe I'll see you at lunch. The...,"

The elevator stopped again, this time on the tenth floor, and opened to Dante much to Trinity's surprise.

"Oh! Good morning, Mr. Venturi," Roger beamed.

"Good morning, Miss Fallon. Roger. What floor are you heading to?"

Dante's deep voice rumbled through her and filled the elevator. She murmured her hello, but was distracted. Dante called her Miss Fallon rather than Mrs. Fallon. Eugenia must have told him explaining the reason for her absence the week before, or it was a Freudian slip. If the latter were the case, it would be one strange coincidence. It was also somewhat strange she hadn't heard from Dante all last week. He had been so attentive to her and then nothing. He was probably busy, she mused.

"Fifteenth," Roger answered.

Dante hit the fifteenth button, then Private Forty-one even though she already pressed it.

"So, um, Trinity, the cafeteria is on the first floor. Maybe I'll see you at lunch."

She smiled polite and nodded, happy when the elevator doors closed after him. There was no way she was going to eat with Roger. It wasn't that he wasn't nice, because he seemed to be. It was just far too soon to be making male friends. Actually, she didn't want any male friends.

"How are you, Trinity?"

How could she forget Dante was in the small space with her?!

"Fine," she gulped.

"How was your weekend?"

Huh? He didn't know? So his address of her name was a mistake? Where did he think she was last week? What did Eugenia tell him? How weird. Maybe he was just being polite by avoiding the subject entirely. Should she tell him?

"A-actually, I n-n-need...," Trinity squeezed her eyes shut. She needed to stop stuttering, "to speak with you." Why was it so hard to talk? What was wrong with her?

"Of course."

Dante waved her on until they were both inside of his office and gestured for her to have a seat while he took his own. "What's up?"

"I'm not sure Eugenia told you, but my husband died last week. It's why I was out," she swallowed.

Dante steepled his fingers together, gently swiveling in his chair with a blank expression. So he did know. He was simply being polite in the elevator.

"I'm sorry. I didn't know. I was out of town all last week. My condolences."

Wow. She misread his expression just then. He really didn't know. It was because he had been out of town. That explained it. Even so, he sure looked like he knew. Although, she didn't know Dante. Not really. Sure she spent the evening with him once, but that was dinner with other people. Oh, then there was the time she spent telling him about David, with a few times after that. But, still, it hadn't been nearly enough time to learn a person's mannerisms. Right?

"I-I'm not sad."

"Of course not. I imagine you feel relieved."

Trinity looked down at her hands. "Mr. Venturi...,"

"Dante," he corrected.

"D-dante, I don't have to take up your home anymore. I can move back into my house."

He looked thoughtful, "Do you like your house?"

"It doesn't matter if I like it or not. I shouldn't be monopolizing your time or property."

Dante smiled. "Monopolizing? You're not."

"I am. You can't rent the property out because I'm in it."

"I don't care. Trinity, I'd much rather have you living closer to work than where your house is located."

"How do you...how do you know where I lived?"

His brow wrinkled amused, "Your application."

"Oh yeah. Sorry. I'm paranoid, I guess."

"Yes, about that. Trinity, I may be overstepping but how would you feel about seeing a therapist?"

Her eyes shot up to his surprised. "A therapist?"

"You've been through more than what anyone should ever have been put through. Perhaps it would help to speak with someone you don't know to get it off your chest and help you heal. Our insurance is excellent. You wouldn't have a bill."

"I-I'm not past the probationary period here. The lady in human resources told me I have another month to go before I am offered health insurance."

"Pff. Nonsense. I'll see to it you're added immediately."

Trinity stared at Dante in disbelief. "Why are you helping me so much?"

"Why not? Do you believe you're not deserving of it?"

"Yes, as a matter of fact, I do. You don't know me. I haven't earned anything."

"And you don't know me. I suggest you take me up on my offers while you get back on your feet."

"And when I get back on my feet? Then what? What do you want?"

She knew she just asked some bold questions judging from Dante's face. Oh well. If he decided helping her was a mistake, she could always go back to the house she owned. She could find a job and make a new plan.

"I want you to keep working. I want you to climb the ladder here in this company. You're smart. I need smart people."

Smart? She wasn't smart. If she were smart, she would have found a way out of her situation without having been rescued.

"You think you're not smart," he watched her intrigued. "Let me assure you, you are."

"You wouldn't have thought that last week. The day David died."

"Why do you say that?" he frowned.

"I was upset that night...,"

"Naturally."

"I drove to the morgue to see him."

Dante's hands lowered to his desk, his expression turned stoney. "What did you say?"

His voice was so quiet, she strained to hear him. If she wasn't mistaken, Dante seemed angered by what she just divulged. As if he didn't quite believe his ears. She blinked a few times, trying to mask her surprise. "I-I-I s-s-said, I went to see him in the morgue. To say...g-goodbye."

Pushing his chair away from his desk, Dante stood and went over to the window to look out. His wide back blocked her view of his face. How puzzling. Why was he so upset? Trinity shifted in her seat uncomfortable. It was suddenly too warm in his office. The space feeling as if it had shrunk.

"What did your husband die from, if I'm not being too invasive?"

He was being too invasive. But how could she not answer him after everything he helped her with? "Um...a drug raid. I think it was a shootout. I could see he had been shot in his arms."

"And they let you into the morgue? I'm sorry, but I'm surprised by that," Dante turned to face her, his frown deeper than before.

"I am too actually. Although, they did tell me that it wasn't a usual thing. I guess it was because I was pretty upset. In hindsight, a part of me wishes I hadn't seen him. His expression is going to haunt me for a long time," she trailed off.

Dante closed his eyes and let out a long sigh, "I'm sorry you had to see him like that, Trinity. I hope you take me up on my suggestion to talk to someone about this. You don't need to walk around with the heavy burdens you do. As far as your living situation, I truly hope you stay where you're at. I have numerous properties both full and vacant. Truth is, I don't really need the money. If people rent my homes, great. If not, I don't really care. You are far from intruding on the place."

"I do love the townhouse. It's too good for me, but I'm grateful," she smiled kind.

Dante hung his head with a short chuckle. "Promise me you'll stop speaking about yourself like that. You are a very deserving person. You're smart, kind and beautiful. You have your entire life ahead of you. Carpe diem. Remember?"

Trinity's eyes lit up. She did remember. That phrase helped her get this job. Ms. Jewell had been impressed with her. But, wait. Did she hear right? Did he just call her beautiful?

"Y-you think I'm beautiful?" she blurted.

"Of course. I told you so the night of our dinner. Did you forget?" he asked amused.

Trinity blushed, then her face fell. It was guilt. She shouldn't be flirting or speaking so casually so soon after her husband died. It wasn't right.

"You can smile. You have every right. I'm sorry but, pardon my French, the fucker deserved to die. I'm glad you're free of him."

Dante's language shocked her. He was so put together and polished, she hadn't expected the curse word to come out of his mouth. Somehow, it made him more attractive. As quickly as that thought entered her mind, she dismissed it. She didn't know how to feel free enough to think pleasant thoughts. It would take some time to get used to the idea of no longer being under threat.

Another thought came to the forefront of her mind. Was Dante this giving to his other employees? She better ask while she had the courage. "Dante, I have a question."

"Go ahead." He sat back down behind his desk. "Is it about your pay? Hasn't Ms. Jewell talked to you about it?"

"Oh, um, no. But, that isn't my question."

"It should be. I never do one bit of work without knowing what I'm being compensated for. As you know, the position you're training for is

Ms. Jewell's. While you're in training you'll earn a salary. It's base pay is seventy-five thousand a year. We give raises twice per year, depending on performance."

Seventy-five thousand?! Holy shit! She would definitely be able to afford to live on her own with that kind of money.

"T-thank you, Dante, but I don't have experience."

"That's why Jewell is sticking around for another month to train you. I don't want anyone else to take the position."

"Oh."

"Now what was your question?"

"Are you this nice to everyone?"

"No."

She waited, but he didn't elaborate.

"Oh. Okay," she whispered more so to herself.

"Before you head out, Trinity, I wanted to mention, I have a fundraiser I've been invited to. It's a silent auction. I'd like you to be my date for the evening. I'll need you to keep track of what I bid on and such."

"A-alright. Are you sure you don't want Ms. Jewell to accompany you. I don't have experience with that sort of thing."

Dante stood and came around his desk to open his office door. They were but a foot apart. Trinity tried in vain to ignore the gallop of her heart. Standing this close allowed her a personal view of his dark dark eyes. They were so dark, it was hard to see the detail of his iris. A slight wave of dizzy caused her to blink herself back to reality.

"All the better to attend. It's excellent experience," he smiled reassuringly.

Was that a dimple? And how were his teeth so damn perfect? "Oh, okay. When is it?"

"This Saturday. It's black tie so have Eugenia help you with a gown. I suggest you go after lunch today to give yourself time to find something on such short...,"

"Uncle Dante! Oops," Gio barreled into the office nearly tripping over Trinity if it weren't for Dante shoving him backwards and nearly off his feet.

Dante rolled his eyes, watching his nephew regain himself. "I would suggest you walk next time, Gio. Gio, this is my new assistant, Trinity Fallon. Trinity...,"

"Woah. You're hot."

"Gio! What the hell is wrong with you? Sta' zitto!" Dante smacked his nephew on the back of his head, sending him a few feet forward.

Trinity's eyes grew. She had to stifle a laugh, biting her lip. How interesting to see Dante like this. He was always so composed. Her attention was then stolen away by Gio who slapped at his uncle's hands before frantically smoothing his hair back and straightening his tie.

Gio didn't seem to be much older than herself. He was handsome and looked a lot like Dante. However, Dante was far better looking than his nephew.

"I apologize for my nephew. He's still growing his brain," Dante said already having regained his composure.

"I'm sorry," Gio said sheepish.

"No worries. Nice to meet you."

"Are you a college student?"

"No," Trinity blushed embarrassed. She should be in college. Had she the proper parental guidance, she would be. Instead, she was finding her way by sheer luck.

"She's already been interviewed, Gio. Sit down. I'll be with you in a second. I need to finish up with Miss Fallon."

"Oh, sure. Steal her away and keep her for yourself. You're such a cock block, uncle."

"You're treading on thin ice, Gio. Trinity, shall we?" He held his hand out and guided her into the hall.

"He's thirty, Trinity! Don't let his good looks suck you in! He's old!" Gio shouted.

Dante slammed the door shut and paused a moment before looking at Trinity with an apologetic smile. "I'm trying my best to groom him. It's a daunting task."

"It's fine," Trinity laughed. "He's very funny. You're lucky to have him."

"I'm not so sure," Dante joined Trinity's amusement. "Oh, and forget you heard the age comment. I don't like to think of myself as old."

"What's this I hear?" Ms. Jewell came walking up the hall toward them.

"Gio being Gio."

"Ah, yes. Well, we love him anyway," she smiled kind, nodding at Trinity.

"Good morning."

"Good morning, dear. I'm so glad you're finally starting with us. I'm excited to teach you everything I know. I'll take it from here, Mr. Venturi."

"Excellent. Trinity, if I don't see you until Saturday, I will be picking you up at seven. Have a nice day, ladies."

Trinity watched Dante walk back to his office and close the door. His walk was confident. It probably helped that he was so tall. He had to stand well over six feet.

"You're going to find those two are very comical together."

"Is his nephew a college student?"

"He is. He will be graduating next year."

"Oh. I thought he was more my age.

"He's exactly your age. He's very gifted."

"I don't think Mr. Venturi agrees," Trinity laughed.

"Not at all. Gio loves taunting him. Now," Ms. Jewell clapped her hands, "shall we begin?"

-#-

Dante paced his office. What the fuck happened? An unknown officer was supposed to come to Trinity's house and tell her the man was dead and that was to be the end of it. How had David Fallon's body been recovered? He called Michael and Andrew into his office. Heads were gonna roll.

Both men came in at the same time and sat. Judging from their expressions, they knew why they were there. Except, their expressions weren't guilty.

"Whose idea was it?"

"It was both of ours, boss," Andrew said.

"Explain."

"If there wasn't a body, there would be risk of an investigation launched by his cop friends. Mrs. Fallon would have been questioned. We didn't think you would want that. We also didn't think you would want his cop friends constantly sniffing around her door or ours. Even if the departments are on the payroll. So, we felt it best to give his body over to the few we could trust along with a story on a recent case. No one would question it."

"What about his partner? Was he a personal friend?"

"We looked into it and it didn't appear that he was."

"So what case? Where?"

"Third ward. There's constant wars in that area and we found out the third precinct was working with the first on a particular drug bust. It was perfect."

"Normally, your little plan would have been fine. This time, not so much," Dante's jaw ticked.

The men exchanged a confused glance.

"She went to the morgue, and they let her see my handiwork."

"Shit. Didn't see that coming."

"Yeah, me neither, boss. Sorry."

"Needless to say, I'm not too pleased. Don't ever change plans again. Not without my knowledge. Understood? Good. Go."

Unbelievable. He could see their reasoning. It made perfect sense. Who could predict she'd go to the morgue? Dante shook his head. She was not only beautiful but courageous too. What she did took a lot of balls. He admired her for that.

If only she could see how wonderful she really was.

Chapter 15

The mirror in the bedroom really was the best. The light hit it just right. Trinity twisted and turned admiring the gown Eugenia helped her pick out at the Versace store. Eugenia had asked Trinity if she lived under a rock after she mispronounced it. Oh well. The black cross-back bustier, floor-length gown was made of silk and fit her like a glove. It was a miracle alterations weren't needed.

Her black Louboutin stilettos were a sandal style, with thin straps around her ankles and across her toes giving her an extra five inches of height.

Eugenia explained an updo hairstyle would look best for the entire look and promptly set to working on sculpting an elaborate bun complete with wisps and curled tendrils cascading down. The style reminded Trinity of a Greek goddess.

If that weren't enough, Eugenia went further and did her makeup too. She lectured about how a smokey eye and red lippy was very appropriate for an evening look. When she finished, Trinity's jaw dropped. Was that her? Woah. She always thought she was pretty good with makeup. Not anymore. Eugenia was the master. She took a selfie. There was no way she'd ever look this good again without Eugenia's help. Might as well save it.

After twirling a few times, Eugenia dubbed her belle of the ball without having seen any of the other ladies. She said she didn't have to see any of them to know Trinity would stand out as the most beautiful. Something about her high cheekbones and naturally full lips. Trinity puckered in the mirror. Her lips were full? Was that good? According to Eugenia it was. She also had gone on and on about Trinity's eyebrows being virgins and perfect for shaping, whatever that meant. She wiggled her eyebrows in the mirror trying to emulate Maleficent to no avail.

No matter all the funny comments Eugenia made, making her laugh endlessly, she was definitely ready for tonight. Ready and nervous. Hopefully, she would represent well and make a good impression. The last thing she wanted to do was embarrass Dante at a function he had been invited to, or anywhere for that matter.

"Oh no. Where's my clutch?" Trinity tossed around tissue paper and boxes finally finding her black sequined bag. Thank the lord. Now to see if her phone would fit inside of it. Yup. She also needed to get her driver's license, lipstick, credit card and some cash into this thing. Please fit. The bag resisted until it was forced to snap shut. Relief. Everything fit...barely.

Alrighty! She was ready to go. Now all she needed was her ride, or was it date? Was it a date? No. Dante told her this night would give her experience. She was probably getting paid to go. That's good. She needed the money. The twenty dollars she shoved into her purse wouldn't go very far if she needed to use it.

The doorbell rang at seven sharp. One thing about Dante Venturi, he was always on time. Punctuality, was important to him it seemed. Thank goodness she was ready. Trinity peaked to ensure it was him and shook her hands out. Why was she so damn nervous? This was work. There was nothing to be nervous about. Just because he looked drop dead gorgeous didn't mean anything. It didn't affect her. At all. She swung the door open.

"Good eve...," Dante blinked once then twice before clearing his throat, "evening, Trinity. You look...stunning."

A rush of heat colored her cheeks. "Thank you. You look very handsome." Very handsome? The man wasn't very handsome. He was beautiful and sexy all at the same time.

"Thank you. Shall we?" He held out his arm.

Trinity closed the door and locked it before looping her arm with his. A thrill went through her when her bare arm touched the soft fabric of his tuxedoed arm. She could feel strength in him as he ensured she didn't fall down the steps with her long gown. That fact alone had her feeling warm. Too warm. Distracting herself, she brought her attention to a black limo. She had never been in a limo before. The heat in her belly changed to a flutter of excitement.

Once in, she noticed the creamy leather seats, a little bar and moonroof. She could literally lay down comfortably and nap in here. Hell, she could live in here. It was awesome! She wished she could take a picture, but didn't want to look foolish in front of Dante.

"Would you like champagne?"

"I better not. I'm working."

"This evening isn't just work, Trinity. You are allowed to enjoy yourself," he smiled. "It's Saturday night, after all. Anyway, I'll be introducing you to a lot of people. I hope you don't mind if I introduce you as my date."

"I-I don't mind." It was a date then? A work date. Yes. That was it. This was a work date. Of course it was. Duh. But he could have brought a real date if he wanted. It probably wasn't that hard to keep track of everything he was going to be bidding on. How much could he possibly buy?

"Good."

"Why didn't you bring a date?" Trinity asked curious before she could stop herself.

"I did." Dante gestured to her.

"T-this is a date?" Why was she so hung up on this? Didn't she just reason this was a work date? But she knew why. It was hearing Dante's confirmation. His matter of fact voice. As if he spared no thought. At least not like she did.

"You look too beautiful not to be called my date, Trinity. You're definitely my date. You have to be."

"W-why?" she asked breathless.

"Gio will be there. There's no way he's claiming you as his date when you're my date," he emphasized.

Trinity couldn't help it and busted out laughing. "You two are very funny. I didn't know I was a trophy?"

"Far from it. Unlike my nephew, you have a brain."

"That's not what Ms. Jewell said. She told me how gifted your nephew is. He's my age and graduating very soon."

"Don't get any ideas. Gio isn't for you," he sobered. A shadow of irritation crossed his face.

Trinity's lips parted. How could he be so bold, and irritated, as to tell her who wouldn't be good for her? She wanted to be just as irritated as he was, but it was too difficult with the look on his face. "Is that so? And who would be?" she teased.

"Me, of course."

Okay. She definitely wasn't expecting that answer. She had only been joking around. But, Dante didn't look like he was teasing in return. He looked...serious. The flutter in her stomach came back.

"I've gone too far. I apologize," he smiled.

Trinity smiled back, but felt confused. Eugenia was right. She knew back when she prepared Trinity for the dinner Dante hosted. Eugenia said Dante was interested, but it was too hard to believe at the time. Hell, it was hard to believe now. Why would he be interested in her? She was damaged goods.

"Dante, I don't understand. Why...me?"

"Why not you? You're beautiful, kind, smart, courageous, tenacious...,"

"Stop. Please. I'm not any of those things."

"Yes, you are. I can go on and on, Trinity."

"I'm...broken," she looked away.

Thankfully, the car stopped and the door opened to her escape. The driver helped Trinity out of the car, but Dante came around and took over. Once again, he took her arm into his and escorted her up the stairs to a set of double glass doors. Her body needed to stop reacting to him. To stop breathing in his delicious cologne. No! It wasn't delicious. Stop sniffing him! Trinity pressed her nails into her hand. Focus. Focus on the building.

It was a good focal point. The building was a very large and very fancy hotel. The entrance boasted a shiny front desk, but that's not what took her breath away. What did was the ceiling where a gorgeous mural was painted above depicting the heavens. So beautiful! If she could, she would stand and stare up for a few more minutes. Dante kept them moving. She couldn't wait to see what else there was. Never in all her life was she ever in a place like this.

Dante squeezed her hand a little and guided them to the hall where the auction was being held. Heavy chandeliers hung in the large room creating sparkling patterns on the ceiling, setting the room aglow with its soft light. The carpeted floor cushioned her feet, easing the tension of her heels much to her relief.

Numerous tables were set up against the illuminated walls with many auction items laid out for perusing. The rest of the room was delegated to dining tables for the guests. Each table was covered in white linen and china with an elaborate and numbered floral centerpiece. Dante took her over to a head table where they received their table number.

"We're number one. Of course we are," Dante smirked. "Shall we look at all of the items before we sit?"

"Sure."

Trinity wasn't sure what types of items she was expecting to find, but it certainly wasn't what was laid out. Expensive looking jewelry, watches and art pieces were displayed. Wow. A tennis bracelet caught her eye as she regarded everything. It sparkled under the lights. It was beautiful. Whomever won that item would sure be lucky.

"Do you like that bracelet?" Dante startled her.

"It's lovely. Everything here is," her eyes went to a framed painting. "Do you like art?" she pointed, steering away from Dante's question.

"I do. I'm an avid collector actually. That piece there is Native American by a man named Eanger Irving Couse. It's called The Treasure Jar. I have a print. It's my favorite."

"I can see why. How much does that print go for?"

"That one is the original. I'm quite surprised to see it in all honesty. I thought it was in a museum. But, to answer your question, some of his work has been known to go for over one million at auction."

"What?" Trinity breathed. "One million?"

"Easily."

"That's crazy. Who would pay that?"

"I would. In fact, I'm determined to have it."

Trinity's eyes grew. "Seriously?"

"Seriously."

"Dante!"

A man's voice had Dante spinning around till he found its source. His jaw flexed.

"Gabriel. How nice to see you," Dante said, his smile tight.

Trinity didn't miss the tick working in Dante's jaw. So this man was someone her boss-date didn't like. Note taken. How interesting. She wondered what the tension was about. Trinity blinked. Since when was she nosey?

"Aren't you going to introduce me to this gorgeous creature?"

"I don't see a creature anywhere around, Gabriel, but I wouldn't mind introducing you to my date. Miss Fallon, this is Gabriel. Gabriel, Miss Fallon. My date."

"Au chante, mademoiselle," Gabriel took Trinity's hand and kissed it.

"I don't...sing," she smirked, gently pulling back her hand.

"That means I'm delighted to meet you, dear."

"Ah. You meant, enchanté. I understand, now. Pleasure to meet you as well, sir." Trinity hadn't meant to sound sassy. The words just flew out of her mouth. What the hell was going on with her? Dante was going to fire her for sure. Why couldn't the floor split open and swallow her?

Her dark thought was interrupted by Dante's deep laugh. His deep sexy laugh to be exact.

"Better luck next time, Gabe."

The man shrugged with a smile, "I didn't know she's French."

"I'm not," Trinity smiled, relieved Dante wasn't angry with her.

Gabriel stared at her. His eyes roaming her face. "No. Of course not. You look Italian. Am I correct?"

Dante regarded her with thoughtful eyes. Jeeze. Talk about nerves.

"This time you are correct, sir."

"Then you're perfect for each other." Gabriel slapped Dante's back and meandered back into the crowd.

"Something we have in common then," Dante grinned. "You speak French?"

"Un peu," she pinched her fingers together. "I took four years in high school, but have forgotten most of it."

"Impressive nonetheless. Do you speak Italian?"

Was that hope in his voice?

"No. Silly, isn't it?"

"Not at all. Especially if your parents don't speak the language. And, It's not typically offered in school. I could teach you."

They were interrupted a few more times by random people before it was time for them to be seated for dinner. They were seated at a table with two older couples and a man who didn't have a date. Trinity couldn't help but notice his eyes were on her.

She shifted in her seat a little. Why did he have to stare at her? It was so incredibly awkward. How was she supposed to comfortably eat her meal. This sucked. Suddenly, the older woman sitting next to her patted her hand and leaned in.

"You ought to get used to it. Especially since you're dating Mr. Venturi. You're the belle of the ball it would seem," she whispered.

"Oh, no I'm...," Trinity looked around. Most eyes were on her. How was it that Eugenia's words were echoed just now?

"Are you a model?"

Trinity laughed, "Far from it."

"You should be, honey. Just remember, hold your head high and ignore the oglers. They wish they had what Mr. Dante Venturi has," she patted Trinity's hand again and winked before turning back to her husband.

Great. Was that why everyone was staring at her? They thought she was dating Dante? She wasn't! Why couldn't they just mind their own business? Even if she was, why would it matter? Why would they care?

As if Dante sensed Trinity's distress, or overheard the old woman, he squeezed her hand and leaned in. "Try to ignore everyone, Trin. Don't let good food go to waste because of an impolite person." Dante smiled at the man staring at Trinity. "Mr. Grett, where's your date?"

Trin? Did he just call her Trin? He shortened her name to form a nick-name? What did that mean? Were they friends? Ugh! She needed to phone a friend.

The man chuckled, "I wasn't as fortunate as you."

"You are right about that."

"Won't you introduce us?"

"I'm eating, Mr. Grertt. Perhaps next time."

If she hadn't been keeping a tight rein on herself, her jaw would have hit the floor. How rude Dante was! Jeeze. She felt her cheeks heat up but didn't dare look at Mr. Grett, whoever he was. Apparently, no one of importance. Especially when the first court arrived. All her apprehension for eating in front of people evaporated.

After the first course arrived, several others followed. Each better than the last. It seemed to be a trend dining with Dante. Only the best food was served. Never in her wildest imagination would she ever dare to dream finding herself in the situation she was currently in. It was as if the heavens opened up and decided to smile down upon her. Maybe.

Soon after the meal, the bidding began. To Trinity's surprise, Dante bid on many items. She wondered if he would win the painting he wanted. After he placed his bids, he excused himself telling her he would be right back and left her standing alone. Great. Now what was she supposed to do?

"Holy mother of God, Trinity. You are absolutely breathtaking. I swear to God, my uncle is hoarding you. It's definitely not fair."

Trinity knew that voice. It belonged to Gio, Dante's nephew. His remark brought a smile to her face. Gio was very easy to like.

"Gio! Thank heavens. I was feeling so awkward."

"Where the heck is Uncle Dante?"

"I'm not sure. He said he would be right back." Trinity looked around.

"I bet he's striking a deal for something he wants. He always does that."

This time Trinity's jaw did drop. "He can do that? It's not fair to others."

"Who said anything about fair? What Uncle Dante wants, he gets. It's just how it is. But don't feel too bad. He'll pay far more for whatever it is than what anyone here could afford. So, in a way, it's kind of fair?" Gio shrugged.

"I guess if you put it that way." It was a weird way of thinking, but whatever.

"I'm so mad I missed the dinner. Did they have steak?"

"They did. And, yes, it was the most delicious thing I ever ate."

"Damn it. This is my mother's fault. She insisted I bring my sister since I don't have a date. So embarrassing."

"Oh, your sister is here?" Trinity glanced around.

"Unfortunately. She's mingling. I'll introduce you to her later."

"Is she older or younger?"

"Younger. She's sixteen and a real brat," Gio laughed.

Trinity swatted at him. "Gio! You shouldn't speak about your sister that way."

"Oh, God, don't touch me. If Uncle Dante sees that, he'll think I'm trying to steal you away."

Trinity stiffened. Memories of David's jealousy ran through her brain making her feel slightly nauseated. Was Dante the jealous type?

"Trinity? Are you alright? I was only joking. Uncle Dante is too confident to worry about me. Actually, Uncle Dante is too confident to worry about anyone."

A breath she was holding released. Thank the lord. Not that she was hopeful for a relationship with Dante. It was just, she didn't need to be around anyone who was jealous.

"But, on a serious note, Uncle Dante is really impressed with you."

"Really? How? I haven't even done anything yet. I'm not even sure I can do Ms. Jewell's job."

"Pff. I can't even do my job that great. Don't worry. Just think of Jewell's job as a professional organizer. You'll be fine. It also helps that he's into you."

"Into me?"

"Yeah. Duh. Haven't you seen the way he stares at you? You're all he talks about."

"But I'm married. I-I was married."

"I know. I'm sorry to hear. But, the bastard got what he deserved."

What? What did Gio know? Why would he know anything about her husband? "You know about my husband?"

"I mean, like I said, Uncle Dante talks about you a lot. I mean, not with other people. Just me. Since I'm family. He never talks about his private business with anyone other than family. And even then, there's exceptions to that rule. He's very particular. We were all raised that way. Kinda have to be." He rubbed at his neck and cleared his throat looking around at nothing in particular.

Okay? This conversation was the weirdest she ever had. She could barely follow it. On the other hand, Gio was a little fountain of information despite it being somewhat cryptic.

"Gio, did your uncle tell you if he had any plans for me?"

"Plans? What do you mean?"

"Like, plans," Trinity shrugged trying to send him a telepathic message.

"Ohhh, plaaans. I get it. No."

"Oh. Maybe, don't tell him I just asked that," Trinity laughed nervous.

"No worries." He grabbed two flutes of champagne from a waiter's tray and handed one to Trinity. "Do you see yourself having a relationship with my uncle?" his asked nonchalant.

Trinity sipped from her glass, the bubbles tickling her nose. She didn't see herself having a relationship with anyone ever again. Things were too fresh. But, if this were a fantasy, she would be crazy to say no. How wonderful it must be to live in Dante's world.

"It's too soon for me. My husband literally died last week."

"My bad. I'm sorry."

"It's okay, Gio. My husband was a bad man. So, what about you? Any girlfriends to speak of?"

"I don't keep one girl. I like to play the field. Spread my attention out on many chicks."

Trinity laughed at that. If anything at all, Gio was going to be a great friend to have.

"Then you're not spread very thin." Dante came up behind Trinity, startling her.

"Very funny, Uncle Dante. Very. Funny," Gio smiled with pursed lips and squinty eyes.

Trinity wasn't sure if what Gio joked about earlier was in fact a joke or if Dante really was the jealous type. She had felt relieved when Gio assured her. But now that Dante was back, she felt uneasy. Her eyes darted between them.

"Has my nephew been keeping you company?" Dante grabbed a flute of champagne for himself.

Trinity nodded, but looked down at her shoes. Her heart was racing.

"That's good. I was gone far longer than anticipated. I apologize."

"Gave you a run for your money?" Gio asked.

"They always do. Where's your sister?"

"Hey, how'd you know I came with her?"

"I know everything, Gio," Dante dismissed, his eyes scanning the room.

They continued to talk like nothing happened. Like she had done nothing wrong speaking with Gio so friendly. Risking a peak at Dante, he looked very calm and happy. He was enjoying the banter he had going with his nephew. He really wasn't jealous?

"Go find Mirabella, Gio. I want Trinity to meet her."

"Why? She's a...,"

Dante gave him a don't finish that sentence look.

"Ugh. Fine," Gio whined.

"It's hard to believe you two are the same age. You'd think he was ten," Dante laughed noticing Trinity was preoccupied, "Trin? Are you alright?"

"Um, yes."

Dante smiled confused. "Your mood shifted. What happened? No. Wait. Follow me."

Dante led them out of the room and down the hall to a cloak room. The dim room was lined with coats, cocooning them in and affording privacy.

"Tell me," Dante worried.

"It's nothing, really. I feel foolish for even saying anything at all. We can go back." She pressed against his chest, but he resisted. Damn butterflies.

"No, we most certainly will not. I want to hear what you have to say."

It took several minutes for Trinity to muster the courage to come out with it. All the while, Dante stood patient making the room feel hot and much smaller than what it really was. She needed to escape. She needed air. The only way to obtain it was to spill her guts.

"Gio and I were talking, and he made a joke and I slapped him to stop. When I did that, he said not to touch him or you'll get jealous," Trinity's eyes snapped up. "Oh! He told me he was kidding and that you're never jealous. I guess the word jealous triggered me a little. I don't want to do anything that might jeopardize my job or, or...I don't know," Trinity was wringing her hands tightly and her throat was so dry it was hard to swallow.

There was no way she could look him in the eye. She concentrated on her manicured toes. But her eyes widened at the soft touch of Dante's finger under her chin. He gently brought her face up to meet his eyes.

"Trinity. First of all, Gio is correct. I am not a jealous man. Protective, yes. Jealous, no. If men are looking at whoever I'm with, it makes me feel proud to be with that person. And, as far as your job is concerned, it's secure. Please don't worry."

Trinity nodded.

"Is there anything else?"

Should she ask him about his interest in her? Maybe she should so that he doesn't hope for more. It was best she set him straight now.

"Yes, actually. A few people have said that you might be interested in me. Including you. Is...is that really true?" Trinity dared to look him in the eyes.

"It is." His answer was simple.

"Dante, I can't. Like I said in the limo, I'm damaged. Broken. I don't want you to hope for something that will probably never happen."

"If circumstances were different, would you consider me?" he asked curious.

Maybe it was time to lighten the mood. "No."

"No?" Dante echoed in surprise.

Trinity smiled soft. "I'm joking. Of course I would. But, things are the way they are. I just don't see how they could ever change."

"You deserve every happiness, Trinity. Whether you're with someone or not. I'm not going to push this. I know you're hurting on many different levels. Just know I'm here, and will be here," he shrugged.

"You're too nice to me, Dante. Way too nice. I can't be...," Trinity swallowed hard, "I just don't want to lead you on. I think there are so many gorgeous women here tonight who would look so beautiful on your arm," her watery eyes darted between his. It really wasn't fair to him. He deserved to be happy too. "Gio can take me home."

"You are my date, Mrs. Fallon. And despite my giving you space and backing off, I'm definitely not going to allow you to dump my sorry ass in the middle of the cloak room," Dante laughed. "Come on. Let's go and have some fun and see what we've won. Oh, and I want you to meet Mirabella. Gio is kind of right, she's a bit of a brat. But, we love her."

Trinity laughed. "Okay." She started to follow Dante out, but tugged on his suit jacket. "Wait. I have a request." she watched his eyes change curious. "P-please don't call me Mrs. or even Miss Fallon anymore. My maiden name is Aldi. I'm planning on changing my name as soon as possible."

Dante's lips spread into a dazzling smile, making her heart stop and her stomach flip.

"Trinity Aldi," he tested her name on his tongue. "I like that. It suits you. Very good, Miss Aldi. Shall we?" he held his arm out.

Chapter 16

Just how and when Monday came to be was a mystery. In one breath it was a Friday night, then an awe inspiring Saturday evening full of good food, interesting people and new experiences, and finally Sunday. Not that Sunday was all bad, Trinity mused. It actually served its purpose by providing time to catch up with laundry and house cleaning. Even a little couch potatoing was had. All and all, the weekend suddenly, magically, ended up as one big evaporated blur. Depressing for any fantastic-weekend veteran such as herself.

Saturday night's auction kept replaying in her mind. It truly had been chalked full of revelations and experiences she was still wrapping her mind around. She felt like Cinderella with Eugenia as her fairy godmother, a deer in headlights with Dante, an elaborate painting from all the stares she received, to a teenager again with Gio and Mirabella. A stuffed teenager from having eaten too much.

The weekend's memories were a good distraction while Trinity sat uncomfortable on a vinyl couch in a small office, waiting for her new therapist. Feeling a little nervous, she had no clue how this was supposed to go. The first step was always the hardest, or so she had been told.

At the end of the day, Dante was right as intrusive as his suggestion was. She did need help. She didn't want to feel broken or think of herself in such a way ever again. It was time she started living her life. Simply going through the motions wasn't good enough. She was only twenty for heaven's sake. She shouldn't be working. She should be in college or doing both, rather than trying to pick up the pieces of her life. But she was, and so, talking with someone who didn't know her might help. Either way, she had nothing to lose. An added bonus was that the office visit was fully covered under the health insurance Dante put her on. Insurance was everything.

Trinity owed so much to Dante. He took a chance and gave her a job, a new place to live, clothes and a company car. Even food when she first moved in. It was amazing! Trinity frowned. Not really. She knew why. It was all because he was attracted to her. Did that make him selfish? It was hard to say. Especially since she told him a relationship was never going to happen.

Still. He hadn't taken any of those things away from her. But that was only because he wasn't giving up on her just yet. He asked if she would be interested in him had things been different. Of course she would be. Aside from kind, caring and generous, he was gorgeous. Who wouldn't want to be with him?

Trinity smiled to herself. Perhaps she wasn't as different from him as he was from her when it came to attraction. Her thoughts were interrupted by the therapist coming into the small room and having a seat. If Trinity had to guess, the woman was middle-aged with graying strands of curly hair at her temple. Her skirt was long and wispy reminding Trinity of a gypsy. She looked super relaxed and carefree. A small amount of tension released from Trinity's shoulders.

"Trinity Fallon?"

"Um, yes, but I'm changing my last name. If you could call me Aldi. Actually, if you could just call me Trinity?"

"Of course. It's nice to meet you. Thank you for coming in. I'm Leslie Shaw," she smiled. Her kind, blue eyes sparkled. "I read through your paperwork. It's a very tricky situation you're in, Trinity. You must feel conflicted between relief and grief."

"I'm definitely relieved." Trinity grabbed her wrist and twisted her hand around while she took in the room, having trouble maintaining eye contact. "As far as grief, I feel numb really. It's hard to believe he's gone because I moved out before he died. So, it still feels like he's alive out there."

"That must be very difficult for you to feel like you can't move on."

"It is. And, I'm not exactly sure what moving on means."

"You don't have to know what it means. There's no right or wrong definition."

The therapist moved her attention to the file in her lap. Trinity couldn't help but notice a cozy blanket draped over the woman's chair, and the elegant way she moved her papers around. Despite the ticking clock, she seemed unbothered with time.

"I noticed in your paperwork you're most recently employed by Venturi Transportation. That was before your husband's death?" She picked up a cup of coffee and sipped from it slow.

"Y-yes. I fell into the job unexpectedly actually. My boss gave me a place to stay and set me up when he figured out what David had done to me."

"How did he figure it out?" the therapist looked confused.

"He saw my injuries. He...kind of took me under his wing."

"What a kind person. You must feel very grateful to him."

"I do. It's just a little complicated."

"Oh?"

The ceiling looked interesting. Why was it so hard to look the therapist in the eye? Trinity sighed deep. "My boss made it clear to me that he's interested in me."

"How does that make you feel?"

"I told him I'm broken. That I can't. That I probably never will be right for a relationship. It, honestly, doesn't make me feel too great."

"Understandable. It's important to know you're not broken, Trinity. You can heal, but it's going to take work. Do you like this man?"

"I do. He's easy to like," a warmth spread to her belly. "He's kind and very generous. All of his employees like him too. His personal assistant seems very fond of him. I'm taking over her position because she's retiring."

"I see. Well, listen, you're entitled to live a very happy life, Trinity. There's no reason why you can't. Yes, you survived a trauma. But, it's not the end all of your life. Your healing will take time and work. In the end, it's going to be up to you. No one can force you. No one should. If your boss can't take no for an answer, I suggest you find a new job," her forehead wrinkled. "Your boss really shouldn't be hitting on you, in my opinion. Does it make you uncomfortable?"

"Not at all. He's not creepy," Trinity chuckled.

"No? Are you sure?"

"Very. He's...easy on the eyes."

"Ah," the therapist grinned. "I think there's hope for you yet, Trinity. Don't give up on yourself. Would you like to make more appointments so that we can get to work?"

"I think so." The therapist was extremely easy to talk to, Trinity reasoned.

"Excellent."

"Before I go, can I ask a question?"

"Absolutely."

"Is it bad for me to feel attracted to someone?"

"No. Not at all. You're your own person, Trinity. You make all the decisions and rules. There's no right or wrong."

-#-

The morning therapy session went by so fast. Even though it was kind of a get-to-know-you session, it felt good to go. Trinity was also happy to be back at work. It was already mid-morning, and she sat at her desk entering in data just as Ms. Jewell showed her. It was a relatively easy task, and she was glad for it. Her mind was too preoccupied for anything difficult.

Her therapist told her it was okay to feel attracted to someone. It was okay that she was attracted to Dante. Of course, she had no intention of telling anyone that bit of information. But it definitely felt relieving. It was okay, and there was no need to feel guilty. David was a monster who made her feel horrible. He hurt her, almost killing her several times. Now, he was gone. There was no way he could ever hurt her again.

Even her bad dreams were starting to lessen. It was probably because of Dante. She always thought about him before drifting off to sleep. She suspected he was the reason why she slept so peacefully. Had it not been for him, she would have been stuck in her old life riddled with nightmares.

Hell, maybe David would still be alive to this day. Not that Dante was responsible. But had she been at her old house, and never met Dante, she would have been cooking dinner for David. He would have been eager to come home for it. Maybe, he wouldn't have taken on that risky case and gotten killed. Any little circumstance could have changed her and David's paths really.

Looking around her office, which still needed decorating, she couldn't help feeling relieved. Her therapist was right. This was her one and only life where all of the decisions were hers to make along with the rules. There was no right or wrong about it. It really was a powerful thought.

If she really wanted to, she could be happy. She could have a relationship with a man. Not that she felt ready, but still. She could if she wanted to. The thought felt liberating. Her therapist was pretty good for being able to make her feel so uplifted. Good thing she made more appointments.

"Trinity!" Gio poked his head into her office.

"Hi Gio!"

"Wanna go to lunch?"

"Is it that time already?"

"Yup. I'm dying for some pizza and it's calzone day."

"Ooh. Yes. Count me in. Is Eugenia coming?"

"Are you kidding me? She's out with her supervisor. I think they're already sleeping together. Come on."

When they arrived at the cafeteria, Trinity was surprised to see how many people were in line. What the heck? By the time they got their food, the lunch hour would be over with. Her stomach growled much to her embarrassment.

"Oh my God. What gives? I should assert my authority and skip this damn line." Gio balled his shaky fists.

"Gio! Don't you dare," Trinity giggled.

"Oh, I'm daring. Come on. We'll go in through the back."

Gio grabbed Trinity's hand and pulled her through the crowds. It must be a regular thing he did, because people were yelling at him. How embarrassing!

"What good is it to work for Uncle Dante if I can't bend the rules, people?!" Gio shouted over Trinity's head causing her to duck a little.

A few empty water bottles were launched in their direction. Oh jeez. She hoped a food fight didn't break out.

"Ha! Suckers!" he shouted again tossing a bottle he managed to catch.

Trinity groaned, but then forgot her mortification when they arrived at the kitchen. Wow. There sure were a lot of calzones being prepped for baking.

"Shirley! My favorite cook. How about two calzones for your two favorite people? That blue apron looks dashing on you, by the way."

Shirley looked to be in her eighties with blue hair and crinkled skin. She rolled her eyes. "Gio, you're not supposed to be back here. And who is she?"

"She's Uncle Dante's girlfriend. So it's okay."

"Gio! No, I'm not!"

"Shh. We'll get food if she thinks you are, so shut up."

"Oh boy." Trinity rubbed her forehead.

"What did you say?"

"I said...she...is...Uncle...Dante's...girl...friend!" Gio shouted so the woman could hear him.

Was Gio for real? She never met anyone like him. If she had to guess, she'd say he was probably a class clown. She started to laugh again. She needed to hang around him more often. He really was funny.

Grabbing the tray, Gio held it up in triumph. "Alright! Calzones, dipping sauce, salads and cola! What else is there to life? I am...complete."

"You're also fat!" Shirley yelled.

"I knew you could hear me just fine, grandma!" Gio dodged a calzone Shirley whipped at his head. "Let's get out of here!"

Finding a booth, Gio slid in on one side while Trinity slid in on the other. Gio genuinely looked completely happy with his food. It was hilarious. She couldn't help herself and started to laugh again.

"What?"

"You really love food."

"Yup. Nothin' comes between me and my meals. So I have a few pounds on me? Who cares, right?"

"I don't see anything wrong with it," Trinity shrugged.

"Just you wait. You keep eating here with me, and we can be muffin-top buddies."

"Muffin-top buddies? What the heck is a muffin top?"

"Don't you know? It's when your stomach muffins out over the top of your pants."

"Oh," Trinity faltered. She must really have been living under a rock. She never heard that expression. Was she so paralyzed living with David that she missed out on everything? Even slang?

"So, I'm not gonna be around tomorrow because Uncle Dante has a huge business deal going. I always organize them. I have to act serious. It kinda sucks."

"Aww. Do you not like this work?"

"I do. It's just, I guess, ever since you started, I've been able to have a little fun. I like you, Trinity. I'm glad we're friends."

Wow. She'd never had anyone say that to her that wasn't female. This man-child sitting in front of her was her first male friend.

"I'm glad we're friends too. It's nice to be able to sit and joke around without any expectations on me."

"That must suck. I bet you always have dudes hitting on you."

"I don't know," she shrugged.

"Well, you're totally gorgeous but not my type. So you're safe."

Trinity broke out into a huge grin. "And, pray tell, what is your type?"

"Well, I love, love, love, full-figured chicks. You're, well, you're kind of a twig," Gio cringed waiting for Trinity's reaction.

She couldn't help but laugh, biting into her calzone. "I don't know," she said with a mouth full of cheesy goodness. "I keep eating with you, I might just add a little junk in the backseat."

Gio busted out laughing. "Backseat?! It's trunk. You're hilarious." His eyes closed in bliss as he devoured his calzone.

"How the heck do you eat so fast?" Trinity looked at Gio's empty plate in horror. She hadn't even eaten half of hers yet.

"Oh, I don't waste time. If I would've waited any longer, it would have cooled off. I bet your calzone is getting cold."

"Don't even think about it, mister." Trinity guarded her food. "Eat your salad."

"Boring."

"H-hi, Gio."

Gio looked up at a shy girl who stopped at their table. This girl looked to be just his type. Although, she also looked very nervous.

"Oh, hey, Sarah. How's it goin'?"

"Um, good. How are you?"

"Pretty great. It's calzone day," he pointed at Trinity's half eaten food biting his lip.

"Yeah. Oh, um, hi. Are you new?"

"I am. My name is Trinity. Nice to meet you."

"Nice to meet you. A-are you two friends?"

"Yeah?" Gio's brow cocked as he slid his gaze over to Trinity.

"I see. Well...bye."

"Bye? Woah. She's super weird. What's up with that?" He jerked his thumb in Sarah's retreating direction.

"I think she likes you, Gio. She was trying to ask you if I'm your girlfriend."

Gio's nose wrinkled. "You think?"

"It's kind of obvious," Trinity laughed. "And don't you dare say yuck," Trinity pointed her fork at him.

"What? Yuck to you being my girlfriend or yuck to her?"

"Both."

"I wasn't even gonna say, yuck. Hey. I was wondering about something."

"Hmm?"

"Maribella really liked you and you're my friend now, so we were both kinda hoping you'd come over for dinner this weekend. My mom is supposed to be making lasagna...," Gio's expression turned thoughtful, "although, she sometimes gets lazy. Anyway, it would be kinda cool if you came. We could hang out and play video games or watch movies."

Trinity blinked up surprised. Being invited over to Gio's house was the last thing she ever expected. When was the last time she ever hung out at a friend's house? It had to have been in middle school. How fun would it be to do things like that? Another thought popped into her head.

"You live with your parents?"

"Of course I do. I'm only twenty, remember? I go to school and work. Cut me some slack, woman!"

Trinity laughed. "Sorry. Count me in. What should I bring?"

"Dessert. Let's see, do you bake?"

"Do I bake? Boy, you are in for a treat. I'll bring something that'll make me your new bff."

Gio clapped his hands together and rubbed them with an evil look on his face.

"Ew. Don't do that," Trinity fell into a fit of laughter.

Amazing. Becky had been her one and only friend throughout high school. Eugenia had become her new friend who she valued very much. But, Gio...she could tell he was going to be her very best friend.

It made her smile for the rest of the day.

Chapter 17

The day finally arrived! It was the day of the dinner Gio invited her to, and she needed to do some baking. Pronto. She promised Gio something fantastic. But what? Ooh, she got it! Her very own chocolate chip cookie recipe. Those were always a huge favorite whenever she baked them with her mother, which wasn't very often.

She wondered how her mother was doing. Her parents never checked on her, among other things, and it caused a riff between them. Maybe she would call. Perhaps mend things. Someday.

Trinity let go of the thought and went onto Apple Music. It was only recently she realized Dante paid for a subscription for everyone in the company, thanks to Gio telling her.

Ariana Grande's, Break Free caught her eye. Kind of appropriate to her situation.

"I'm stronger than I've been before!" she sang and bopped around her kitchen grabbing everything she needed to bake.

She loved baking. It was relaxing. She liked to cook too, but not as much as baking. Nothing was more comforting than something warm, gooey and chocolatey.

Mirabella and Gio were going to go crazy for these cookies. Maybe she should bring a copy of the recipe with her. That way they could bake them whenever they wanted. Although, something told her, Gio would never set foot in a kitchen unless he was grabbing food. Just like the other day in the cafeteria. How hilarious and mortifying that was.

She missed Gio the rest of the week. He had to work with Dante and was throwing tantrums according to Ms. Jewell. Hopefully, things would go back to normal on Monday and her lunch buddy would return.

It made her think of Dante. Where did he eat for lunch? In his office or did he go out? Hmm. Maybe she'd ask him. Trinity's stomach sunk. On second thought, better not. He might think she was fishing for an invitation. She didn't want to confuse him.

Brushing off her hands, she popped a sheet of dough into the oven and ran upstairs to look through her closet. What to wear tonight? Trinity tapped her lip. Maybe she would give Becky a try. Now that David was gone, she didn't need to keep her distance. Right?

The phone rang once then went straight to voicemail. Weird. Did Becky press the decline button? Dialing Eugenia, she didn't answer either. Her phone, however, rang a bunch of times before it too went to voicemail.

She was on her own. Actually, no she wasn't. She could shoot Gio a text and ask him. His response was immediate, telling her to wear jeans or whatever. Perfect. As much as she loved dressing up, she longed to be comfy for once.

After Trinity had all of the cookies baked, she packaged them up into an airtight container and went upstairs to get ready. Powder-blue jeans, white t-shirt and a gray comfy sweatshirt with gray slouchy socks. Oh yeah. She looked ultra comfy. Finding a matching hair tie, she pulled her hair up into a high ponytail and quickly curled the tail. A touch of mascara and lip gloss, which was a waste because she was going to be eating, and she was ready to go. She hesitated. Did she need blush? Sucking in her cheeks, she decided a little dab wouldn't hurt. There. Now she didn't look like a zombie.

Assessing herself more closely, she smiled. She looked younger like this. Her appearance reminded her of how she used to look in high school. That was only two and a half years ago. Amazing how fast time flew. Amazing how her life experience was vastly different from practically everyone else's, and not in a good way.

Trinity murmured. Dwelling wasn't going to help, and only ruin her good mood. Tonight was about having fun. She would stuff her face, play video games and watch movies or whatever Gio had in store. She was going to be in good company tonight. For however difficult, she wasn't going to let memories of David haunt her thoughts.

Grabbing up her keys, bag and cookies, she headed out. It took a few seconds to type in Gio's address before hitting the road. It was a surprise to see he only lived twenty minutes from her. Not a bad ride at all. It would give her time to listen to some music and see a new part of town. Actually, looking at the map on the navigation system, it was the next town over.

After a few minutes, the city quickly melded into the countryside. Interesting. This was a wealthier community. The farther and farther she drove, the bigger and bigger the homes were getting. Holy cow. These places were mansions.

Should it really be surprising? Not really. Gio was the nephew to the owner of a giant company that had been in business a very long time. Tonight would be a treat, getting to chill out in a mansion. A female voice announcing the final left turn into Gio's driveway interrupted her thoughts. The drive looked to be pretty long since she couldn't see the house. It took her a minute more before the building appeared to be rising out of the ground against the horizon. Holy crap. This place wasn't just big it was ginormous! Why didn't he warn her?

Another thought plagued her as she parked off to the side away from the house. Was Gio's parents home? Trinity slapped her forehead. His parents probably were. Didn't Gio mention something about his mother making lasagna for tonight? Trinity whimpered. She was a total airhead. What made matters worse was imagining everyone sitting all together at a table. Good lord. She came to his house looking like a total couch potato! What will they think of her? What was she supposed to say to Gio's mother? Oh, hi, I'm going to be your brother's personal assistant. By the way, I don't have an education, I don't know how to act around you rich people and I don't know what I'm doing!

"Great. Maybe I should just go home," she groaned.

"What?"

Trinity screamed, "Gio!" Grabbing her cookies, she got out of the car and swatted him. "You scared me!"

"Sorry. Why would you go home when you just got here?"

"How the heck did you hear me?"

Gio shrugged, "Are those cookies? Give 'em."

Trinity held the container out of reach. "No way. I want Mirabella to have a few before you devour them," her eyes grew emphasizing her point.

"Pff. They that good, huh?"

"Better than good. Wait, Gio. Listen, are your parents home?"

"Yeah, why?"

"It's just...i-i-it's just that...look at me."

Gio's forehead wrinkled. "I am? Beautiful?"

"No. I look like a couch potato. I don't want to make a bad impression," Trinity worried.

"Um, look at me. I am a couch potato. Besides, you look adorable. I may need a huggie a little later."

"A huggie?" Trinity curled her lip.

"Yup. You look too cuddly. Can I have a cookie now?"

"Oh you!" Trinity tried to swat at him again, but he took off running back to the house...mansion. What a giant kid, she thought feeling giddy.

"Trinity!" Mirabella cheered, running out to meet them and enveloping Trinity in a hug.

"Hi Mirabella!" Trinity hugged her back feeling warm.

"Call me Belle or Bella, remember?"

Mirabella took a liking to Trinity right away at the auction and asked to be called by her nicknames. She had indeed forgotten. Bella was very sweet for sixteen years old. Not even she was sweet at that age. And she seemed to be quite close with her brother. Trinity found their interactions fascinating and enjoyed watching them.

"Did you bring cookies, Trinity?"

"I did. Would you like one?"

"Oh, hell no."

Gio held the door open for Trinity and his sister with a frown. Trinity followed Bella in and tried to keep her jaw from falling to the floor. This place was gorgeous. The foyer was all stone from floor to ceiling, a winding staircase boasting a wrought iron railing was nestled into a corner, and a long hallway disappeared into who knew where.

She soon discovered the hallway led to a kitchen with beautiful stone countertops and expensive appliances. The house had a very rustic feel to it. While it was beyond large, it was extremely cozy. Trinity immediately felt at ease.

"Your home is beautiful, guys."

"Thanks. Bella, you can't have a cookie unless I can have one and Trinity already told me no," Gio pouted.

"Kids, pizza will be here in thirty minutes. Gio stop pouting."

Trinity set the cookies down onto the center island, and wished to shrink and die. This must be Gio's mother. Dante's sister. A very pretty, older woman with chestnut-brown hair and expressive brown eyes smiled kindly at her.

"You must be Trinity. You can call me Anna. It's very nice to meet you," she extended her hand.

"Likewise," Trinity whispered with a gulp, her sense of ease evaporating. Why did she feel so nervous?

"Ah. I see what the fuss is about. You brought cookies. Did you make them?"

Trinity nodded her head with a shy smile. If she spoke, she might start stuttering. That was the last thing she wanted to do. Hopefully, this woman didn't think she was rude.

"I might have to try them."

"What?! Mom, that's not fair. Trin made those for us!" Gio yelled trying to take the container.

"My house, my laws," Anna waved a cookie under Gio's nose before sinking her teeth into the confection.

That's when her expression melted. Oh no. Were they bad? Shit! Trinity hadn't tried them. She was so confident they would taste good--they always did--she didn't bother trying them.

"I-I-I'm...," Trinity squeezed her eyes trying to get her words out, "sorry. You don't have to eat it."

Anna's eyes popped open in surprise. "What? Trinity, you misunderstand me. These are to die for."

"Mom!" Gio stomped his foot. "I want one right...now!"

Trinity jumped startled by Gio's outburst. Then, without her realizing it, she busted out laughing. Gio looked so funny standing there in his sweatpants and t-shirt, belly jiggling from all his stomping. There was no way this was the same man she worked with. But, of course, he was. Only Gio could get away with skipping a line full of hungry employees. This boy was serious about food!

Mirabella joined her, laughing even harder when Anna handed her a cookie and not Gio. Gio waved a dismissive hand at his mother and sister hearing the doorbell ring.

Anna rolled her eyes. "Make yourself at home, Trinity. I hope you don't find my son too weird. He never grew up, I guess."

"He's not weird, mom. He's fun!" Bella said protecting her brother.

"If he's not weird, why doesn't he have a girlfriend yet?" Anna countered.

Bella shrugged, "I don't know, mom. He's weird."

Trinity laughed. This family was so nice. She wondered then how Gio's father was. That would be Dante's brother-in-law. She never saw him at the office. Did he work for Venturi Transportation?

"What's all the commotion?"

Trinity gulped. She shouldn't have asked herself the question. Now she was about to get the answer. Crap. Don't stutter, don't stutter, don't stutter.

"Oh, Gio is throwing a food tantrum. Peter, this is Trinity. She's Gio's friend from work."

Peter held out his hand. "Nice to meet you, Trinity. Welcome to our home."

"Nice to meet you," Trinity shook his hand happy he didn't hold onto her longer than necessary.

"You work under Dante, if I'm not mistaken," Anna added.

Trinity nodded with a smile.

"That so? How's he treating you? Well, I hope?"

"He is, thank you," she whispered, thanking the lord her tongue behaved.

Despite not stuttering, Peter's full attention was on her. He was studying her. If she hadn't looked up at the precise moment she did, she would have missed his narrowed eyes. Did she say something wrong? Crap! Where the heck was Gio and Mirabella?

"My son told me a lot about you. You guys seemed to have hit it off," he smiled.

"He's been a great friend to me."

"Only a friend?" Anna's voice was full of hope.

Trinity's head whipped to Anna. Oh boy. "Oh, um, yes. We...we're friends."

Gio saved her from having to explain the dynamic of their relationship, sliding into the room on his socks with a stack of pizzas in hand. Mirabella ran after him with a bunch of other boxes Trinity assumed was garlic bread or whatever other appetizer they ordered. That was a lot of food. Should she offer to pay for herself?

"What are we talking about?" Gio looked at his mom suspicious.

"Your mother wants to know why Trinity isn't your girlfriend," Peter answered exasperated.

Gio clicked his tongue and rolled his eyes. "Mom, me and Trinity are just friends. Besides, Uncle Dante called dibs. I will not break the bro code. Jeez."

Trinity felt her eyes grow. How could Gio say that?! She couldn't help but slide her gaze at Peter who was staring at her. If he wasn't curious or suspicious before, he certainly was now.

"I told him I'm not looking for a relationship," Trinity quickly assured. She better tell them the reason. "M-m-my husband died two weeks ago."

The kitchen fell silent. Great. Maybe telling them was a mistake. But it had to be done. She didn't want any of them thinking she was using Dante or his family for any type of financial gain. She didn't want anything. Now that David was dead, she stood to earn money from the eventual sale of their home and from a small life insurance policy. But she couldn't say all of that.

"Oh my God. I'm so sorry, Trinity. I didn't know," Anna's fingers were pressed to her lips.

"There was no way you would have known. It's okay," Trinity assured.

Anna darted daggers at her son, but Gio only shrugged. Trinity could imagine Anna wasn't too happy Gio neglected to inform her of the important parts. But why would he? He probably told his parents he was having a friend over and that was the extent of it. No need to tell them about her personal life. In actuality, it made her feel good. Gio wasn't a blabber mouth. A good quality to have in a friend.

"I'm sorry for your loss, Trinity. Tell me, how old are you?"

"Dad! Seriously?!" Mirabella stomped her foot.

"It's okay, Bella," Trinity smiled kind, then answered Peter. "I'm twenty, like Gio."

"Do you have children?"

"No."

"Interesting. What made you get married so young?"

Because he pressured. Bamboozled. Hypnotized. What other verbs were there? She wanted to tell them, but this was supposed to be a fun evening. And...she didn't know these people. There was no reason to tell them.

"Young and dumb, I guess. Everyone makes mistakes," she inadvertently whispered.

"That's enough, Peter. Trinity was invited over by Gio to have a nice time, not an interrogation. I'm so sorry, sweetie," Anna's eyes were filled with genuine regret and shame.

"It's okay. Really," Trinity smiled sad.

"Let's go to my room. Can you carry the cola and plates?" Gio handed Trinity a drink caddy and paper plates. "Bella, you grab the wings and garlic bread. I'll take two of these pizzas and napkins. Oh, I'm taking all the cookies too," Gio glared at his mother.

Trinity was about to follow Gio and Bella, but stopped short setting the drinks and plates down. She dug into her purse and pulled out some cash and a sheet of paper she printed before she left her house.

"H-here you go. This is for my share tonight and my cookie recipe. I thought maybe you would like it," Trinity smiled shy.

Anna took the recipe from Trinity, but pushed the money back into her hand. She captured her bottom lip between her teeth upset. "Your money's no good here, honey. But the recipe I'll take. It's very generous of you. Not even my own grandmother would give up some of her recipes," she chuckled soft, then sighed. "Trinity, I'm so sorry. We didn't mean anything."

Trinity had to run her tongue along her teeth to keep from crying. She didn't know why she felt like crying, but she did. Blinking rapidly, she staved off the tears. "It's really okay. Thank you so much for having me ...here."

"Trin! Are you lost?" Bella came back into the kitchen, her smile fading. "Are you okay?" She placed her hand on Trinity's back.

"Yeah, I was just giving your mom my cookie recipe."

"Oh my God! Thank you! Come on!"

Trinity was never more happy to be pulled away.

-#-

Dante pulled up to his sister's house hoping she cooked dinner. After coming home, he decided he needed real food. He worked late and was dead on his feet. He could have easily ordered take out, but he wanted a home-cooked meal. His parents were traveling, so that left himself. He didn't cook. His sister was his only hope, and she never let him down. Good thing he changed into his sweatpants. He didn't need to be constricted when he stuffed his face, a luxury he very seldom allowed himself. But, his sister made a mean lasagna so it couldn't be helped. Please have lasagna, he silently prayed.

"Sissy! I'm dying!"

Anna came out of the kitchen wiping her hands on a towel, chewing something with a happy smile. This was a good sign.

"Durante!" she hugged him tight. "So nice to see your human side."

"Hello and shut up." Dante hugged his sister back, letting his weight fall onto her until she pinched his side. "Fuck! That hurt!" he pouted rubbing his skin.

"You deserved it." Anna stood back and frowned. "You look tired. Get in here and have some pizza."

Pizza? What the hell? He didn't want pizza. He wanted fucking lasagna. Damn it. Oh well. He may as well stay and have pizza with Gio and Bella. They'd be happy to see him. At least Bella would for sure.

"Dante!"

"Hey, Peter," he smiled.

"Here's a plate. Help yourself. Do you want water or a beer? What do you want to drink?"

"Water is fine. I can get it."

"Sit down. How'd it go today?"

Dante rolled his eyes. "It was ridiculous. Buyer wanted to negotiate the price. Can you believe that? Since when? It's always been, here's the shit, here's the price. I don't understand people nowadays."

"You gotta watch 'em. Your father taught you that," Peter waved his hand. "Eh. You'll do good. I'd never make it."

Dante rolled his eyes, "You would if you tried, Peter. You past it up without trying."

"You're smarter than me," Peter shrugged.

Dante bit into his pizza thoughtful, "I do have my concerns with Gio. He's not cut out for the job, Peter. You and I both know it. I'm worried."

Peter shook his head and made a guttural noise, "I know. It's something to discuss in the future, I suppose. I don't know...," he trailed off in disgust.

"Leave him be, Peter. There's no reason why he can't keep doing what he's doing. He doesn't need to be the head of anything. I don't want him to," Anna argued.

"Enough business. Where's Gio and Bella? Aren't they home?"

"Mhm," Anna wiped her mouth. "He's entertaining a guest," she winked at Peter.

"Really? A woman?" Dante asked surprised.

"A gorgeous woman. Outside of my wife, I don't think I've ever seen anyone prettier."

"Thank you!"

Peter nodded at his wife.

"Serious? Who?"

"I can't remember her name? It's different. Real pretty," Peter scratched his head.

Dante set his pizza down and cleared his throat with a shrug. "What does she look like? Maybe I know her."

"Hmm, well, she has very long platinum hair and real pretty blue eyes. Oh! I know. It's Trinity. Yes, that's her name. Trinity," Anna smirked at her husband.

Dante choked on his water. What the fuck?! Trinity? When did Gio swoop in? He used his napkin and composed himself. The last thing he wanted to do was race around looking for her. Actually, that was the first thing he wanted to do.

"Where...are they?" he tried his best to ask nonchalant, crossing his arms.

"In his bedroom," Peter tossed.

Dante narrowed his eyes. His sister and brother-in-law were messing with him. So Gio blabbed and told them he liked someone. What a big mouth.

"If you think I'm going to go racing upstairs, you're sadly mistaken. Nice try." Dante resumed his professional air.

Peter and Anna started to laugh.

"So, what's her story?"

Dante shrugged. "She's a new hire. You can see why I'm interested."

"She told us her husband died two weeks ago."

Images of a dead David Fallon flashed through Dante's mind. It was surprising Trinity would reveal that information. His sister caught on.

"Yes, well, she told us that after your brother-in-law put his foot into his mouth," Anna shot her husband a disgusted frown.

Dante nodded. Not surprising. Peter was always one to interrogate people. It wasn't always the best to have him present during negotiations.

"So, what's up with her? She's only twenty and already a widow?" Peter pressed.

"She was abused by her husband. Badly."

Anna rubbed her temples, "And?"

Dante grabbed another slice and took a bite. "I killed him," he shrugged.

"Aye-yai-yai," Anna crossed herself.

"What? What was I supposed to do? Let him keep killing her? Fuck that."

"You did the right thing, brother. I would have done the same."

Dante smirked. No, Peter, you wouldn't have the balls. "Thanks. Now, I'm gonna go kill Gio."

Dante took the stairs two at a time while his sister yelled at him to not hurt her son too much. As if he could ever hurt Gio. His sister made him laugh. She was always a softie when it came to her son. It explained a lot.

All of his efforts to try and toughen that kid up were sabotaged by his sister. Their mother was the same way. Luckily, for him, he was able to rise above the coddling. There was no room for a soft heart in the game. The reality of his life had rules that were all written in blood.

Fortunately, for his family, he became good at the game. All of their operations were tucked and hidden very neatly inside Venturi Transportation while his clubs served as disguises for his boardrooms when it came to less than kosher negotiations. Not only did he run a tight outfit, he also managed to keep peace between the other families. Things were good.

With Gio being uninterested in taking over, he knew he was in it for the long haul. That was fine with him. The work satisfied certain cravings he knew weren't natural. He shouldn't enjoy killing as much as he did. Shaking his thoughts free, he stopped to listen at the door. The only thing he could hear was the movie. Quietly, he turned the doorknob and opened the door to Gio's dark room.

It looked like they dragged Gio's couch in front of the television. Their backs were to him. All three of them were huddled together. None of them noticed him. They were too engrossed in eating pizza and watching The Nun. He had seen that movie in the theater a couple years ago. This was perfect timing. In a few minutes, the movie was about to go to a jump scare. How fun would it be to scare the shit out of Gio?

On silent feet, Dante crept fully into the room and positioned himself behind his nephew. He held his hands up and right when the moment came, clamped down onto Gio's shoulders causing him to scream like a girl along with Trinity and Bella.

Pizza and popcorn went flying into the air. Trinity launched off the couch and onto the bed, Bella slid down to the floor, clutching her heart, and Gio had Dante's hands in a death grip. Was he crying?

Dante started to laugh and couldn't stop. Tears were coming from his eyes. Holy shit that was great! When was the last time he had that much fun? Gio let him go and pressed a button on a remote, lighting up the room.

"You...asshole!"

"Aww. What? You scawwwed?" Dante asked him in a baby voice and continued laughing.

"Fucker," Gio ran his hands through his hair trying to catch his breath.

"Uncle Dante! You scared me and Trinity too!" Bella bounced up and hugged her uncle. But his eyes were on Trinity who was getting off the bed with a shy smile.

"Hello, Trin. I didn't know you were here."

"Gio and Bella invited me."

"Uncle Dante, you gotta try one of Trinity's cookies!" Bella held up the container which was already half gone.

"I'm assuming there were more of these," Dante reached in and grabbed one for himself. When he bit into it, he closed his eyes. So this was heaven?

"Gio almost ate them all!" Bella slapped her brother in the head.

"You made these, Trinity?"

"Mhm."

"They're probably the best I've ever eaten."

"They're her own recipe too. She gave it to mama so she could make more for us. Wasn't that nice of her?" Bella sighed.

"Very. So...do you guys mind if I join?"

Chapter 18

It wasn't awkward like Trinity thought it would be. They all sat together watching a movie, eating and joking around. It was also an entirely different side to Dante than what she had ever seen before. She couldn't look away.

For one thing, he wasn't in a suit. He wore black sweatpants and a t-shirt, without any shoes. The relaxed look shaved years off of him. He laughed a lot around his niece and nephew and joked mercilessly.

What a warm family. It was so strange to watch. She never experienced a close family dynamic like this one. Not growing up with a sister or a brother always kept her curious as to how it would feel. Now she knew. It felt nice. Loving. It hit her then. She never really felt or experienced...love.

Her parents were never affectionate, and she didn't have siblings to fill the void. David was always hurting her. Becky hugged her from time to time, but it wasn't the same. No wonder she couldn't recognize how wrong her relationship with David had been.

She was too busy trying to feel accepted. Trying to feel loved. Her chest felt tight. She didn't have this. Suddenly, she felt jealous. Not in a bad way, just in a way where she wished this was her life. She should be counting her lucky stars Gio befriended her. At least she could get to watch them interact. Hopefully, without looking creepy.

As much fun as it was to watch, it created longing. Maybe it would be better to leave. She didn't really fit in here. Her presence felt like more of an intrusion. What time was it anyway? A glance at her watch told her it was quarter to eleven. Time really did fly when having fun. She overstayed her welcome. As much as she didn't want to interrupt the banter that was going on, it was time to go.

"Um, I should get going," she said soft not wanting all eyes to be on her, yet they were.

"Aww. Why!" Bella cried.

"It's late. I-I should go," she whispered.

"You don't have to, Trin. You could even stay overnight if you want to," Gio said grabbing a cookie.

Trinity shook her head aware of Dante's eyes on her. She swallowed, "Thank you, but I should really go. Thank you so much for having me. It was really fun." Trinity quickly grabbed her things and hugged Bella. She knew it was probably a weird thing to do, but she couldn't help it. The girl hugged her back just as tight.

"Gimme a hug, bestie." Gio squeezed her hard then let her go. "See ya Monday! Oh, but text me when you get home so I know you made it alive. I'll call you tomorrow!"

No one ever said that to her before. How...different. "Okay."

"I'll walk you out," Dante offered.

They went down the stairs and to the door where Trinity put her shoes on.

"You could take Gio up on his offer, you know."

Trinity glanced up.

"To stay over. That way you wouldn't have to drive home," he clarified.

"I can't do that, Dante. It wouldn't be right. It's not even right that I'm here," she whispered. She didn't exactly know why she was whispering. Maybe because she knew, in the back of her mind, she didn't know where Gio's parents were.

"Why not?"

"This is your family, Dante, and I'm your secretary. I don't want to make you uncomfortable or cross any lines. The last thing you need is to feel strange at the office. I don't want that for you."

"Are you not Gio's friend? He really likes you, Trin. He called you his best friend. He never does that. He has a lot of friends too."

"Of course I'm his friend. It's just...i-i-it's," her eyes squeezed.

"Shh. Trinity, it's okay. You know how I feel about you. You could never make me uncomfortable," he brushed his knuckles over her cheek.

Trinity couldn't help but close her eyes. The gesture was so simple and pure, it shouldn't have caused her to melt like it did. It just felt good to be touched so softly. Tears started to well.

"Come here." Dante took her into his arms.

He enveloped her. His masculine cologne infiltrated and surrounded her being with his person, making her feel the safest she'd ever felt in the entirety of her life. It was too much. Tears spilled onto her cheeks. She had to get out of there. She pushed at him, relieved when he immediately let her go.

"I h-h-have to go," her voice cracked. Without looking back, she ran out the door to her car.

The faster she could get home, the better it would be. She wouldn't go back there either. She needed to stay away from Gio and Dante and their family. She didn't deserve to be in their home clouding it with her dark thoughts. Her therapist was wrong! She was broken.

Tears streamed down her face. Why did her life have to turn out the way it did? Why did she have to get involved with David? Why couldn't her parents have loved her the way parents were supposed to love their children and protect her? Why didn't they ever check on her? Why?!

Now she was this fucked up, broken person. David was the one who got lucky. He didn't have to live on this earth anymore. But she did. She not only had to live here, she had to pick up all the shattered pieces he left behind. Slapping her wheel with the palm of her hand, she let out a frustrated scream.

Wiping viciously at her tears, she looked at the clock. It was almost midnight. Her parents were in the same timezone as her. Who cared if it was midnight. There was no better time to give someone a piece of her mind. She was about to pick up her phone when she thought better of it.

She sniffed loud wiping her nose. What would calling them do? Nothing. They didn't give a shit then and they wouldn't now. They would tell her to come down for a visit just to placate her, knowing she would decline. Pff. She should impose on them, just to make them uncomfortable.

They didn't even know David was dead. They didn't know he beat her endlessly or almost killed her. They didn't know that her and Becky weren't friends anymore. They didn't know she had three new friends, Eugenia, Gio and Bella. They didn't know she had a new job with a great mentor, Ms. Jewell. They didn't know she had the most generous boss in the world, albeit for selfish reasons since he was interested in her. But...who cares? He was still the best. They didn't know any of it.

So what was the use of keeping them in her life? Screw that. She wouldn't give them the satisfaction of hearing from her. They could just die too! She screamed, hitting the wheel again.

When she finally got home, she slammed her car door shut. It felt good to do it. It felt good to make noise. She didn't even know she had it in her to make so much noise.

Trinity fumbled around for her keys, sniffing angrily until she noticed a pair of headlights pull up. Fear spiked through her. She'd better get inside. Her hands shook, dropping her keys. Crap! What if it was someone from the police department? What if it was David's friends, and they were here to hurt her? Her heart started to race.

"Trinity!"

Relief whooshed out of her. Dante. He followed her home? She squinted against the porch light. Yes, it was him.

"Dante?"

He jogged up the few steps and grabbed up her keys handing them to her. "Are you alright?"

"Ye-yeah. What are you doing here?"

"I wanted to make sure you made it home safe. You were upset. Can I come in?"

Trinity nodded, and unlocked her door. Dante closed it behind them sending the deadbolt home.

"Can we talk?"

"Yeah," Trinity kicked off her shoes and set her bag down onto the kitchen table. She didn't wait for Dante to do the same before heading into the living room, flicking on the cozy fireplace and sitting down onto the couch.

"Do you want me to make tea?"

"No." Dante joined her on the couch. He stared at the flames for a few minutes before speaking. "It's okay, you know. I can't imagine what you must be going through, but it's okay to have a good time. It's okay to let other people in. It's okay...to let me in."

"I don't know," Trinity looked away with a sniff.

"You're not expected to know everything. But, from my standpoint, I'm telling you it's okay to be in my home or Gio's. You're not intruding, Trin. Gio invited you over tonight because he wanted your company. So did Mirabella. If you don't accept their friendship, you'll miss out. Even from me. I like you as a person. I've never pitied you."

"Haven't you?" Trinity looked sharp. "Isn't all of this for your own benefit?" Trinity swept her hand over the room.

"I don't understand," Dante shook his head.

"You told me you're interested in me. Here comes a damsel in distress. What better way to be a hero," Trinity clenched her teeth.

It was wrong of her to say. It was hurtful. She just couldn't control her tongue. Even if she bit it. Looking up at Dante, she was surprised to find no anger in his expression. Not even pity like he said. Instead he looked...amused? Slowly a wide grin broke out.

"What is so funny?" she demanded.

"You are. If you knew me better, you'd know I don't need to play the hero to woo you, Trin."

"Is that so?"

"Yes. Have you no eyes?"

Trinity scrunched her nose. "What do you mean?"

Dante rolled his and stood up. "Look at me." With a wrinkled t-shirt, sweatpants bunched up on his calves and messy hair, Dante stood before her with an expectant expression. "Well? What do you see?"

"I...," she bit the inside of her cheek.

"Uh! I'll tell you. Sexy. Sexy is what you see. Duh! I don't need words or actions. I just need my body to stand here before you to win you over. Simple." He plopped back down onto the couch slinging his arm over the back of it.

Trinity's mouth fell slack. Was he for real? How dare he mess with her bad mood. She didn't want to laugh. She didn't even want to smile. But that's what he was making her do. And where was the serious, debonair boss of hers? Who was this amusing man? He was right. He was sexy. She closed her mouth.

"I'm sorry. I'm sorry for the way I acted. It wasn't right."

"Please. Don't apologize, Trin. Never apologize to me. Deal?"

"Deal. Thank you for making sure I got home safe."

"Tomorrow's Sunday. Do you want to do something with me? Not a date, but as friends," he hurried to say.

"What?"

"A client of mine gave me tickets to the aquarium. They expire soon, and I'd like to use them. Come with me."

The aquarium. She'd always wanted to go there. She even asked David once to take her, but he complained it cost too much and didn't have time. Now was her chance!

The offer was suspicious because it definitely sounded like a date, but he clarified it would be only as friends. It was probably fine. As long as she clarified it too just so that he wouldn't get his hopes up.

"I would love to go. As friends."

"Great. How about I pick you up at nine? That way the crowds will be lower and we can take our time."

"Okay."

"Wear sneakers. It's a big place."

-#-

Cute baby pink canvas Vans? Check. Cute baby pink jeans with heart pockets and rolled cuffs? Check. Cute heather-gray crop sweater? Check. Hair down and curled into soft waves. Light pink gloss and black volumizing mascara. Check, check and check. She looked pretty. Trinity turned this way and that, checking all angles of her outfit. Her butt looked good in the new jeans too. Not that she was hoping to impress.

This wasn't a date. She shouldn't have put so much effort into her appearance. Why did she? It was automatic, she supposed. Plus, it was a great chance to wear the new outfit she ordered. It was so cute. She looked soft and romantic. Oh great. She hadn't planned on looking romantic. Especially since this wasn't a romantic date. It was only two friends going out to the aquarium to look at fish swimming around, and only because Dante had free tickets he didn't want to waste. He probably couldn't find anyone else to go with, so he asked her.

Gio and Bella could have went with, but he did only have two tickets. Trinity rolled her eyes at herself. Gio could certainly afford to buy his own ticket. He had a great job working with Dante. She had a great job too, she smiled at her reflection. It felt damn good.

Ms. Jewell took a chance on her and things seemed to be going well. She was learning. David never acknowledged her capable of learning new things. He dissuaded her from going to college after high school telling her it was too hard, too expensive and a waste of time.

Brushing her dark thoughts aside, she grabbed her new mini-backpack purse and threw her wallet, lip gloss and keys into it. Dante would be arriving soon. She couldn't wait. Her phone was fully charged and ready to take a ton of pictures.

Right on time her doorbell rang, and she opened the door to a very attractive Dante. He was wearing a pair of black jeans. She smirked. She never saw him in jeans before. Only suits and sweatpants. He had on a fitted white polo shirt the showed off muscles she didn't realize he had, and black sneakers to complete his outfit. Her eyes went back to his arms a moment too long, and her cheeks reddened.

She didn't need to worry about being caught checking him out. He was busy himself. Black eyes traveled the length of her body. If she hadn't been paying attention, she would have missed how fast he assessed her. Very sneaky, she thought.

"Good morning. You look, forgive me, but you look very huggable," he smiled.

Trinity blushed remembering Gio's word for hug as huggie. "Thank you. Pink is my favorite color."

"Duly noted. Shall we?"

Heading over to the aquarium early was definitely a good move. The traffic was lighter than normal, and they arrived in short order finding a prime parking space.

Trinity was so excited, it took all of her concentration not to jump up and down in her seat. She felt like a little girl. She settled with bouncing her legs a little.

Dante looked over at her and smirked, "You're too cute, do you know that?"

"W-what?"

"I can see you're excited," he nodded at her legs.

Stilling herself, she blushed. "I've always wanted to come here. Thank you so much for picking me."

Dante turned the car off and bit his lip looking through the windshield. "Trinity, why wouldn't I pick you?"

"I...I don't," Trinity sighed. "A place like this is for when you do something good, and you get rewarded. I haven't done anything good. Bella would have been the better choice. Even Gio for how hard he works."

Dante closed his eyes, clearly taking a few deep breaths. Trinity watched him confused. Was that wrong? Her parents always told her that if she had done very well on her report cards, they would take her places or buy her things. Of course, she never really earned high marks so she never reaped any rewards.

He asked her if she wanted to come out today as friends because he didn't want to waste the tickets. He should have chosen Bella. She would have loved to see this place, she assumed.

"Trinity, that's not right. You don't have to earn the ability to go anywhere. If I invite you out, it's because I want to be in your company. Bella and Gio can come here on their own anytime they want or we can go together any other time. This time, I wanted you here with me." Dante took a steadying breath. "I know I told you we're here as friends, but I really want to call this a date. I really do. You don't have to have any worry about me touching you or doing anything you don't want me to do. But, I really want to think of it as a date," he glanced at her.

"Okay," she whispered with a blush.

If she were to ever move forward, now was the time to take a risk. To feel uncomfortable in the moment and see where it leads. Her therapist told her it was okay to feel attracted to a man. If that was the case, then it must also be okay to go on a date. Dante said he wasn't going to touch her. He wasn't going to hurt her. He only wanted to enjoy her company in this building. There was nothing wrong with it.

His eyes snapped up hopeful, "Really?"

"Let's go before I change my mind," Trinity got out of the car before Dante could open the door for her.

The aquarium was huge. The first thing they noticed was two large open pools home to stingrays and little sharks. The other thing they noticed was a slightly weird smell coming from the tanks.

Trinity wrinkled her nose, but ignored it. She wanted to touch them. They looked so soft. And, they were. The animals swam near the top of the tank where people leaned over to touch their silky bodies. A smile spread across her face. The way they glided through the warm water looked as if they were flying. So effortless, so magical. Beautiful.

Trinity was a little reluctant to touch the sharks, but Dante didn't have a problem. He even fed them. That's where she drew the line. Touching them was enough for her.

Exhibit after exhibit housed so many different creatures from octopus to jelly fish. Huge tanks home to coral and colorful saltwater fish captivated Trinity's attention the most. A favorite part of the exhibit was a tunnel where one was surrounded from top to bottom and sides by a tank of fish darting over and under. It was like standing in the middle of a dream.

After a few hours, their tour was at an end and Trinity was starving. She wondered if she could ask Dante to stop at a fast food restaurant or something so she could have lunch at home rather than having to cook anything. She was way too tired to move.

"There's a really good burger place not far from here. Would you like to have lunch there?"

"Oh no, that's too much, Dante. This morning has been so great. I couldn't ask for more."

"You might not want more, but I do. I'm starving." Dante stretched with a yawn. "It's your choice if you want to watch me eat or join because I'm not driving you home first," he said bored.

"Dante!" Trinity laughed realizing he was teasing her.

"Oh, so you will order a burger for yourself? Scandalous. Absolutely scandalous. Actually, I didn't know young ladies such as yourself even ate."

"Stop," she laughed. "I actually love to eat. A burger sounds great right about now because I'm starving too."

"Your wish is my command. So demanding. Sheesh."

"Dante! Stop teasing me!" her cheeks blazed.

"Why? It's fun. I like your blush. It's very pretty and it compliments those cute jeans."

"Oh my lord." Trinity pressed her palms to her face. He was really embarrassing her. But, this banter felt nice.

Dante was comfortable to be around, and he was smart. He knew all about the aquatic life at the aquarium and told her a bunch of facts. He even took her into the gift shop and purchased a pink fish Squishmallow stuffy. She squeezed it thinking about the fact no one ever bought her something like this. Her parents always told her stuffed animals were for infants.

Was this how people were everyday? What she witnessed between Dante, Gio and Bella, their playfulness, was that normal? Was this date normal? She had nothing to compare it to aside from David. He never actually took her on any dates unless one considered sitting at Burger King a date.

She didn't have any more time to think on it as Dante came around to open her car door and escort her into the restaurant. The place was full of people waiting for a table. Little kids held balloons and darted around their parents playing and yelling. It was pretty loud here, but Trinity didn't mind.

Dante went up to the hostess and said a few words. Much to Trinity's surprise, they were taken back to a table right away. Woah. Did they just skip all those waiting customers? She wanted to ask, but didn't dare. As selfish as it was, she was starving and secretly happy to be seated.

Dante didn't waste time announcing he was having a Papa burger with fries and a chocolate milkshake. That sounded great but glancing at that meal, she had to work to keep her eyes from bugging out of her head. Twenty dollars for a burger?! Since when? Much to her dismay, many of the meals were in the same price range. Jeez. Wasn't there anything here for under ten dollars? Ah. A kids meal was nine. It had a cheeseburger, fries and soft drink. She'd probably get full off of it. She didn't need much.

"I think I'll just have the kids meal," she said closing her menu.

Dante looked up from his menu even though he was already set on what he was having, and raised his brows. "So...let me get this straight. I'm having the papa burger meal, and you're having the kids meal?"

"Y-yes?"

Dante placed his menu down, then leaned forward a little bit clasping his hands in front of himself. "Trinity?"

Trinity leaned in looking around confused. "Yes?" she whispered.

"Are you...by chance...a little?"

"I think I am."

He leaned back in his chair crossing his arms, mildly amused. "Really? I never pegged you for one."

Trinity looked down at herself. She never thought of herself as big. Was she big?

"I'm not going to lie, I wouldn't mind being your daddy," he smirked biting his lip.

Realization struck. She had seen a romance novel online once about men who were daddies and women who were their little girls. Was Dante joking around with her? He did purchase a stuffed animal for her at the aquarium when he saw her eyeing it. And she was wearing all pink, and what had he said to her? Oh yeah. He called her huggable. Oh no! He had the wrong idea!

"Relax. I'm teasing you. You're easy, Trin," he laughed, his straight teeth on display.

"Oh you! That was not nice."

"Pick whatever meal you want, Trin. You'll regret not trying something off the main menu. The kids meals aren't that great."

"Oh yeah? How would you know?"

"I have a few smaller children in my family. After ordering kids meals one time, we switched to regular meals. The kid meals are pretty skimpy."

"Ah."

"Dante!"

Dante's head snapped up with groan. Trinity searched around to find the familiar voice. Her face lit up when she saw Mirabella and Gio. They were waving like maniacs, both of them holding baloons.

"It's Gio and Bella!" Trinity waved back.

"Don't encourage them, Trin."

"Yay! Here they come."

Trinity made room for Gio and he slid in pulling her arm to him where he quickly tied his balloon around her wrist. Bella slid in next to Dante bopping him in the head with her balloon while he groaned and smacked it out his face. Bella ignored her uncle, giving his arm a hug then grabbing his menu with a giggle.

"How did you find us here? And why do you two buffoons have balloons?"

"Ha! That rhymed. I tracked you," Gio supplied looking over the menu with Trinity.

"We're on a date."

"A date, huh? Trin, did you know you were going on a date?"

"Not at first."

Gio laughed, "Thought so. Anyway, me and Bella were hungry."

"So? You couldn't go somewhere else?"

"That wouldn't be fun, Uncle Durante."

"Don't call me that," Dante rubbed his forehead in frustration.

"Your full name is Durante?" Trinity asked.

"Yeah. I don't use it. I go by Dante."

"We use Dante too, but mama calls him Durante to get on his nerves," Bella chimed in.

They were interrupted by the waitress who took their order, her eyes lingering on Dante a little longer than what was polite. Trinity wasn't surprised. It didn't escape her notice many women stared at him throughout the day. She had to admit, it felt pretty good to be the one on his arm.

"I'm so glad you guys found us," Trinity smiled.

"Why? Date not going good?"

"Oh no. It's been so fun. We went to the aquarium and saw so many cool things!" Trinity's eyes lit up. "Dante even bought me a Squishmallow."

"A Squishmallow?! I love Squishmallows. Aww, Uncle Dante. I want one!" Bella whined.

"You went to the aquarium?! What the hell, Dante? I would've liked to go," Gio complained outraged.

"Yes, well, I'm not dating you two. Lord give me strength," he rubbed his face.

"I'm glad you took Trinity out on a date, Uncle Dante."

Dante smiled, but caught a look from Gio who nodded. His smile faltered. "Will you excuse me a moment, Trinity?"

Dante left the restaurant with Gio trailing behind him. He kept walking until he was by his car where he unlocked and climbed into it.

"Sorry to intrude on your date, uncle. I had to find you."

"What's going on?"

"The deal we negotiated with the Luca family didn't go so hot. When the shipment arrived, they claimed we padded our price."

"Well I didn't," Dante shook his head.

"Yeah, well, they think you did."

"So the deal fell through?"

"For us, yeah. For them, not so much."

"What do you mean?" Dante's jaw clenched.

"They kept all our product and told us...they told us to go fuck ourselves."

Chapter 19

nger has been known to elicit the color red to the mind's eye. It was true. Anger was red, and he was seeing it. How could another family, one his father maintained peace with for well over twenty years, decide to upend all that work? To steal from his family? To steal, not just thousands, but millions of dollars worth of product? It blew Dante's mind.

A family meeting would have to be called. Immediately. A plan would have to be configured and implemented. No matter what the plan ended up being, there was going to be bloodshed. Loud or quiet, it didn't matter. Blood was going to spill, and it wasn't going to be his family's blood.

If Dante didn't regain control quickly, he'd lose not only his reputation and respect but his position within the state. His family controlled the state. His family decided who, what, why, when, where and how. He'd be damned if another family was just going to come in and take that away.

There was only one guess as to why this was happening. Vincent Luca, the head of the Luca family chose a successor. Meaning, the man was either retiring or dying. It was more than likely the latter. Vincent enjoyed his power too much to just give it away. So who did he choose as the family's new capo dei capi? His nephew, Nick Luca. And the young blood was already making decisions before the old man was in the ground. Foolish kid.

Dante found it all amusing the similarity he shared with Vincent. Nick was Vincent's closest male heir, much like Gio was for himself. The commonality didn't sway Dante's plans for Nick.

Gio did good coming to find him. Maybe he pegged him wrong. Maybe he was cut out for the job. While he was a jokester and seemed to have taken a deep liking to Trinity, it was that happy-go-lucky attitude which camouflaged the real reason for seeking Dante out. Gio's actions would be rewarded. The only thing the kid had left to do was learn how to take out the garbage. This was the perfect opportunity.

Dante headed into the restaurant where he found Gio back to that happy-go-lucky self, joking around with the girls. As much as they were laughing, Trinity's expression faltered for a brief moment. It was so slight had he blinked, he would have missed it. She was smart. She knew something was wrong.

Thanks to David Fallon, she was an expert at reading facial expression and mood. Too bad he couldn't use her talent in some of his meetings. It wasn't a bad thought. He could bring her in on some of his legit deals and ask her opinion on things to see her talents in action. He'd give it some thought on another day. Now was not the time. He smiled at his group.

"After lunch I'll have to drop you back home, Trinity. Gio and I have an emergency meeting at work."

"Do you need help with anything? I could go in with you," concerned marred her brow.

"Thank you, but no."

"I-if it's important, maybe we should have our food wrapped up to go. Bella can come home with me, and I could drop her off later," Trinity suggested.

"Oh! Yes! I want to do that," Bella bounced in her seat.

"Are you sure you don't mind, Trinity? It can wait."

"Not at all. Bella and I will have a lot of fun. I have new makeup we can try," Trinity turned to Bella with a smile.

Bella breathed in excited.

"No way. Bella is not allowed to wear makeup until she's thirty," Gio warned.

Trinity looked to her lap. "I'm sorry. I didn't know."

Gio's expression dropped. "Trinity, I was only joking. You girls do whatever it is you want to do."

"Yeah we will. Gio's not the boss," Bella stuck her tongue out at her brother.

"Gio...go to the office," Dante grated. "I'll drop the girls off and meet you there."

-#-

How could Gio be so stupid? He knew Trinity had been abused. That she was healing, or trying to. He would speak with him later about his stupidity. In the meantime, he needed to speak with his father and grandfather. Sure they turned things over to him but when shit like this happened, he always included them.

Dante walked through his quiet building. It was always his most favorite time. When no one was around, he could think. Free from the bustle of people running around, free from hearing his name being called and free to be able to get work done. Sundays were his Monday. When he organized for the week ahead.

When he reached his office, he was surprised to see his nephew, father and grandfather sitting around chatting.

"You guys are fast. Where's Peter?" Dante asked taking a seat behind his desk.

"He's out with mom. I told him it was fine for him to stay with her."

"Why?" Dante asked irritated. Even though Peter wasn't born into the family, he was his sister's husband. He needed to start stepping up. The man was a milquetoast. Useless.

"They're shopping. You don't want to piss your sister off do you?"

Fair enough. Anytime Anna was pissed, things didn't go well for himself or his brother-in-law and nephew. It was better to let things alone. Although, it still irritated him.

"So, Nick Luca fucked us over?" Dante's grandfather, Marco, asked.

"Seems so," Dante rubbed his forehead.

"Did we even know Vincent was going to name him? What's wrong with your generation, huh? Our families worked so hard to build trust, to build an understanding. Now look at it," Geno complained.

What the hell? His generation? He wasn't the one who caused the problem. Why was his father always like that? Always including him on shit that wasn't his fault. Unbelievable. He should have handled this on his own.

"This certainly isn't my fault, dad."

"Let him alone, Geno," Marco slapped his son's head. "Your boy's doing a fine job."

"The fuck? A cosa serve?" Geno smoothed his hair back into place. "All I'm saying is that we're the one who established the businesses and these kids don't seem to care. Nothing's how it used to be," he waved his hand disgusted.

"I've worked very hard at maintaining the integrity of our businesses, dad. If you don't like how I do things, by all means, reclaim your throne. I don't give a shit," Dante grated.

Marco waved a dismissive hand at his son, "Ignore your father, Dante. So what's the plan?"

"The Luca family made a mistake naming their successor. I'm guessing Nick fucking us over was some sort of display to show they're still in the game."

"It was totally unnecessary. Vincent's not even dead yet. Ignorante!" Marco remarked in a crackled voice.

"I agree."

"We gonna knock him down a peg, Uncle Dante?" Gio asked.

"No. Knocking him down a peg is like swatting a fly. It always comes back. Instead, we'll knock him off the fuckin' peg."

"It's the only way, kid," Geno agreed with a loud sniff of his nose and a satisfied nod of his head as he adjusted himself in his seat.

Dante turned to Gio and crossed his arms. "You're good at paperwork, Gio. And, you did good coming to find me. But if you're gonna be in this business for the long haul, it's time you learned all the ins and outs."

Gio's face paled. He knew what Dante was referring to. Dante nodded at his father and grandfather. They agreed. Peter didn't have a say in it. He wasn't there. Anna didn't have a say in it either. It was none of her business.

They allowed Gio to rest under Dante's wing. But Dante's wing wasn't angel white. It was nero infernale...hellfire black.

"W-what does that mean exactly?" Gio cracked his knuckles nervously.

"Exactly what you think it means," Dante answered simple.

Marco stood up and patted his son on the back. "Let's go, Geno. Let the boys handle things. We're in the way now."

Geno nodded and stood up, stopping short of Dante's desk. "Do it tonight. Do it quick. Fix this shit."

Dante's jaw flexed, his eyes met his father's, "Have I ever let you down?"

Geno reached over making the sign of the cross and kissed his fingers, "Dio ti benedica."

"God bless you too, dad. Tell ma I'll call her later," he yelled out after his father left the room. Dante squeezed the bridge of his nose, "He drives me fuckin' nuts."

"Dante? Please tell me you're not gonna make me do what I think you're gonna make me do," Gio swallowed.

It was precisely what he thought. Gio needed to learn. How the hell was he supposed to be an appropriate successor if he couldn't even shoot his gun at a real target? There was no way around this. The kid had to do it.

"It'll be fast."

"You're serious," Gio frowned. "You're really gonna make me kill Nick Luca?"

"Yes. I am."

"I can't, Uncle Dante. I just...can't."

Dante slammed his fist down onto his desk, causing Gio to jump. "There is no can't!" he roared jumping up out of his chair. He came around his desk and grabbed Gio by the shirt and hauled him out of his chair. He was so close, their noses touched. "You think Nick will spare you?! You think he would hesitate?! No! No, he wouldn't and he won't," Dante let Gio go to slump down in his chair. "The first fuck over was a message. The second won't be, and it'll be you. It won't be me. It'll be you first."

"Wh-what? Why?" Gio's eyes watered.

"Because they know I have no one to name as my successor but you. How fun it will be for them to watch our family scramble with your death."

"But what about Geno and Marco?"

"Two old men? They would love that. An empire easily quashed after my death." Dante relaxed back into his chair. "Your death is their fun. My death is their business. It leads to the fall of our empire and the rest of the family as we know it. I'm not wrong. This stops tonight, Gio."

"By my hand."

"Yes, nephew. By your hand."

"How?" Gio whispered.

"I'll have Andrew find out where he is. Wherever it is, we'll go in and shoot him," Dante shrugged.

"What if it's in public?" Gio worried.

"There's always bathrooms." Dante called Andrew on his phone and instructed him before hanging up.

Gio looked green. It wasn't surprising. The first one was always the hardest and the most remembered. Gio would get over it and move on with a little time. Once he got over this hurdle, nothing would stop him. He would prove to be a well-trained successor.

Tonight's mission would not only guarantee the safety of his and Gio's life, but their entire family as well. Dante thought of Trinity. If she were to become any more entangled with him, he didn't want to risk harm to her. She endured enough.

Dante was happy Andrew got back to him relatively quickly. Nick Luca appeared to be enroute to the hospital. Probably going to visit his uncle. Perfect.

"Come on. I know where he's heading." Dante pulled open his desk drawer and removed a pistol, then opened his credenza where he rummage around till he found a silencer and handed them to Gio. "Screw that on," he said pulling out another for himself.

"Now?!"

"Yes, Gio. Right now. He's on his way to the hospital to visit his uncle. We'll take him out there."

Dante moved fast through his building with Gio trailing behind him. Adrenaline coursed through his veins. He would have loved to be the one to take out young Nick Luca himself, but Gio really did need to learn. A glance back at his nephew revealed his shaking hands. The kid went from green to gray. Not good, yet expected. He'd get over it.

Back in the car, Dante was happy Gio hadn't passed out. Dante drove through the city traffic with ease darting from lane to lane until he reached the hospital. He would park inside the parking structure rather than on the street to avoid anyone noticing him leaving the building. One never knew how many eyes were watching.

Finding a space to park on the first level was a miracle he was grateful to have been graced with. He wouldn't need to take an elevator to walk straight into the hospital's first floor. His only caveat was not knowing which room Vincent was in. Easily solved.

"Before we get out of the car, here's how this is gonna go. We'll stop at the giftshop first."

"Why?"

"Gio, it's always customary to bring the one you're visiting flowers. Hasn't my sister taught you anything?"

"But I'm not visiting Vincent," Gio whispered.

"No, you're not. But you are visiting Nick. You'll need to have your gun in your hand without anyone noticing it, hence the flowers," Dante's eyes emphasized his meaning. "We'll walk to the floor Vincent is on. If we see Nick in the hall, you point, shoot and keep walking. If he's inside the room, we go in and you point, shoot and walk out. We walk slow, no matter what."

Gio rubbed his shaking hands down his face. "Do I say anything? To Nick, I mean?"

Dante shrugged. "That's up to you. Everyone has their own style. Just don't miss. I've taken you shooting plenty of times. You're a good shot. You got this."

"There's so much that can go wrong. What if there's metal detectors? Then what?"

"There isn't any. At least not the last time I was here."

"When was that?" Gio worried.

Dante shrugged. "I don't know. Last month, I think. Forget about it."

"I wish I had something to calm me down," Gio shook his hands out.

"What do you mean?" Dante frowned.

"I don't know. A joint maybe?" he looked hopeful.

"Are you smoking?"

Gio shrugged guilty.

"There's no room for that shit in this business, Gio. You run it straight. Totally sober. No drugs. No alcohol. I don't care how nervous of a person you are. You run it straight."

"Yeah," he whispered. "Let's get this over with."

Dante slapped him on the shoulder and got out of the car. They went to the gift shop and purchased two large bouquets of dense flowers. Afterwards, they ducked into a nearby bathroom happy to find it vacant. Dante helped Gio situate his weapon while he did the same for himself.

"Front desk is next."

Dante squared his shoulders and casually walked up to a middle-aged woman chewing gum and working on a crossword puzzle. It didn't take long for her to notice him and beamed with a bold smile.

"Can I help you?"

"We're here to visit my uncle. Vincent Luca. I'm not certain the room number."

"Of course. Let me just look him up. Ah. He's on the second floor, hospice care, east wing, room twenty-four. I'll get you visitor passes. What's your names?"

"Vincent and Nick."

The woman laughed, "Someone's named after their uncle. And another Nick? Too cute."

"It's an Italian thing," Dante smiled taking the passes from her. "Thank you."

"Sure thing, honey."

Dante nodded to Gio and they headed to the stairwell happy they only had to walk one floor up.

"How am I supposed to put the pass on with one hand?"

"You're not going to put a pass on. Just put it into your pocket," Dante rolled his eyes. "Room twenty-four won't be far in. There will probably be a ton of hospital staff walking around, so let's hope Nick is inside the room alone. If he isn't...let's just hope he's alone."

There would be no way Gio would be able to kill more than one person. If Nick wasn't alone, Dante would kill anyone else in the room save Vincent. The man would die sooner or later. Let him watch his family die first. Served him right. Fucking bastard for letting his stupid nephew run things.

Rounding the corner, it was as predicted. The hallway had a few nurses bustling around, a doctor walking by and a maintenance man fixing a door. It was a lot. They would need to maintain calm. Dante pulled Gio to a stop just short of the door. He peaked in. Sure enough, Nick was inside. But so was another person. He couldn't see well enough to tell who they were. Dante glanced around. None of the staff were paying them any mind which was a good thing.

"There's two people inside besides Vincent. Nick's sitting in front of the window. A straight shot. You're going to walk in first, and kill him. Don't wait for any last words. You'll then turn around and walk out slowly. You'll keep walking until you get to the car. I'm gonna take out the second guy. Do not worry about me. Do not turn around and look for me. Just walk. I'll be right behind you. Do you understand?"

Gio nodded. Dante watched a resolve settle over his nephew's eyes. This was a good sign.

"Good. Let's go."

Everything happened so fast it was slow motion. Gio opened the door and walked through with Dante behind him to close the door. Nick's face fell along with the flowers in Gio's hand while the gun made a loud cough rather than a telltale bang. As instructed, he turned around and exited the room leaving Dante behind.

The other man stood up. Dante still didn't recognize him, and chalked him up to being Nick's friend as he held his hands up in surrender. There was no such thing as mercy in this game. Dante dropped him without any final words. He set the flowers down onto a small table situated next to Vincent's bed and hung the call button up behind him, away from his hands. The man's eyes were wide and filled with horror.

"Don't die yet, Vincent. I want to talk to you." Dante stood at the end of the bed knowing he didn't have much time. "Did you know Nick stole my product? Millions of dollars worth?"

The older man shook his head in denial, his eyes going to his dead nephew. Dante followed his gaze.

"He's gone, Vince. Gio got him in the head. It's really a shame, you know? Marco and Geno established peace, I've maintained it and your family fucked it up. Honestly. But, not to worry. While your family's little empire has come to an abrupt end, your women and children will be spared."

"Kill me," Vincent rasped.

Dante looked surprised. "Kill you? You haven't even said goodbye to your wife and daughters. No, Vince. I'm not going to kill you. Besides, I'm sure you'll want to have some alone time with your nephew." Dante looked at Nick's lifeless body and decided to help Vincent out. He positioned the armchair in front of Vincent's bed, then dragged Nick's corpse over and hoisted him up and onto the armchair pulling his lopsided head back to rest against the pillowed headrest.

"There. Perfect for a heart to heart." Dante swiped his arm across his brow. "Well, I've overstayed my welcome. Till we meet in hell, Vincent Luca, I bid you a goodnight."

Dante pulled the door closed softly and walked down the hall taking note of the name on the next door over. A one Beatrice Cole. He shoved his hands into his pockets and started to whistle. A nurse smiled at him, and he returned it with a slight nod.

"Excuse me, sir?"

"Yes?" Dante stopped and smiled again, making the nurse blush.

"I don't see you have a visitor's pass."

"Ah. I was just visiting Bea. I'm sorry," he grinned embarrassed. "I meant Beatrice. I've always called her Bea."

"Aww. Are you her grandson?"

"I am. How did you know?"

The nurse ducked her head shy. "Lucky guess."

Dante held his hand out. "Thank you so much for taking care of her. I'm embarrassed to confess it's been really difficult for me."

"It's our pleasure. She's such a sweetheart. And mourning is nothing to be embarrassed about. It's natural."

"Indeed."

"Did you check in at the front desk? We have to make notations in our files."

"I did. I must have walked off without my pass. I was so anxious to see her."

"Oh, not a problem. Happens all of the time. What's your name?"

Dante started to walk away with a grin. "Mr. Cole. A pleasure." He kept walking disappearing around the corner where he picked up his pace till he reached the stairwell.

How no one entered Vincent's room in the entire fifteen minutes he'd been on the floor, was nothing short of another miracle. His phone was buzzing and he knew it was Gio. He looked and sent him a two word response while he continued on his way.

This was a splendid job well done. There was no drama or screaming chaos. It was clean. Nick and whomever wouldn't be discovered for yet another five minutes or so. Plenty of time to get back to his vehicle without any irritating delays. Of course, somewhere along the line, cameras probably caught his and Gio's image. For anyone else, it would cause issues. However, it was hardly a problem when one owned the police.

He resumed the tune he was whistling with a smile.

Chapter 20

Having Bella over was so much fun. They played with makeup and listened to music while discussing high school crushes and cliques. While they were four years apart, Bella's stories made Trinity feel so care-free. How good it felt to just let go and relive being a teenager for one afternoon. It was so enjoyable, Trinity couldn't stop thinking about it all week.

Bella was so easy to like, and becoming a fast friend. So was Gio and Dante. Trinity wondered about how it would feel to be a part of a family like theirs. One could dream. In fact, she had fantasized about it many times. She knew it was wrong to think of Dante and his family in that way. It was just too hard not to. They were so full of love. Fantasizing about the Venturi family would be her guilty pleasure. No one had to know.

Trinity put on some music while she started getting ready for work. Rum-maging through her closet, she pulled out a black pencil skirt with match-ing heels and a burgundy silk blouse. Her platinum hair fluffed around her shoulders in large waves. It was a good hair day.

Smiling, she went downstairs to grab her coffee, keys and purse. A week passed since her date with Dante, and she hadn't seen him since that

Sunday afternoon. Ms. Jewell told her he was out of town. During that short time, she focused on her job.

Ms. Jewell started leaving her on her own to perform various tasks during the week. It definitely boosted her confidence. It was kind of exciting. Things felt like they were looking up. She had a new job, new friends and a nice place to live.

Little by little, she thought of David less and less. Realizing this was her new life helped tremendously. With that realization came a personality she didn't know she had. While she was still rather reserved, she started to notice decision making was coming easier and easier.

She also started thinking the idea of dating Dante wasn't such a bad one. He was beautiful, confident, kind and generous. Sure, the last time she spoke to him was when he dropped her off at her house on Sunday. Sure, he hadn't called...or texted. Still, a girl could dream. She had her therapist to thank for it too. Her therapist insisted it was okay to start fresh and it was okay to explore relationships. It was okay to take risks. It was okay to live.

Those thoughts always made her smile. Too bad her parents weren't receptive to her. It would be nice to earn their pride. Maybe she would call them or even visit. What if they had changed? She could always start with a phone call. If she didn't like how it went, she didn't have to waste money on a plane ticket.

The only other thing nagging her mind was Becky. She knew she should really forget about her once and for all. How many times did she keep telling herself the relationship was over with? How many times did she settle it in her mind? No matter how many, her thoughts still plagued. Why didn't she want to be friends with her anymore? Especially since David was no longer around. It was really strange. Maybe Becky was only ever friends with her because she felt sorry for her. It was a good possibility.

Checking her Instagram showed Becky was doing just fine without her. She posted a few pictures of herself and another woman Trinity didn't recognize. A few of them were at bars and the shopping mall. The images made her frown.

"Boo!"

Trinity jumped out of her skin startled. "Eugenia!"

Eugenia giggled. "Stuck in your head, huh? Whatcha thinkin' 'bout? Ooh, I bet I know. A dreamy pair of dark brown eyes?"

"Shh," Trinity looked around. "Are you going up with me?"

"Yeah. I have a stack of papers for Dante to sign."

The women stepped into the elevator.

"He's not even here. He's been out of town."

"I know. I thought it would be great to have this stack ready and waiting for him when he got back."

"Nice," Trinity laughed. "So are you free for lunch? I was all by myself last week."

"Girl, you know I can't. My boss lunches with me, duh."

"You're bad."

"No badder than you," Eugenia nudged Trinity.

"I'm not doing anything with my boss that's anywhere near what you're doing with yours," Trinity poked Eugenia in the arm.

"Pff. Jealous?" Eugenia busted out laughing.

"Girls. Up to no good, I see. Where are you going with those papers, Ms. Eugenia?" Ms. Jewell stopped them in the hall.

Eugenia pointed at Dante's office door with an innocent expression.

"No. You give those to me. Back down to your floor, dear."

"Aww. You're no fun, Ms. Jewell. Trinity invited me up here anyway."

"No, I didn't!" Trinity protested.

"Eugenia, you know your credibility with me went out the window a long time ago."

Eugenia braced her hands on her hips, "When?"

"When I caught you in the broom closet with the janitor."

Eugenia snorted with a laugh, covering her mouth. "He was so hot. Tattoos all over. Uh! I miss him. Byee!"

Trinity and Ms. Jewell watched Eugenia sashay back into the elevator. Ms. Jewell shook her head.

"Are you two friends?"

Trinity blushed, "Yes."

"She's a very good woman. You picked a great friend to have," Ms. Jewell smiled. "Are you ready to run Dante's office for yet another day?"

"Yes! I got this."

"Of course you do, dear. I'll check back with you before you leave for the day."

The morning was going flawlessly. It really was a great day. Until lunch. She was standing in line, alone again. Eugenia wasn't kidding. She disappeared with her boss again. Trinity hoped she was being careful.

"Hi Trinity."

Trinity looked up. "Hi Roger."

"You remember my name?"

Sure she did. At the time she met Roger, she was so certain she would never lunch with anyone or make friends. Things were different now. She nodded.

"Impressive. So, how are things going? Find your sea legs yet?"

"I have, thanks. I really enjoy it here."

"Nice! Hey, wanna join me for lunch?"

"Sure."

They found a table and sat. Roger was nervous, Trinity could see. She could also see he was attracted to her. It was something she was beginning to notice more and more. The male attention, that was. She received many good mornings, good afternoons and good nights. However, no one ever peaked her interest more than Dante.

"Tell me about yourself, Trinity?"

Aside from the a la carte line, today's special was spaghetti. Roger wasted no time digging in and slurping up his noodles. Trinity couldn't tear away from his sauce-stained lips. He looked like a little kid who needed a bib.

"Roger, I already interviewed for the job. Don't tell me I have to do it again?" Trinity smirked. Another new trait she noticed about herself was that she could be bold and joke around at the same time.

Roger laughed, "Aww, come on. You can tell me one thing about yourself at least," he shifted in his seat. "Okay, okay, I'll go first," he pointed at her with a meatball perched on the end of his fork. "I love to dance."

This raised her eyebrow. Roger loved to dance? She hated judging people, but with his checkered pants and pocket protector, he looked like he had two left feet. She suddenly felt guilty for the thought.

"Really? What kind of dancing?" She had to know.

"Salsa. I know, I don't look like I can dance," he sniffed. "It's written all over your face. But! I can. And...I'm good." He ran his fingers through his curly hair, fluffing it out.

Trinity laughed holding up her hands. "I believe you!"

Roger's face fell. "Dang. I was hoping you wouldn't."

"Why?" her nose scrunched.

"Cuz then I'd say, if you don't believe me, come out with me Friday night and I'll show ya," he clicked his tongue with a wink.

"Smooth, Roger. Real smooth," she giggled.

"Thanks. So, what do you say? Would you like to go dancing Friday night?"

"Like a date?"

"Yeah."

"I would, but I'm not dating right now." She didn't want to tell him she went on a date with Dante. For one, she wasn't sure if Dante would be mad if people knew they had a date. And two, Roger really wasn't her type as bad as the thought sounded in her own mind. Yikes. It really was a bad thought. She just couldn't help it. Roger wasn't Dante.

"I see. Well, that's no problem. How about we go as friends?"

Where had she heard that line before? Oh, yeah, Dante. He tricked her. She didn't want to be caught in the same web.

"I'd only go if I could bring some friends."

"Sounds good. You can bring a friend, and I can bring a friend."

Trinity rolled her eyes. "No, Roger. That's a double date. I'm bringing more than one friend, and I'm not telling you how many or who."

"You're a tough negotiator, you know that?"

"Of course I know that. Duh."

Roger stretched his hand out over the table and shook Trinity's. "Deal. As friends."

-#-

She sure had a lot of friends. Not really a lot, but more than what she had ever had in her whole entire life. She had Eugenia, Gio, Bella, Dante and now Roger. Maybe Roger. Tonight would tell. If he got fresh, she'd kick him to the curb. Sort of. Instead, she'd just tell him to back off nicely.

Thank goodness Eugenia and her boss, Parker, and Gio were all going tonight. Gio didn't know it, but Trinity invited Sarah. Maybe they'd hit it off. She never tried to be a matchmaker before. Hopefully, she didn't crash and burn.

Eugenia decided they needed to get ready together so she could help Trinity with her makeup and outfit. Secretly, Trinity hoped she wouldn't pick out too revealing of an outfit. It was almost seven. Eugenia would be arriving soon.

They were all meeting at La Notte. At least it was a familiar place even though it held both good and bad memories for her. Trinity pushed it out of her head. She would only choose to remember the good.

A few minutes later, Eugenia showed up with a few dresses in one hand and a huge makeup bag in the other. Oh boy. Tonight was a full glam kind of night, she could feel it.

"I have got a dress for you," Eugenia dropped everything letting out a large sigh. "I need something to drink, girl!"

Trinity shook her head with a laugh getting Eugenia a water.

"So you're dressing me up like a hooker?"

"Oh yea. Not to worry. I'll be slutting it up with ya."

"Couldn't I just go in my sweats? Look how comfy I am?"

Eugenia gagged. Then gagged some more. "That answer your question? Now brace yourself and behold! Tonight, you are going to be the lady in red. Ooh, mysterious," Eugenia waved her hand over the dress like a fortune teller over a crystal ball with a laugh. "Red dress, red shoes and red lips. Uh! To die for! I'm gonna wear green."

"Green," Trinity curled her lip.

"Yeah. Why not?"

"You can't stand next to me then. We'll look like a Christmas tree."

"Oh, shit. You're right. Hmm. I'll wear...blue?" She pulled the dress out and held it up.

"Much better. Now we'll look very patriotic."

Eugenia clicked her tongue. "Stop it! We'll be fine. So, who's this Sarah chick you invited?"

"Gio's type. I think they'll hit it off."

"Nice. Dante coming?"

"He's still out of town, I guess. I haven't talked with him," Trinity shrugged.

She wasn't going to lie, it stung a little he hadn't contacted her. Not only didn't he contact her, Gio had been silent for the entire week as well. She was surprised he texted her back and agreed to come out. Maybe they had a really busy week.

Whatever. It wasn't like she was actively dating Dante. Not officially at least. And she certainly wasn't his girlfriend, even though the idea was starting to appeal to her more and more.

Either way, it was okay. She had a great life now, and she wasn't going to be ungrateful for anything. There was no room to feel greedy. If she was meant to be with someone, it would happen. Maybe it would turn out to be Roger. Trinity whimpered.

"What is it?"

Trinity shook her head and sat down for Eugenia to work her magic. Heavy tapping, brushing and smoothing went into Eugenia's work on Trinity's face. It was hard to keep her head still at times. Good thing this lady wasn't a makeup artist. She was definitely heavy handed when it came to her application technique. Jeez!

"Done. You look like you belong on the cover of Maxim."

"Oh boy. Eugenia, I don't want to look like that. I don't want people to notice."

"Hush your butt. Go try on the dress I bought."

"How much was it?"

"Free. Go."

"Eugenia! You're not supposed to use the company's credit card for your shopping pleasure. Dante's going to kill you," Trinity argued.

"If he saw you, he'd thank me."

"Yeah, well, he's not coming tonight."

"Pity. I mean, I feel really bad for you, Trin. Being stuck with Roger and all. Why did you even tell him you'd come out?"

Trinity shrugged, "He wants to prove he can salsa. What was I supposed to say?"

"Can you salsa?"

"Hell no," Trinity laughed. "Especially not in the heels you brought."

"You'll be fine. Go."

Eugenia was right. She did look like she belonged on the cover of Maxim. What the heck was wrong with her friend? She couldn't leave the house looking like she did. The red bodycon was like a second skin, clinging to all the right places. One of the right places being her chest. Her boobs were supported perfectly, creating a generous cleavage. The waist was tucked tight, giving her butt the attention it deserved, and the matching stilettos elongated her legs found only in men's dreams.

Exercise was to credit for her body, but genes played a big part too. She always found it easy to build muscle. Her body was one thing she was proud of but also conscious about. Men always stared. She was still getting used to feeling proud rather than embarrassed and small for it.

"Girrrl! Damn. Now you look like you belong on the cover of Playboy. If I wasn't screwing my boss, I'd date ya. You are fine! It's really a crime. Ha! I rhymed."

Trinity laughed. "You don't look so bad yourself, hot stuff." She wasn't lying. Eugenia was beautiful in a dress very similar to her own. No wonder Parker scooped her up.

"Shall we?"

When they reached the club, there was a line out the door. Actually, there were two lines. One for people who were on a list, and the other for people who weren't. Eugenia called ahead and put all their names down. They wouldn't need to pay a cover since they worked for Dante. The benefits to knowing someone, Trinity mused.

The bouncer's eyes lingered on Trinity, and Eugenia gave him a look. Was Gio and Parker inside already? What about Roger and Sarah? Maybe they were. Maybe they should have all met outside first. Eugenia tugged on Trinity's arm.

Eugenia was so confident. She knew who she was and what she wanted. It was admirable. Trinity definitely felt more sure of herself around the woman. That confidence crumbled away as Eugenia pulled her upstairs.

"Are we supposed to be using the VIP lounge?"

"Why the hell not? Dante's not even here. Why let the room go to waste? Besides, Gio's in there already," she giggled.

Should have known. Of course he was. Thank goodness. Gio smiled when he saw them, but his face dropped when he focused on Trinity.

"What are you wearing?! How the hell am I supposed to enjoy my night?"

"What do you mean?" Trinity asked knowing exactly what he was talking about.

"What do I mean? Look at you," he groaned. "Dudes are gonna be hitting on you left and right. Ugh! This blows. I had the worst week ever, now I gotta be your bodyguard."

"Hush your butt. That's not gonna happen."

"Seriously," Gio gave a deadpan look. "That's not funny, Trin. I'm so not happy with you right now."

Trinity cringed, "You're gonna hate me even more. I kind of invited, Sarah."

"What?! Why? I don't even like her," Gio stomped his foot. "This night is getting worse and worse!"

"Shut up, Gio. Trinity looks awesome thanks to my outfit and makeup choices, not including her natural beauty. And, give Sarah a chance. She's shy."

"Fine," he flopped down onto a couch. "So where's your admirer?"

"Who?" Eugenia asked.

"Roger. He's in love with, Trin, you know."

"He is not. He just wants to prove his salsa moves."

"Pff. Yeah. Salsa moves on you."

"Who cares. What's Roger gonna do? He's a nerd." Eugenia waved away Gio who was trying to exhibit salsa moves with his arms, and failing.

"Hey! Keep your mitts to yourself!" Parker grabbed Eugenia away from Gio.

Soon everyone showed up including Roger who wouldn't stop staring at Trinity. So Gio was right. One night of dancing wouldn't hurt anything. Hopefully.

Trinity was happy when they all agreed to hit the dance floor. Roger hadn't been lying. The man could move. He was crazy good, and able to show Trinity a few moves. She had to admit, it was fun. A lot of fun.

Soon, she had forgotten about everything and let loose. Most of the night was dancing with Roger since he was the only one who could properly dance. And dancing with him kept other men away, weirdly enough. It also helped she had a few drinks in her. What better way to loosen up than with some liquid courage.

Trinity noticed Sarah showed up, and Gio was entertaining her. They looked like they were having a good time. Gio didn't look too bored, and Sarah seemed to be in awe of him. Maybe they would work out.

"Do you want another drink, Trinity?" Roger yelled by her ear.

"Sure."

There were a lot of men around, and Roger noticed. "Maybe you should come with me to the bar. I don't feel comfortable leaving you standing here by yourself. You might get kidnaped."

"I doubt that, but okay," she laughed.

"I'll watch her."

Was she always startled? Were her eyes forever growing? Dante. She spun around. Yup. It was him. He looked...delicious in a black suit and deep wine-colored tie. A man couldn't get any more handsome. The room melted away.

"Dante," she said breathless.

"I've missed you. Dance with me."

A slow song was playing, and she fell easily into his lead. His body pressed softly against hers as they swayed to the music. Roger was a great dancer, but there was something about Dante that made her blood warm up.

"You look gorgeous, Trin."

"Thank you. Did Gio tell you I was coming tonight?"

"No. I'm here most Friday evenings to check on things. Imagine my surprise when I saw you...on Roger's arm no less. He's a lucky man."

"He is?" Trinity asked confused.

"Are you not on a date?"

"No," Trinity laughed. "Eugenia, Parker, Gio and Sarah are here too. Besides, Roger's not my type."

"Ah. Who is your type?" Dante spun Trinity, then brought her back against him.

"Maybe...you are." That answer had to be the alcohol talking. Her cheeks started to flame. How could she be so bold as to say that?!

"I already know I am. I'm just waiting for you."

"How long would you wait?"

"The rest of my life. You're the one, Trin. I know you are. I want you to be mine. You know this."

"I didn't hear from you all week."

"Miss me?"

"Maybe," she whispered.

Dante looked down into her sapphire eyes. Before she knew what he was thinking, his lips brushed over hers so softly it felt like a feather was brushing against her skin. Back and forth, ever so slow, till he nipped at her once then twice before claiming her lips in the most tender kiss she ever experienced. The feeling left her wanting more when he pulled away too soon.

"Be mine, Trinity," he rested his forehead against hers swaying them back and forth.

Carpe diem, she thought.

"Yes."